"I thought you were a nightmare, but you're real, aren't you?"

Haley questioned.

"Not every woman considers an evening with me a nightmare," Adam countered.

Haley flopped her hand onto her forehead. "I'm happy for you, truly I am, Mr.—" She looked up at him. "I'm sorry, what did you say your name was?"

Annoyed, Adam sat up straighter. "Don't you remember anything that happened?"

"On the contrary, the point where you announced our marriage is forever etched in my mind." Haley shook her head slowly. "As if I'd been run through with a sword—a rusty sword—a dull, rusty sword with ragged edges."

"You must remember…." Adam frowned and waved his hand across the bed.

Haley shrugged helplessly. "No."

"Not even when you and I…"

She shook her head.

"Or when you—"

"I did something?" Haley's eyes bulged. "What did I do?"

"You did it three times—I'd think you'd remember!"

Dear Reader,

Multitalented author Judith Stacy is back this month with a delightful new story called *The Marriage Mishap*. When virtual strangers Adam Harrington and Haley Caufield wake up in bed together and discover they have gotten married, Adam quickly realizes that it's the best thing that's ever happened to him. Haley is not so sure, and her new husband has to figure out how to keep them married long enough to convince her that their wedding blunder can lead to wedding bliss. Don't miss the fun.

In *Lord Sin* by Catherine Archer, a rakish nobleman and a vicar's daughter, whose lack of fortune and social position make her completely unsuitable, agree to a marriage of convenience, and discover love. And in Elizabeth Mayne's *Lady of the Lake,* a pagan princess surrenders her heritage and her heart to the Christian warrior who has been sent to marry her and unite their kingdoms.

Our fourth title for the month is *Cally and the Sheriff* by Cassandra Austin, a lively Western about a Kansas sheriff who falls head over heels for the feisty young woman he's sworn to protect, even though she wants nothing to do with him.

Whatever your tastes in reading, we hope you enjoy all of our books, available wherever Harlequin Historicals are sold.

Sincerely,

Tracy Farrell
Senior Editor

Please address questions and book requests to:
Harlequin Reader Service
U.S.: 3010 Walden Ave., P.O. Box 1325, Buffalo, NY 14269
Canadian: P.O. Box 609, Fort Erie, Ont. L2A 5X3

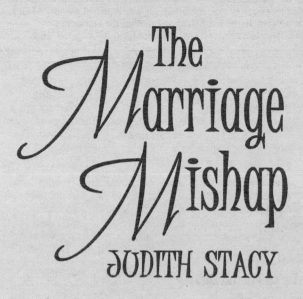

The Marriage Mishap

JUDITH STACY

Harlequin Books

TORONTO • NEW YORK • LONDON
AMSTERDAM • PARIS • SYDNEY • HAMBURG
STOCKHOLM • ATHENS • TOKYO • MILAN
MADRID • WARSAW • BUDAPEST • AUCKLAND

ISBN 0-373-28982-0

THE MARRIAGE MISHAP

Copyright © 1997 by Dorothy Howell

d in U.S.A.

Books by Judith Stacy

Harlequin Historicals

Outlaw Love #360
The Marriage Mishap #382

JUDITH STACY

began writing as a personal challenge and found it a perfect outlet for all those thoughts and ideas bouncing around in her head. She chose romance because of the emotional involvement with the characters, and historicals for her love of bygone days.

Judith has been married to her high school sweetheart for over two decades and has two daughters. When not writing, she haunts museums, historical homes and antique stores, gathering ideas for new adventures in the past.

To Judy and Stacy—
the most supportive, understanding daughters
on the planet.

To David—
I couldn't have written a romance without you

Chapter One

Sacramento, California
1894

Whose shirt was she wearing?

Haley Caufield lifted her head off the pillow and squinted down at the strange white linen shirtsleeve draped over her hand. Her breath caught. It was a man's shirt.

Curled on her side, she craned her neck and peered over the satin coverlet. Bright morning sunlight streamed through the lace curtains across the room, piercing her eyes and sending a dull ache reverberating through her head. The room came into focus: marble-topped table, green velvet settee, beveled mirror.

Ribbons of fear threaded through her. Nothing looked familiar.

The bed behind her suddenly shifted of its own volition, and an arm snaked beneath the covers and around her waist. Fingers brushed her bare belly and settled between her breasts.

Haley froze. She pressed her lips together to hold in the scream that burned her throat. Someone was in bed with her!

The arm tightened and pulled her across the bed, molding her against a hard chest; muscular thighs eased against the backs of her legs. Haley's heart slammed into her ribs, pounding with an intensity that escalated the dull ache in her head to a pulsating throb.

Slowly she pushed her thick brown hair aside and looked back over her shoulder. A man!

A little whimper slipped from her throat. Panic overwhelmed her. A strange shirt, a strange bed, a strange room—and a man. What had she done?

Haley turned her head away, her mind spinning. How could this have happened? She'd never been on an unchaperoned outing before, never allowed a man to so much as kiss her—not even Reginald Farnsworth.

The image of her mother flashed before her eyes, and Haley nearly groaned aloud at the memory of her dire warning about coming to Sacramento alone. The entire twenty-three years of Haley's life had been spent safeguarding her reputation. How could she face her mother again? The woman still brooded over the Farnsworth episode. What would she say if she found out about this?

Haley cringed. If her mother ever discovered the real reason she'd come to Sacramento, she'd probably never speak to her again.

The hand between her breasts shifted, and Haley tensed. A wave of nausea swept over her. When word of this scandal got out, she'd be ruined.

Haley pressed her fingers to her lips, afraid she'd

be physically ill. The deep, even breathing of the man behind her echoed in her aching head. As if nothing were amiss, as if the world hadn't just come crashing down, he lay sleeping, oblivious of everything.

A glimmer of hope blossomed in Haley's mind. Maybe, just maybe, she could slip away without waking him, and no one would ever know of this debacle.

Holding her breath, Haley reached beneath the covers and closed her hand around the man's forearm. The coarse hair covering his thick, heavy muscles felt foreign against her fingers. Carefully she lifted his arm and dislodged his hand from between her breasts. Hope flickered. This just might work.

"Not so fast."

Haley gasped as the man quickly captured her waist and rolled her onto her back. He pushed himself above her on one elbow. Dark stubble covered his firm chin and square jaw. Tousled black hair hung over his forehead. Deep green eyes assessed her lazily, playfully. Haley swallowed hard.

"You're not trying to get away from me, are you?" He dipped his head and nuzzled her neck.

Haley's mind reeled as strange sensations assailed her. His lips, soft yet demanding. His body, powerful against hers. She wanted to push away, but was afraid to touch him. He exuded an animal strength.

Haley licked her dry lips. "Well, yes, I have to go now."

He lifted his head and frowned down at her. "All night includes the following morning."

What was he talking about? Haley shifted away, but he tightened his grip on her. She forced a smile. "Actually, I don't think it's morning any longer."

He shrugged indifferently. "I don't give a damn what time of day it is. I'll pay you extra."

"Pay? What are you—?"

He lowered his head to her neck again. "After last night, you're worth any price."

Haley gasped, and her body went rigid, blocking out the feel of his mouth on her skin. "You think I'm a...a..."

He lifted his head again. "Look, honey, I'm not paying to hear you talk."

Haley swatted at him. "Get off of me! Get your vile, disgusting self off of me this instant!"

He pushed himself higher on his elbow. "What the hell's wrong with you?"

She thrashed wildly, kicked back the covers and sat up. "How dare you say such a thing to me! I've never been so insulted in my entire life! Where did you ever get the idea that I am one of those...those...soiled doves?"

A wry grin tugged at his lips, and he gestured with his hand. "Well...."

Haley looked down and gasped in horror at the sight of her shirt hanging open, her bare breasts peeking out. She grabbed the fabric and pulled it tight against her.

"Call yourself what you like, honey, but it's getting late, and I've got things to do today. Come on."

She slapped his hand. "Don't touch me!"

"Maybe you'd better explain what you're doing in my bed." He leaned back against the pillow and dug his knuckles into his eyes.

Haley felt her cheeks burn at the sight of his wide chest, covered with crisp, dark hair. A new wave of humiliation washed over her. "This is your room?"

He gazed around, then pushed his fingers through his hair and shrugged. "No, I guess it's not. Is it yours?"

"Of course not!" Hot indignation burned in her. She couldn't bear another second of this.

Haley scrambled from the bed, clutching her shirt closed as a fresh tide of embarrassment engulfed her. Her gown lay on the floor, beside his trousers. One of his socks rested atop her stocking. Her petticoat hung from a chair, with his undershirt draped over it.

Mortified, Haley bent to retrieve her stocking, then remembered that the shirt she wore barely covered her thighs. She froze and glanced back over her shoulder. He lay propped against the pillow, the sheet barely covering him, one arm resting casually over his drawn-up knee, watching her and looking comfortable and relaxed, as if he woke every morning of his life in a strange bed with a strange woman beside him.

Cautiously she bent at the knees and snatched up her stocking, then rushed around the room, grabbing her clothing. Then she dashed into the bathroom and slammed the door.

Her head throbbed painfully and her stomach rolled as she stood by the sink, trembling. How could this have happened? She'd had only one thing on her mind when she left San Francisco, and that would be scandalous enough if word ever got out.

She had no notion of where she was or how she'd gotten here, but one thing was certain. She was leaving immediately, and would never lay eyes on that man or this place again.

Haley dropped her bundle of clothing on the tile floor—evening wear from the wedding she'd attended yesterday with Aunt Harriet. Haley shuddered at the thought of going out in public now, with no hat, no gloves, exposing her bare shoulders at midday. What would Aunt Harriet say?

She didn't care. She would get to the safety of her aunt's house and bribe the kitchen servants to let her sneak inside. She'd climb up the rose trellis, if she had to.

As Haley frantically sorted through her clothing, her heart sank into the depths of her churning stomach. Not everything was here. In her haste, she'd left some of her clothing in the other room. And that would mean parading around the bedchamber again, with those deep green eyes scrutinizing her every movement. Haley slumped against the wall.

A soft knock sounded on the door. Haley jumped. It was him. What if he came in after her? What if he wouldn't let her leave?

His deep voice came from the other side of the door. "You left your handbag. I thought you'd need it."

Haley tossed the tangled mass of hair off her shoulder. She needed her handbag desperately. Drawing in a deep breath, she stood behind the door and opened it slightly.

Her purse passed through the opening. "I found it on the table."

She cleared her throat. "Thank you."

"This was by the door." A silk stocking appeared.

She pulled it from his fingers.

"On the bureau." Her corset dangled in the opening.

She gasped and snatched it away.

"Under the covers." Pink ruffled drawers passed through.

Haley stared, horrified, at the garment and mumbled a fervent prayer that the floor would open and swallow her whole.

"That's all I found...so far."

It was enough. Haley pushed the door closed and dug through her purse. She found her comb and twisted her hair into a simple chignon. The fasteners on her gown were nearly impossible without help from her maid, but she closed as many of them as she could. She dared not look at herself in the mirror. Pulling herself up to her greatest height, Haley walked into the bedchamber again.

Jingling coins drew her attention to the window. Hands thrust deep in his pockets, the man stood looking outside, his profile outlined by the bright, sunlit sky. He wore tan trousers and a sleeveless undershirt that molded itself to his tight belly and wide chest; dark hair curled above the scooped neck. His shoulders were straight, his arms muscular.

Haley held up the white linen shirt she'd brought from the bathroom and willed herself not to blush. "This must belong to you."

He accepted it and dropped it on the table in front of the window. "I think we're at the Madison."

"A hotel?" Haley peered out the window at the trolley cars, horses and carriages on the street below. Her stomach rolled violently. "We're at a hotel?"

He nodded. "Do you need help with your gown?"

Stunned by the familiarity of his offer, she looked up at him sharply. "No— I..."

He stepped behind her. "We can't have you walking through the lobby with your gown undone. People might get the wrong idea.''

She felt his hands against her back as he closed the fasteners. Her skin tingled at his touch.

He stepped away and slid his hand into his pocket again, jingling his coins. ''Do you want me to have breakfast sent up for you?''

Haley pressed her palm against her stomach. ''No, no, I don't think I'll ever be able to eat again.''

''Head hurt, too?''

She looked up at him. ''Yes. How did you know?''

''You have a hangover. What you need is another drink.'' He rubbed his forehead. ''And so do I.''

Her back stiffened. ''I do not drink. Why, I only took one sip of champagne yesterday to toast the bride and groom. After that, I only drank the punch.''

''You were at the wedding?''

''Yes, I was.''

He gazed down critically. ''As an invited guest?''

Her chin went up a notch, and she clamped her mouth shut. He didn't need to know that her aunt was a friend of the bride's family. Nor did he need to learn that she had arrived in Sacramento less than a week ago, escaping the fiasco in San Francisco that had turned her own mother against her and set her on an unexpected path.

He shrugged. ''Well, remember not to drink the punch at any more weddings. It's the best way to avoid a hangover—and a lot of other things, too.''

Haley pinched the bridge of her nose and drew in a deep breath. So, she'd gotten drunk out of her mind and fallen into bed with a strange man. How humiliating.

Pulling together the last shreds of her dignity, Haley looked up at him. "I'm leaving, Mr.—"

He gave her a stiff bow. "Adam Harrington, at your service, madam."

"Harrington?" Haley thought she might faint now. He was a member of one of the oldest, most prominent families in Sacramento, and she'd behaved like a common streetwalker. With all the aplomb she could muster, Haley turned to leave.

"Wait. Let me see you home."

"I hardly think that would be proper, Mr. Harrington." When he grinned, she realized how ridiculous she sounded, and that made her angry.

"You'll at least need money for a hansom cab." He searched through his trousers, then picked up his coat from the chair and went through the pockets.

Her chin went up. "Mr. Harrington, I have no idea how I came into these circumstances, but I am fairly certain it couldn't have happened without some help on your part. So you can rest assured that you have done more than enough for one day. In fact, I would say that if I never lay eyes on you again in my life, that would be too soon." Jaw set, Haley marched across the room.

"Excuse me?"

Annoyed, Haley stopped at the door. "What?"

"Would you happen to be Haley Caufield?"

She turned and saw him reading from a crumpled paper he'd removed from his coat pocket. "Yes, I am."

"Haley Carissa Caufield?"

A chill swept up her spine. "Yes."

"You might want to wait a minute before leaving."

She sighed heavily. "Why would I want to do that?"

He looked up at her. "Because, Miss Caufield, it would seem that you and I are married."

Chapter Two

"Breathe… That's right. Just keep breathing."

Haley lifted her head, and the room spun around her before strong hands pressed her onto the pillow again. She blinked, and a face came into focus, freezing the image in her mind. She moaned. "I thought you were a nightmare, but you're real, aren't you?"

Adam sat down on the edge of the bed. "Not every woman considers an evening with me a nightmare."

Haley moaned again and flopped her hand onto her forehead. "I'm happy for you, truly I am, Mr.—" She looked up at him. "I'm sorry, what did you say your name was?"

Annoyed, he sat up straighter. "Don't you remember anything that happened?"

"On the contrary, the point where you announced our marriage is forever etched in my mind." Haley shook her head slowly. "As if I'd been run through with a sword, a rusty sword—a dull, rusty sword with ragged edges."

"You must remember…." Adam frowned and waved his hand across the bed.

Haley shrugged helplessly. "No."

"Not even when you and I...?"

She shook her head.

"Or when you—"

"I did something?" Haley's eyes bulged. "What did I do?"

"You did it three times—I'd think you'd remember," Adam grumbled, and rose from the bed.

"Well, do *you* remember?" she asked challengingly.

He glared at her with wounded pride. "And who says marriage doesn't have its tender moments?"

"Are you sure we're really married?" Haley sat up, and the room spun again. Adam grasped her shoulders and steadied her; his hands felt strong.

His gaze captured hers. "Maybe you should lie down."

That was how she'd gotten into this mess in the first place. Haley looked up, and for an instant felt lost in his green eyes, brilliant as emeralds and nearly as mesmerizing. She pushed his hands away and scooted to the edge of the bed. "Where's that paper you found?"

Adam took it from the bedside table. "Executed by Judge Williams himself, and properly witnessed by Harry and Laurel Oliver."

"The newlyweds?" Haley opened the paper and read the words, saw the signatures and the official seal.

"I've known Harry Oliver for years. He works at the courthouse." Adam shrugged. "I don't know how it can get any more legal than that."

"We got married at someone else's wedding?" Haley curled her lips distastefully. "Is that *done*?"

Adam plowed his fingers through his hair. "It must

have been at the reception, because I remember the ceremony."

Haley's gaze came up quickly and met his. "You don't remember, either? I thought it was only me."

Adam shifted, and his gaze wandered across the bed. "Parts of it, I remember very well."

Haley's cheeks pinkened. "At least this explains how I got here."

Adam crossed the room and retrieved his shirt. "And how I got here, as well. Believe me, Miss Caufield, I'm not in the habit of deflowering innocent young women."

Haley looked back at the bed, then sprang off it. She smoothed down her gown, reaching for any modicum of dignity she could muster. "This can't be happening."

He looked back at her. "Some women would be pleased to find themselves married to me, Miss Caufield."

She ignored his claim. "We have to do something."

Adam shoved his arms into his shirtsleeves. "Such as?"

Haley touched her finger to her chin. "Harry and Laurel, the newlyweds. They witnessed the whole thing. Let's talk with them."

"Honeymooning in New York. Won't be back for two months, maybe more."

"Then how about this judge? Maybe he—"

"I doubt Judge Williams will take too kindly to having his word questioned."

"Is it too late for an annulment?"

His gaze roamed the bed, and he drew in a big breath. "I would say it's far too late for that."

"Then that only leaves..." Haley's stomach pitched.

"A divorce?" Adam's gaze met hers as he closed the buttons on his shirt. "Now there's a scandal our families will enjoy."

Haley pressed her fingers to her lips. Another scandal. Her mother had nearly disowned her over Reginald. What would she do if she found out about this?

Haley stepped closer. "It wouldn't be a scandal if they didn't know about it."

"You're saying you really don't want to be married?" Adam frowned as he shoved his shirttail into his trousers.

The haughty, indignant arch in his brows wound Haley's stomach into a tighter knot. She pulled herself up straighter. "I suppose that comes as a surprise to you, Mr.—Harrington, was it?—but I have definite plans for my own future, and they do not include a husband."

Adam pulled on his waistcoat and jacket, and stuffed his cravat into his pocket. "I don't think either of us is in the proper frame of mind to make such a decision."

"My mind is quite made up, Mr. Harrington. And I'll thank you to keep this entire unfortunate incident to yourself. I'm leaving." Haley headed for the door.

"Wait." Adam followed her across the room.

She grasped the doorknob and looked up to find him standing over her. His height was overwhelming. She barely reached his shoulder. "What?"

He reached over her head and held the door closed. "Isn't a husband allowed a goodbye kiss?"

Haley's knees nearly gave out. A heat, an aura, engulfed her as Adam eased closer. His gaze captured hers, and all rational thought left her head. He folded his arms around her and pulled her against his chest. She felt the strength in his arms, tempered by the gentleness of his touch.

"Well?" A tiny grin pulled at his lips.

She tried to protest, but couldn't speak the words. Visions, images, flashed in her mind.

Adam touched his mouth to hers, kneading them together gently until she parted her lips. He moaned deep in his throat as his tongue met with hers in an intimate exchange. She was sweet, giving, exquisite...just as he remembered.

Desire coiled in his belly as further recollections surfaced in his mind. He pulled his lips away and kissed a hot trail down her cheek, nestling against her neck. She tasted good. He wanted more.

"We don't have to call off the marriage right this minute," he whispered against her ear. "Another hour or two wouldn't make any difference. How about it?"

Adam lifted his head and looked down to find Haley staring at him. Her lips were wet and swollen with his kiss, and her body was nearly limp in his arms. But her eyes, deep blue eyes, were wide with fright.

They'd made love all night, done wonderful things with each other, and he didn't understand her reaction. He wanted to be mad, but couldn't. Instead, he stepped away and pulled in a deep breath.

"Well, at least let me walk my wife down to get a cab."

Befuddled, Haley stepped aside as he opened the door and walked with him down the carpeted corridor. The air was cooler here, and it helped clear her mind—enough for her to worry that they would be seen in the hotel together.

At the head of the grand staircase that descended to the lobby, Haley stopped. "I'd rather go down alone."

Adam peered down the stairs. The double doors at the main entrance were only a short walk across the lobby. Several men sat on the settees and others stood near the front desk. Haley in her evening gown— modest as it was—certainly would catch their attention. And suddenly he didn't like the idea of those men ogling her.

He shook his head. "I'll see you to the cab."

Haley started to protest, but he closed his hand over her elbow and led her down the stairs. She took heart in the strength that radiated up her arm.

Crossing the lobby, Haley kept her head down, though she could feel the stares of everyone there. At least she was new in town and almost no one knew her; the chances that she'd be recognized were slim.

She lifted her gaze for an instant, calculating the distance to the doorway. Only a few more feet and she'd be safely out of the Madison Hotel, safely away from the man clinging to her elbow, safely on the path to salvaging her reputation, not to mention getting her plans back on track. Her spirits lifted. No one would ever know.

Aunt Harriet stepped into the doorway.

Haley dug in her heels and pulled back. What was her aunt doing here at the Madison on a Sunday afternoon? Her first instinct was to run, but the man at her elbow anchored her in place. She pulled against him.

He held tight and looked down at her. "What the devil is the matter with you?"

Her breath came in quick puffs as her aunt's gaze fell on her. She watched in horror as the older woman's expression turned from surprise to anger.

Suddenly Aunt Harriet was surrounded by three other women. Haley's knees trembled. They were her aunt's friends, the cream of Sacramento's society. How could she explain away what was so painfully obvious? Her gaze swept the lobby as she looked for an escape route, a place to hide—anything.

Adam looked at the women, then down to see the terror on Haley's face. "I take it you know that woman," he whispered.

She worked her mouth, but no words came out.

The three women spotted her, and recognition bulged their eyes. They bent their heads together, whispering, then craned their necks at Aunt Harriet.

Haley clamped her hand around Adam's arm. "She's my aunt. And those old hens are her dearest friends."

Adam looked at the women, then back at Haley. "She's your aunt? Harriet Covington is your aunt?"

She bobbed her head quickly and gazed up at him, desperate. "What are we going to tell them?"

Adam couldn't hold in the grin that pulled at his lips. He slid one arm around her waist and bent until his mouth brushed her ear. "We could always try the truth."

Haley wanted to slug him. "I told you, I don't want anyone to know about this—this mess."

"Would you rather tell them we simply spent the night together?"

Aunt Harriet advanced on them, her wrinkled

cheeks pink with anger, her body rigid with well-practiced containment of her emotions. Behind her, the three other ladies stared, wide-eyed.

Her gaze raked them both. "What is the meaning of this?"

"Mrs. Covington, it's good to see you again. Haley tells me you're her aunt." Adam smiled smoothly.

She looked up at him for the first time, and recognition drew her mouth into a tight bow and bobbed her brows to her hairline. "But— I— You— Well, Mr. Harrington?"

"We were just on our way to see you, Mrs. Covington, weren't we, dear?" Adam gave Haley a squeeze, and a squeak slipped through her lips.

Aunt Harriet glanced back at her three friends who were hovering within earshot. She pulled herself up straighter. "Mr. Harrington, I must ask for an explanation."

"Believe me, Mrs. Covington, the whole thing came as quite a surprise to us all. Isn't that right, dear?" Adam looked down at Haley, a gracious smile in place. "Go on, tell your aunt."

Haley would have collapsed onto the floor long ago, had it not been for Adam's strong arms around her. She felt the hot glare of her aunt, the nosy exchange of her friends, who must be dying to spread this juicy piece of gossip unfolding before them. But which was the worst scandal? Marrying a stranger in a drunken stupor, or getting caught sleeping with one?

Haley lifted her chin, collecting her pride as best she could. "Aunt Harriet, Mr. Harrington and I got...married last night."

Aunt Harriet gasped in a most unladylike fashion. Her three friends circled her, whispering and offering congratulations. Several moments passed before Haley realized they were all pleased with the news.

"Well, well." Aunt Harriet's cheeks had pinkened. "This is quite exciting, Mr. Harrington. Quite exciting."

Haley didn't understand it, but at least no one was mad at her or would spread unsavory gossip. She didn't want to linger, though, to hear the questions about the wedding details that were sure to follow.

"I'll see you later, Aunt Harriet, and we'll talk more then."

"Certainly, dear, of course." She gave her a proud smile. "And Mr. Harrington, we'll want to have you over for supper very soon—your father, as well, of course. We should all get to know one another better, now that we're related."

Adam nodded cordially. "Good afternoon, ladies."

Arm anchored around Haley, he crossed the lobby, leaving the women to stare after them. He looked down at Haley. "See? I told you not everyone considered marriage to me a horrible prospect."

She would have slapped that smug grin from his face, had she not been certain Aunt Harriet and her friends were still watching. Haley clamped her mouth shut and went out onto the street in front of the hotel, the bright sun stabbing her eyes. Adam hailed a hansom cab. The driver jumped down and opened the door for her.

"Well, Mr. Harrington, it was nice…meeting you."

He closed his hand around her elbow. "What's that supposed to mean?"

"I told you already." She eased her arm from his

grasp and sighed heavily. "Surely you're not thinking we should stay married?"

He shrugged. "Now that your aunt knows the truth, what else can we do? The news will be all over the city by nightfall."

That much was true. Haley pressed her lips together. "But I don't know a thing about you."

Adam stood a little straighter and tugged at his waistcoat. "Adam Oren Harrington. I own a business, which, I'm proud to say, is quite profitable. I'm thirty-four years old, in good health, have few vices, and all my teeth." He stretched out his lips, displaying two rows of even white teeth. A little grin tugged at his mouth. "Well? Does that meet your expectations for a husband?"

He looked so comical, Haley couldn't help giggling. "On the surface, yes."

"And what else would the lady like to know?"

Haley studied him for a moment. "You don't know a thing about me."

Adam took her hand in his. Slowly he brushed his thumb over her palm and captured her gaze. "I'll be at your aunt's after supper tonight. We'll discuss everything then."

Ripples of warmth radiated up her arm. She ignored them and pulled her hand away. "I've already told you, Mr. Harrington, I have plans that do not include you. Plans that—" *Could cause a worse scandal?* Haley held her tongue.

Adam folded his arms across his chest and watched as her bustle disappeared into the cab. He passed money to the driver, and the cab pulled out into the street.

One thing he'd learned long ago was to keep his

options open. Snap decisions were often regrettable decisions. Uninformed decisions were disasters. True, he knew nothing about his new wife now. But by the time he arrived at her aunt's home tonight, he'd know everything he needed to know about Miss Haley Carissa Caufield.

"Oh, thank God it's you."

Haley plopped down on her aunt's mauve settee and touched her hand to her forehead.

Seated across the marble-topped coffee table from her, Jay Caufield settled deeper into the wing-backed chair. "Who were you expecting? Your new husband, maybe?"

Her gaze came up quickly. "How did you find out so soon?" She'd left her aunt at the Madison only hours ago.

"Good news travels fast," he said, though his tone indicated that he considered it anything but.

"Please, Jay, don't play games with me." She'd taken a bath and tried to nap, but she hadn't been able to sleep, images of her mother, her aunt and her new husband tormenting her.

"It's all over town. Your aunt was at the Madison for one of those ladies' club luncheons, spewing the news like a champagne bottle just uncorked." Jay rose, his slender frame rigid. He threaded his fingers through the pale blond hair at his temple. "How could you have done this? Look, cousin, don't you realize who Adam Harrington is?"

Haley offered him a weak smile. "Aunt Harriet and her friends were quite pleased by the news."

He laughed bitterly. "I'm sure they were. But she's your aunt on your mother's side. Social position is what they live for. I'm your real relative, Haley. Our fathers were brothers. You should have discussed it with me before you up and married a Harrington.''

"Well, where were you last night, anyway?" Haley sat up straighter. "Maybe none of this would have happened if you'd been with me."

He shifted and looked contrite. "I had to leave. Elizabeth was getting all goo-goo-eyed, talking about bridesmaids and gowns, jockeying to catch the bouquet. I had to get her out of there.''

"You coward. Elizabeth is a wonderful girl. You should marry her."

Jay held up his palms. "We're not discussing me. We're discussing you and your fiasco.''

"My latest fiasco, don't you mean?"

Jay just stared at her. Aside from Aunt Harriet, only Jay knew the reasons behind the Farnsworth incident. Though her mother had taken her from Sacramento when she was only thirteen, Haley and Jay had corresponded regularly. He was three years older than she, and they'd been fast friends growing up together. Jay was as close as a brother would have been, had her mother tolerated her father long enough to produce other siblings.

Jay sank into the chair again. "I didn't think you even knew the Harringtons.''

She shrugged. "I don't know them. I just...woke up with one.''

Stunned, Jay's eyes bulged. "You mean, you two got married—" he snapped his fingers "—just like that?"

She nodded. "I don't even remember the ceremony. Neither does he.''

"But...how?"

She sighed resolutely. "Something to do with the punch, I think."

He chuckled lightly, then laughed, and laughed harder, until he grabbed his belly and threw back his head. "This is too much, Haley, too much!"

She sat forward on the settee. "What's so funny?"

He wiped his eyes with the back of his hands. "When old Martin Harrington finds out what his son has done, he'll hit the roof. I tell you, it's almost worth it to have you married to that family."

Haley flung out her hands. "What's wrong with the Harringtons, anyway?"

Jay sniffed and got himself under control. "Nothing. Unless you're trying to compete with their construction company for work in this town."

She gasped. "The Harringtons own a construction company? But you and I—"

"Exactly. You don't remember, since you were so young, but our fathers had a devil of a time holding their business together in the face of the Harringtons' stiff competition—every construction firm in the area had a tough go of it. The Harringtons finally rolled over most everybody. Only a few firms, like ours, remain."

"So what you're saying is..." Haley shuddered. She didn't even want to consider the possibility.

Jay nodded. "In a way, the Harrington Construction Company was responsible for your father's...demise."

"His drinking, you mean."

"Well, yes."

And that had led to business problems that compounded the marital problems, and eventually landed

Haley at her grandparents' home in San Francisco, with her mother estranged from her father.

Jay shrugged. "Maybe, if things had been different, your parents—"

"It wouldn't have mattered." Haley rose from the chair. "She'd married beneath herself. I heard it a thousand times."

"He worked like a dog to make himself worthy of her."

Haley walked to the mantel, sadness sagging her shoulders. Her father had died young, leaving his brother—then Jay—to run the business. "It was never enough, was it?"

"No," Jay admitted. "He never stood a chance."

She turned and faced him again, drawing in a fresh breath. "So, you and I are left as the sole owners of the Sacramento Building Company."

Jay rose slowly from the chair. "We are. For now. I guess you got my letter."

"I did. And that's what brought me here to Sacramento in the first place." Haley shook her head sadly. "Jay, you can't mean it. You can't close the Sacramento Building Company."

"I've been beating a dead horse for years now. It's no use, Haley, I simply can't go on. Harrington Construction has work locked up in this town. I haven't sent you any profits from the business for some time now, but I suppose the amount was hardly noticeable, compared to the money your doting grandfather Hasting heaps on you."

Haley smiled. "You've done a wonderful job with the company. Your father would have been proud."

"I do the best I can. Outbidding Harrington for jobs in this city is tough. We're small potatoes compared to them. Come down to the office, sometime, I'll show you around...while there is an office, that is.''

Haley threaded her fingers together. "No, Jay, I'm not going to let this happen. I'm a partner in the business, and I have a say in what happens to it. Closing Sacramento Building is the last thing our fathers would have wanted. We'll find a way to keep it going.''

"Well, not tonight, I'm afraid. I've got to run.'' Jay clasped her elbow and kissed her cheek as the mahogany mantel clock chimed the hour. He rolled his eyes. "Dinner at Elizabeth's parents tonight—this is getting out of hand.''

"But—''

He was gone, and she was left standing alone in Aunt Harriet's parlor, still contemplating the mission that had brought her to Sacramento.

But before she could do it, she'd have to find a way to get rid of Adam Harrington.

Chapter Three

He'd actually shown up. Haley was surprised, and a little annoyed.

She paused at the bottom of the staircase. From the parlor, she heard his deep voice, then Aunt Harriet's high-pitched laughter; her aunt, it seemed, was quite taken with her new husband.

She crossed the foyer and entered the parlor. Adam was on the settee, his long legs crossed behind the marble-topped coffee table. Aunt Harriet sat in the damask wing-backed chair across from him, hanging on his every word.

He seemed too big for the room, too strong, too muscular, out of place amid the lace, ruffles and delicate furnishings. Though he wore a dapper navy suit, there was a ruggedness about him. His face and hands were tanned, a stark contrast to the crisp white shirt he wore.

Adam stopped in midsentence and came to his feet when she walked in. His gaze riveted her. "Good evening."

Clean-shaven now, he looked different from the way she remembered from this morning. His black hair was combed carefully into place, not tousled and unruly. But those deep green eyes hadn't changed at all. They riveted her now as they had this morning, and made her feel as if she were once again wearing his shirt, instead of a proper gown.

Aunt Harriet smiled up at Haley. "Come in, dear, we were just having a lovely chat."

Haley stopped beside her aunt's chair, in no mood for a lovely chat. "If you don't mind, Aunt Harriet, I'd like to speak with Mr. Harrington alone."

Aunt Harriet wagged her finger. "No, no, dear, not so fast. I want to hear all the details."

"Details?" Haley felt Adam's gaze on her, bringing a flush to her cheeks. "What sort of details?"

"Everyone is asking. What was it that brought you two together so quickly, so unexpectedly?" Aunt Harriet clasped her hands together and gazed up at her.

Haley shifted uncomfortably, her mind working feverishly. She didn't think her aunt wanted to know the exact flavor of the punch, the thing truly responsible for bringing them together. But for the life of her, Haley couldn't figure out what Aunt Harriet was asking.

"Now, now, dear. No need to be shy. You either, Mr. Harrington." Aunt Harriet looked back and forth between them, then smiled sweetly. "It was love at first sight, wasn't it."

"Oh, *love.*" Relieved, Haley touched her hand to her chest.

Aunt Harriet clasped her hands together. "Was that it, Mr. Harrington? Love at first sight?"

He cleared his throat. "Yes, of course."

"Good." Aunt Harriet settled back in the chair. "Tell me all about it."

Adam's eyes widened. "Tell you about it?"

"Yes. I want to hear the whole romantic story." Aunt Harriet pursed her lips slightly. "I don't have to remind you that a marriage of this nature, so sudden, is just the sort of thing some people might misinterpret. We must make certain there are no misunderstandings. I want to assure everyone that nothing short of a deep, abiding love sparked between the two of you at the very first moment you laid eyes on each other."

Haley gazed at Adam. He seemed as startled as she. Then a little grin pulled at her lips. "Go ahead, Mr. Harrington. Tell her."

His eyes narrowed slightly.

"Well, Mr. Harrington?" Aunt Harriet asked.

Adam straightened and tugged down on his jacket. "It was just as you said, Mrs. Covington. As soon as I saw your niece there was a spark, as you put it. And immediately I felt a—a..."

"A deep and abiding love?" Aunt Harriet prompted.

"Yes. Exactly." Adam gazed across at Haley. "Without a doubt your niece is the most beautiful woman I've ever seen. I knew my life would never be complete without her."

A spasm of warmth waffled through Haley. Adam seemed so sincere that for a moment she'd almost believed him herself.

"And you, Haley?" Aunt Harriet asked. "Were you surprised when you found yourself married to Mr. Harrington?"

The vision of Adam naked, propped up in the bed

at the Madison Hotel, looking at her with those deep green eyes of his flashed through her mind.

"Surprised? Yes, Aunt Harriet, I was surprised."

"And in love?"

Haley pinched the bridge of her nose. She couldn't stand another word of this conversation.

"If you don't mind, Aunt Harriet, Mr. Harrington and I have a few things to discuss."

"Oh, of course. And don't worry. I'll be certain everyone knows the true circumstances of your marriage."

Harriet made a quick exit, closing the double parlor doors behind her.

The room seemed to shrink, the sudden quiet making the walls close around her. Haley finally lifted her gaze to meet Adam's. She wished she could read his thoughts.

She was beautiful. He'd known this morning that she was pretty, though admittedly his first impressions of his new wife had not been formed by the features he noticed now—the delicate arch of her brows, her red lips, the deep blue of her eyes and the sooty lashes fluttering against her porcelain skin. The cream-colored dress she wore, with its leg-of-mutton sleeves, emphasized her tiny waist, yet was not able to minimize the fullness of the breasts he remembered so well. Recollections flooded his mind, causing the rest of him to react. Slow heat coiled deep inside him. Adam shifted away and stepped behind the wing-backed chair.

"Have you thought of a way for us to get out of this, Mr. Harrington?"

"No. But, truthfully, I didn't try."

"Why not?" Anger flushed her skin—or was it his gaze? "Are you suggesting we remain married?"

He shrugged. "Why shouldn't we?"

She planted her hand on her hip. "Has it occurred to you, Mr. Harrington, that we don't love each other?"

He uttered a cynical laugh. "Did you think you'd marry for love?"

Obviously, he hadn't. But she had, despite what everyone had told her; she'd proved it, too.

"Who's to say we won't grow fond of each other?"

"Grow *fond* of each other? Frankly, Mr. Harrington, I had something more in mind."

His innards flamed. He dug his fingers into the back of the chair. God, he wanted this woman. "We are already married. We can't just ignore it."

He sounded so reasonable, Haley wanted to hit him.

He shrugged. "There's no reason why marriage should interfere with anything we're already doing."

Her back stiffened. "Interfere?"

"Yes. I'll continue on with my business, and you'll continue on with whatever it is women do all day. Only you'll do it from my home instead of your aunt's. What's so wrong with that?"

"What's wrong with it, Mr. Harrington, is that it sounds like a business arrangement, instead of a marriage. I won't be a party to this sham."

"We took vows, legally and morally." Surely they had; he'd have felt better if he could remember some of it.

"Legal, moral... Words, Mr. Harrington, nothing more. I want a divorce, and that's final."

Haley whipped around and headed for the door. "Miss Caufield."

The stern tone of his voice stopped her. She turned on him. His face was set in firm lines, tight with controlled anger. But he didn't frighten her. He only caused her own anger to grow.

He stepped from behind the chair. "I won't put my family through the shame of divorce. And you, I'd think, would not want a scandal." His eyes narrowed. "Again."

She felt as if he'd slapped her face. He knew. Somehow he'd learned of her debacle in San Francisco. Damn him...

Whatever had happened to her in San Francisco must have been the scandal of scandals, Adam realized as he watched the color drain from her cheeks. He wished he'd had more time to find out exactly what it was. He'd taken the private detective's word that it wasn't serious. Maybe he'd have Oscar check into it further, just for the hell of it. Regardless, the Harrington name would shield her from whatever infraction of the rules of etiquette she'd committed in the past.

Haley drew in a deep breath. The look of smug superiority on his face rankled her. He was getting his way, and he knew it. But the part she hated most was that he was right, and there was nothing she could do about it.

"I don't seem to have a choice, do I?" Haley's chin went up a notch as she clung to her pride.

Adam pulled his watch from the pocket of his waistcoat and flipped it open. "I have to be home in one hour. I'll send for your things in the morning. Pack what you'll need for tonight."

"Tonight?"

He tucked his watch away and looked across the room at her. "I want my wife in my home tonight."

"You sound as if you intend to install me there, like a piece of furniture. Should I plan to stand stationary, so that you can hang a picture over my head?"

What a spitfire. Adam's belly warmed again, just when he'd gotten himself under control. He couldn't wait to get her home.

A slow smile spread across his face. "I assure you, having you stand stationary is the furthest thing from my mind. I have other plans."

She took a step closer. "I have plans of my own, Mr. Harrington."

"As I said, I don't feel this marriage should unduly interfere with our lives."

"You can count on it." Haley flung the words at him and marched from the room.

Despite her best efforts to exceed her husband's deadline, Haley was packed and ready to leave within the hour. She looked around the bedchamber that had been her home for only a few days and felt a pang of sorrow at leaving. Or was it remorse? Haley pushed the thought away and slumped down on the pale green coverlet.

"I reckon that's about it, Miss Haley."

"Thank you, Chrissy." She watched the maid close the latches on the trunk. Petite, with a head full of auburn curls always escaping her white cap, the young maid had attended her since her arrival at Aunt Harriet's. Haley would miss her bubbly personality, marked so strongly by her Georgia accent.

"Lordy-day, Miss Haley, I hope you don't mind, but I caught me a look at that new husband of yours." Chrissy shook her head appreciatively. "He's as handsome as Texas and as big as a bull on an auction block. Marriage to him is gonna be more fun than Christmas morning."

Haley sprang off the bed. "Thank you, Chrissy. That will be all."

"Oh, sure." She turned, but paused with her hand on the doorknob. "I just want to say, Miss Haley, I'm privileged to have looked after you here. I kinda wish you weren't going. But I hope good things come your way."

Suddenly Chrissy seemed very dear to her. The thought of going to a strange home, knowing no one, loomed, daunting, in her mind.

A soft knock sounded on the door. Chrissy opened it, and Aunt Harriet stepped inside. She gazed at the trunks, then at Haley. "Mr. Harrington is waiting."

"I'm ready. No, wait, Chrissy, don't go yet." The young maid stopped in the doorway, and Haley turned to her aunt. "I'd like to take Chrissy with me, if you don't mind. Just until I get settled."

Aunt Harriet considered the matter for a moment, then nodded. "Yes, that will be fine. Run along, Chrissy, and pack a bag. Mr. Harrington is growing impatient."

Chrissy squeezed her arms together, holding in a squeal of delight, and hurried away.

Slowly, Aunt Harriet closed the door and turned to Haley. She drew in a deep breath and folded her hands together primly. "Haley, there is something we must discuss. Sit down."

"What's wrong?" Haley perched on the edge of the bed.

"Your mother should be speaking with you on the subject, but since she's not here, I feel I must take matters into my own hands." **She** nodded slowly. "I think that's what she would want me to do."

Haley had no idea what her aunt was going on about, but if it delayed her departure, it was fine with her. "Yes, I'm sure Mother would agree."

"It's about relations." She pursed her lips meaningfully. Color rose in her cheeks. "Marital relations."

"Oh. That." Haley didn't know how to tell her aunt that she was about twenty-four hours late with this little talk.

She drew herself up, forcing herself to go on. "You are a well-bred lady. Your mother has seen to that. You're expected to act a certain way, conduct yourself with proper decorum, regardless of the circumstances."

She'd spent hours in etiquette classes, and many more reading from the volumes of books available on the subject. None of them, however, had mentioned the subject that was causing Aunt Harriet so much distress.

"Husbands, well-bred gentlemen like Mr. Harrington, expect their wives to behave as ladies." Aunt Harriet's brows pulled together. "At *all* times."

Haley sat up straighter, and her gaze wandered across the bed. "They do?"

She nodded wisely. "They do."

"But—" Now she was confused. What she could remember of last night, and what she knew of the condition she'd found herself in this morning and

Adam's response to it, she couldn't have behaved in anything near a ladylike manner. But he'd seemed pleased by it. "Are you sure?"

"Yes. You mustn't abase yourself in such a manner. Mr. Harrington is expecting to marry a dignified, properly groomed lady, and that is what you must be."

Certainly, Aunt Harriet would know. Haley's mother wouldn't have entrusted her to her aunt's care had she not been the epitome of gentlewomanhood. After all, it was Aunt Harriet whom her mother had relied on to take Haley out of San Francisco until the Farnsworth scandal died down.

Haley rose from the bed. "All right, Aunt Harriet, if you say so."

"A lady at all times. Remember that." She pointed a stern finger at her. "We mustn't risk falling into disfavor with the Harringtons."

That was hardly Haley's highest priority, but she kept the thought to herself as she followed her aunt out the door.

Adam waited in the foyer, consulting his pocket watch as Haley descended the stairs. He looked mildly annoyed as he tucked it in his waistcoat, and that pleased her.

The servants took her trunks to Adam's carriage, and her aunt made a show of kissing her cheek and wishing her well as Adam assisted her with her cape and ushered her out the door. Chrissy went ahead and climbed up top with the driver.

The spring evening was cool, and the interior of the carriage was dark as they settled into seats facing each other. Light from the street lamps cast dim shadows across the carriage as they made their way through the city. Haley felt Adam's steady, unnerving gaze upon her as she stared at the passing scenery, pretending not to notice him.

At length he drew a silver case from his inside jacket pocket and took out a cigarette. Sulfur filled the carriage as the match sprang to life, illuminating his features before he tossed it out the window. Smoke coiled around his head.

"Isn't there anything you want to ask me?"

She jumped at the sound of his deep voice coming out of the darkness. "Such as?"

He shrugged. "Such as…my family, my home."

"I assume you have both."

He chuckled. "A new house, actually. I designed it myself. Just moved in a few months ago." He took a long drag on the cigarette and blew the smoke over his head. "You'll run the house now, of course…thank goodness."

And didn't it occur to him *that* might interfere with her life?

"Wouldn't it have been easier to simply hire a competent housekeeper?" She waved away the smoke coiling toward her.

"I have a staff, all quite capable. But you'll have a vested interest in the place. That's what I want. Do with it whatever you like. I'm told it needs a woman's touch."

So, there it was. Her first assignment in her new life. It didn't sit well with her, but it was a role she had trained for most of her life.

He stretched out his legs, long, muscular legs that took up most of the space between the seats. Haley scooted sideways to avoid him. Again, she waved away the white, hazy cigarette smoke. "Must you smoke in here? It's a nasty habit, you know."

Adam studied the glowing tip of his cigarette, then tossed it out the window. "Don't you want to know about my family?"

No, she wanted to get out of this carriage and get back to her own family. "Certainly."

"One brother, one sister. Both younger. They live with my father." Adam shifted uncomfortably on the leather seat and gazed out the window for the first time. "You'll meet them...later."

"You didn't ask, so I assume you discovered all you care to know about me."

Adam grinned and gazed at her once more. Oscar routinely worked for Harrington Construction, handling sensitive matters. He was well compensated for his efforts, and so hadn't minded a rush assignment on a Sunday afternoon.

"Only the basics," Adam admitted. Enough to know she made the perfect wife.

"But not everything."

His brows drew together. "No, not everything."

She shot him a scathing look. "Rethinking the marriage, Mr. Harrington?"

"No." He leveled his gaze at her across the dim carriage. "But don't get any ideas. If you're thinking it's a way to get out of this marriage, you're wrong. I won't tolerate a scandal."

Her chin crept higher. "And neither will I, Mr. Harrington."

"Don't you think it would be all right if we were on a first-name basis now, Haley?"

Hearing him say her name sent a chill up her spine. Recollections of him breathing the word against her ear last night floated up in her mind, along with all sorts of feelings she couldn't capture and certainly couldn't name. She looked away. "I suppose... Adam."

He grinned. "There. That wasn't so bad, was it?"

It wasn't bad at all, but she didn't say so.

Haley looked out the window. The streetlights had disappeared, and by the sway of the carriage she could tell they had left the city. Presently, Adam sat forward.

"We're home."

Haley's stomach tingled. Home? Her home was in San Francisco, with her mother and grandparents.

The carriage stopped, and Adam helped her to the ground while the driver and Chrissy handled her trunks.

Haley clutched her handbag as she gazed at the house. Every etched and stained-glass pane was lit in the three-story structure, setting it ablaze against the night sky. A large porch wrapped the entire first floor, and an onion dome and a witch's hat punctuated the roof. Fashionable gingerbread and scrollwork decorated the house, which was blue with white trim, she guessed—it was hard to tell in the dark. Mature trees in the yard and flowers and shrubbery against the house scented the air pleasantly.

The front door opened, and a small, neat man with a carefully trimmed gray mustache stepped outside.

"Good evening, sir," he droned.

Adam ushered her into the foyer. "Bernard, this is my wife."

The butler gave her a stiff bow and a cursory glance. "Good evening, Mrs. Harrington."

"See to her things." Adam pulled his watch from

his pocket and consulted it. He turned to Haley. "If you need anything, ask Bernard."

And with that, he disappeared down the hall.

"Mr. Harrington is particular about his schedule," Bernard offered in a monotone.

"Certainly," she responded, as if that explained being dismissed like yesterday's news.

"Follow me, please."

She climbed the sweeping staircase behind the butler. Chrissy stepped alongside her, her eyes wide. "Well, somebody slap me—will you just look at this place? You've just got to keep me here, Miss Haley. No offense, but your aunt's house smells like camphor all the time."

Haley didn't answer. She wasn't certain she'd stay herself.

Chimes from the parlor's mantel clock echoed up the stairway, causing Adam to stop and pull out his pocket watch. Fast. Two minutes fast. He couldn't abide an inaccurate timepiece. Bernard would have to be told to see to the clock's repair.

Adam started up the stairs again, then froze. No, Bernard would not have to handle it. He had a wife now to see to those things. A little smile pulled at his lips, and he climbed the stairs.

In his room, he poured himself a glass of bourbon from the decanter on his bureau and sipped it, his gaze riveted to the connecting door to his new wife's suite. He'd sat at his desk downstairs for hours, trying to concentrate on the McKettrick plans. He'd set aside that time specifically to work on them, but he hadn't gotten much accomplished; they hadn't interested him to begin with.

Adam crossed the room and passed through the sitting area to stare at Haley's closed bedroom door. No light shone beneath it. No sound emanated from within. Surely she was sleeping by now; she'd looked exhausted when he picked her up—beautiful, but exhausted.

Quietly he opened the door and light from behind him beamed into the room. She was a bulge under the coverlet, curled on her side facing him. He heard the light, even breathing of her slumbers and wished to hell he'd tossed the McKettrick plans aside and come upstairs as he wanted to. But Haley represented an important element of a long-range plan. No need to rush with her; she'd be here forever.

Adam leaned his shoulder against the door casing and took another sip of the bourbon. He wished he could remember actually marrying her, or at least what had led up to his doing such a rash thing. He remembered being quite captivated by the sight of her, and asking friends if anyone knew her. The Olivers' wedding ceremony had been stoic, as expected, and the reception predictable until the old guard left. Things had gotten completely out of hand after that. Vaguely he recalled reciting vows, images of Harry Oliver and Judge Williams fading in and out.

Adam looked down at the bourbon and swirled it in the glass. He must have had more than his usual too much last night.

He might have kept her regardless of her background, after spending last night rolling around in bed with her. That much of the evening he remembered with great clarity. But after Oscar informed him of her social standing, he could hardly believe his luck. No more women throwing their eligible daughters and nieces at him. No more teas, receptions or piano recitals to sit through in his search for an acceptable wife. Now he had her. And without the bother of the endless engagement parties, the wedding preparations, the ceremony and all the silly hoopla that went with it.

And no chance that the bride would change her mind.

Adam tossed back the last of the bourbon and drew in a deep, satisfying breath. He had it all. His new home and his wife. He was on his way. What could possibly go wrong now?

Chapter Four

Haley pushed her hair off her shoulder and peered over the thick coverlet. Morning sunlight sifted through the white gossamer drapes across the room. She blinked and rubbed her eyes. Another strange room.

She fell back on the pillow and lifted her arm. At least this morning she had on her own nightgown.

"Morning, Miss Haley."

She pushed herself up higher on the pillows and saw Chrissy sorting through her clothing at the bureau. "Is it?"

She smiled brightly. "I know you slept like a hound in the shade. Would you just look at this place? I talked to the other servants this morning and learned that Mr. Harrington designed this whole place himself and had it built just like he wanted it. Marble all the way from Italy, paintings from France. Why, those stained-glass windows downstairs came all the way from England. The whole other end of this floor is the nursery. And there's four bathrooms—four! Can you believe it?"

Haley gazed at the lace canopy over her head and

the pristine white eyelet quilt covering her. A delicate blue-and-white print paper covered the walls, and a deep blue carpet stretched the length of the large room. The furniture was cherry. A new scent clung to everything, as if the room had been waiting for her.

"You'd better get up, if you're wanting to have breakfast with your new mister." Chrissy approached the bed. "Everybody says he's as fussy as a hen with one chick when it comes to his schedule. That Bernard fella? He's got the mister's whole day written down on paper—carries it around with him all the time."

"Lovely…" Haley got out of bed and stretched.

"Over there, that's a bathroom." Chrissy pointed across the room. "And the other door is a sitting room. It's got a big ol' desk in it, and chairs softer than goose down. Your mister's bedroom is on the other side." She giggled. "But you probably know that already, huh."

Haley headed toward the bathroom door, ignoring the maid's insinuation. She knew nothing more of her husband than she had when he abandoned her in the foyer with Bernard. If he'd come to her room with romantic notions during the night, she'd slept through them.

Her feet slowed on the thick carpet. What if he had come? She remembered little of the night before, at the Madison. Had he been here last night and she'd forgotten that too? Haley shook her head. Surely, one of these nights she would remain alert and aware of his overtures.

She stepped onto the cold tile of the bathroom floor grinding her fists in her eyes. She yawned loudly and stretched, rising on her toes, reaching toward the ceiling.

"Good morning."

She squealed and spun around. Adam. He stood before the mirror at the sink, his shoulders twisted so that he could look at her. A white towel wrapped his hips; long, muscular legs showed below it, bulging arms above it. Foamy shaving soap covered half his face.

The breath went out of her. "I—I didn't know…"

A shudder passed through Adam, reverberating until it slammed low in his belly. Oh, God, she was beautiful, all tousled and rumpled and disheveled. Just the sight of her made him want to—

He grabbed another towel from the rack by the sink and held it in front of him, trying to look casual. He gestured with the razor in his hand. "The bath joins our rooms."

She glanced through the open door and saw the same rich blue carpet as in her own room, and a heavy cherry four-poster bed made neatly with a blue quilt. Adam's bedroom. She felt her knees weaken.

"I designed it that way. I designed this whole end of the house as a suite for my wife."

He gestured with the razor again, and she saw the dark hair beneath his arm, the curls across his chest, the line that arrowed into the towel below his navel.

"It's…magnificent," she breathed.

"That tub?" He pointed to the claw-footed white porcelain bathtub. "I had it specially made in Philadelphia. It's seven feet long—the only one like it in the country. The whole house is wired for electricity. As soon as Sacramento Electric Power and Light figures how to generate current more than five miles at a stretch, we'll have it."

"Sir, it is now 6:42." Bernard appeared in the doorway to Adam's bedroom. "Oh, begging your pardon, sir."

"I'm going to work," he explained to Haley.

"I see." She thought she might actually explode at any second from the extreme heat boiling inside her.

"I'll be finished here in—"

"Seven minutes, sir," Bernard intoned.

"Seven minutes." Adam gestured toward the tub. "Unless you'd like to go ahead and…"

Her skin tingled, and parts of her felt suddenly heavy. "No, no, I'll wait." She backed toward the door.

He took a step forward, clutching the towel. "I'll have Bernard work out a morning schedule for us."

"Fine." Haley escaped into her own room. As she closed the door, she caught sight of Chrissy craning her neck.

"He's quite the looker, if I can say so, ma'am."

Haley frantically fanned herself with her palms. Why was it so *hot* in here? "Open a window, Chrissy."

"I'm going over to your aunt's house this afternoon to get the rest of your things." Chrissy hoisted the window and gave Haley a look over her shoulder. "Edward is taking me."

"Edward?"

"Mr. Harrington's driver, the one who brought us over here last night." She smiled. "We got to talking and all. He lives right here, got a place all to himself over the carriage house. Well, now, let's get you ready. I know you don't want to keep your new mister waiting.''

But he didn't wait. Haley found Adam in the foyer, talking with Bernard, readying to leave.

"Have the gardener continue on the rose beds."

Bernard nodded sedately as he assisted Adam into his jacket. "Yes, sir."

"And notify the staff that all decisions concerning the house should be directed to Mrs. Harrington." He nodded toward Haley as she joined them.

"Of course, sir." Bernard cleared his throat quietly. "Today is the twelfth, sir."

Adam tugged down on his starched cuffs. "Yes."

"Tomorrow, sir? Master Kip?"

He nodded. "Of course. Take funds from the household account, Bernard, and get him something. Have it sent over."

"Suggestions, sir?" He passed him his leather valise.

"Whatever you think is appropriate. How old is he now?"

"Thirteen, sir."

Haley felt like an intruder eavesdropping on an old ritual. "Somebody's birthday?" she ventured.

Adam and Bernard both looked at her, unaccustomed to the interruption in their routine.

"My brother, Kip. His birthday is tomorrow."

Haley brightened. "Really? Is your family having a party for him?"

Adam paled slightly. "No."

"Well then, let's have a party for him here." Haley warmed to the idea. "We'll have your family—isn't that what you want, Adam?—and…some friends. I'll have the cook bake a large…"

Her words died when Bernard turned away, as if embarrassed for her, and Adam drew in a deep, steadying breath.

"We don't celebrate Kip's birthday," he said quietly.

Haley clasped her hands together. "Why not?"

He eyed her sharply. "Because our mother died when he was born." Adam pulled the pocket watch from his waistcoat. "Two minutes behind schedule," he mumbled, and looked at Haley. "See that the parlor clock is repaired today. If you need anything, consult with Bernard. He is always apprised of my schedule."

And with that, Adam left her standing in the foyer.

"Would madam care for breakfast?"

Bernard had a way of looking at her without seeming to actually see her. "Whatever Mr. Harrington had."

"Including the spirits, madam? Mr. Harrington has a Bloody Mary with his breakfast."

She frowned. "No."

Bernard bowed slightly and silently left the foyer.

Haley exhaled heavily in the still, silent house. Sitting in Adam's monstrous bathtub this morning, she'd mulled her situation over and, try as she might, Haley could think of no good reason to leave, and several good reasons to stay. For one, it would put the Farnsworth incident behind her, and for another, this marriage would appease her mother, and might even bring her back into favor.

Haley walked into the dining room. But, more than anything, marriage to Adam was just the excuse she needed to stay in Sacramento, which was what she'd wanted all along.

Seated alone at the dining room table, listening to the ticking of a clock somewhere in the house, Haley thought that perhaps it wouldn't be so bad. After all, Adam had kept his word.

She certainly hadn't interfered a bit in his life, just as he'd promised.

Leather creaked beneath him as he eased into the chair across from his father's massive desk, and smoke from his cigar coiled in front of him. Adam blew out a gray, hazy cloud. "Trouble this weekend?"

Martin Harrington reared back, puffing. "Damn vandals. I'd like to get my hands around their necks."

"What happened?"

Martin sat forward and dragged his hands through his silvery hair. "Spilled paint, nail kegs overturned. Nuisance stuff again."

Adam shrugged. "Probably just kids."

"It better not be the trade unions. If I find out it is, they'll sure as hell be sorry." Martin clamped the cigar between his teeth. "How are the McKettrick plans coming?"

Adam blew out a heavy breath. "Fine."

"I want to get there first. I don't want McKettrick looking at anybody else's ideas. I want this bid to—"

"I know. I know." Adam sat straighter in the chair. "You know I don't want to do this project."

"It's money in the bank. Big money. I want it."

They'd discussed it a half-dozen times already; it wasn't the first time Adam and his father had disagreed. "We'll get it, Martin."

He hadn't called his father by anything but his first

name for years, since he came to work at the firm. It suited them both.

"We'd better." Martin rose and walked to the window, his footsteps echoing on the hardwood floor. Folding his hands at his back, he stared down at the street below; the view from his private office on the second floor of the Harrington Building allowed him to look down at much of the city, the docks and the Sacramento River. A long moment dragged by. Finally he said, "Well, who is she?"

Adam tapped his cigar in the ashtray on his father's desk, surprised he'd waited this long to bring up the subject. "Don't you mean, *what* is she?"

He threw a look over his shoulder that offered no apology, and turned to stare out the window again.

"Her grandfather is Cyrus Hasting of San Francisco. I think you're familiar with the family. Banking, real estate, shipping, railroads."

He grunted—a sound Adam interrupted as favorable.

"Her mother's a widow, prominent in social circles."

Martin snorted distastefully.

"She's here visiting her aunt on her mother's side, Harriet Covington."

"Damn. Too bad old Ben Covington died already. We could use another supporter in the legislature."

Adam puffed on his cigar again. "All in all, an acceptable pedigree."

"Oscar check her out?"

"He did."

"No skeletons in her closet?"

Adam shifted in the chair. "None I'm concerned about."

A long moment dragged by. "Well, it's about damn time you got yourself a wife. I don't know what the hell you were waiting for. Bring her to dinner tonight."

Dinner at his father's house was definitely not the evening he had planned.

Martin looked over his shoulder. "I want to meet her."

"I don't think it's a good idea. Gwen—"

"I'll handle Gwen." Martin turned. "Bring her over. I want to meet the woman who'll give me my grandchildren."

"Good evening, sir."

Adam passed his valise to Bernard. Maybe it was his imagination, but the house seemed to smell sweeter tonight. He'd certainly been more anxious than usual to get home.

"Where is Haley?"

Bernard inclined his head toward the back of the house. "In the solarium, I believe, sir."

"Is she ready to go?"

"I'm sorry, sir, I don't know."

He frowned. "You told her, didn't you?"

"Yes, sir."

Adam passed through the arched doorway and headed down the hall toward the solarium, but caught sight of Haley in his study. "What are you doing in here?"

She looked up from her seat behind his desk. "Good evening to you, too."

Light from the gas jets bathed her in hues of pink. Adam rubbed his forehead and stopped in front of the desk. "What are you looking at?"

"Don't you know?" She glanced down at the blueprints laid out before her. "You're designing them, aren't you?"

"I just didn't expect to find you in here."

She sat back. "Is this room off-limits?"

"No," he said quickly. "This is your home now. As I said, you can do with it what you choose."

"Good, because I'd like to—"

"Don't tell me." Adam held up his hand. He'd had his fill of settling servant squabbles, looking at household budgets and worrying over windowsills being dusted in the past few months. He hadn't thought having a large house would be such a burden. "Just do whatever you want."

Haley shrugged. "Well, if you're certain."

"I'm certain."

"What are these things, anyway?"

Surprised at her interest, Adam stepped behind the desk. "Plans for some new houses."

She tilted her head one way, then the other. "They are?"

Adam leaned forward and ran his finger down the lines on the paper. "See? These are walls. These represent windows and doors, bedrooms, parlors."

"Oh." She looked up at him. "Aren't they rather small?"

Her breasts swelled the bodice of her gown, noticeable now because he was looking down on her. Adam's breath caught. "No, they're not small at all. They're full and soft and—"

"The houses are full and soft?" Haley stared down at the blueprints again.

"The houses—oh yes, the houses." *God, what had he just said?* "Actually, they are small, but that's what McKettrick wants. He's expanding, building a new factory and he wants to provide housing for his workers.''

"And they want to live in these tiny little houses?"

She looked up at him again, and Adam felt his knees weaken. He turned away quickly and grabbed a decanter from the table beneath the window. "It's a lot of houses, all generally small. That's what McKettrick wants."

"Well...I suppose." Haley folded her hands in her lap.

Adam poured himself a bourbon, and a little smile tugged at his lips. "Did you have a visitor today?"

"Yes, I did. Mr. Havermeyer stopped by this afternoon."

Thoroughly pleased with himself, Adam sipped his drink and turned to her. "Well? What did you pick out?"

The neat little bearded man had shown up in her parlor with a case full of jewelry. Pick whatever she wanted, he'd said. All her husband had insisted upon was that she have a gold wedding band.

"Nothing."

"Nothing?" Adam frowned. "You need a wedding band, Haley. It's hardly proper for you to be seen in public without one. And I told Havermeyer to let you have whatever else you wanted. I expected you to be pleased."

Haley sat back in the deep leather chair. "Had I been married to Mr. Havermeyer, I would have been very pleased to pick out a wedding band with him."

What was wrong with this woman? He'd sent a jeweler displaying exquisite gems and she'd not wanted anything? What kind of nonsense was she talking, anyway?

Adam tossed down his bourbon. "Are you ready to go?"

"Go where?"

His jaw tightened as he gazed down at her. "To my father's for dinner. I sent word to Bernard for you to be ready when I got home."

"I don't take instructions from servants."

She said it so sweetly that a moment passed before the meaning sunk in. Anger coiled in his chest. "This is how I have my household set up. Bernard handles my schedule."

"Then perhaps Bernard will go to dinner with you tonight." She rose sedately and crossed the room. At the door, she stopped and looked back at him. "I am prepared to go...this time."

Stunned, Adam stared as she sashayed from the room.

They didn't speak as they rode to his father's house in town. Adam smoked four cigarettes, one after another, tossing the butts out the window, stealing glances at his new wife across the darkened carriage.

He had a way with women, or so he'd always thought. He could be generous, thoughtful, kind— even charming, when necessary. Women fawned over him. Mothers, aunts and grandmothers pushed their daughters, nieces and granddaughters at him. Certainly they all thought him a handsome catch. The Lord knew, enough eligible young women had been paraded in front of him.

Adam's shoulders squared as he gazed at Haley in the shadows. So what was wrong with this woman?

Nothing he did made any difference. The house he'd given her, the jewelry he'd offered hadn't affected her in the least. Haley seemed totally immune.

Adam grunted and turned away. Not only had he been unable to charm her, he couldn't even get her to *like* him. And if he couldn't get her to like him, how was he ever going to get her into bed with him?

Adam slouched on the leather seat and lit another cigarette.

Darkness had descended over the city when the carriage stopped outside the Harrington's large home. Adam escorted her up the walk and spoke to the butler who greeted them.

There was a settled look about the house, as if it had been there for years, just as it sat tonight. It was immaculate, almost as though no one lived there. It gave Haley an eerie feeling.

Adam introduced her to his family, and they spoke politely before settling around the dining room table. Almost immediately, Adam and his father began discussing business.

At the head of the table, Martin Harrington was a commanding sight, tall and straight despite his silver hair. Beside Adam sat his sister, Gwen, dark-haired and green-eyed, like Adam. With her mother gone, Haley wondered why Gwen wasn't seated at the foot of the table, as the mistress of the house should be. Nearing thirty, there was a hardness about her. Probably a pretty girl once, lines and creases showed in her face. Or was it something else that had aged her? Haley pretended not to notice that Gwen was on her fourth glass of wine.

At Haley's right sat Kip, tomorrow's birthday boy. Small and thin, he pushed his food around his plate.

Though with his light brown hair and blue eyes he hardly resembled his older brother and sister physically, Haley found a connection; he looked as bored as the rest of them.

Finally something in the conversation caught her ear. Haley perked up. "The McKettrick plans? Adam and I were discussing them this evening."

Everything in the room stopped. All eyes riveted her. Adam blanched. Kip and Gwen looked at her as if she'd just suggested they all disrobe and wallow in the rice pudding. Martin looked as though he'd been violated.

Haley's stomach hardened into a knot. She smiled. "The plans looked very interesting. Have you seen them, Mr. Harrington?"

"No, I haven't." He shoved a spoonful of pudding into his mouth and looked away.

"You've seen the plans? The treasured, gold-plated McKettrick plans?" Gwen rolled her eyes with mock envy and lifted her glass. "A reason to celebrate! More wine!"

Martin glared at her.

"Can I be excused?" Kip dropped his napkin beside his plate, as if he'd been waiting for an opportunity to escape.

"Eat." Martin barked.

"I don't like it." Kip slapped his fork down.

Martin pointed at him. "I don't care what you like—"

"It tastes like garbage! I want to be excused!"

"Not until you finish your meal."

Gwen looked across the table at Kip. "Oh, go ahead. You can leave."

Martin's jaw tightened. "The boy needs to eat. He's skinny as a rail."

"Well, you certainly know what's best, don't you, Father?" Sarcasm dripped from each taunting word. Gwen banged her spoon against her glass. "I said, more wine!"

A doorbell chimed through the house. Martin slammed his spoon on the table. "Who the devil is that, coming to call at the dinner hour?"

"I'll see!" Kip ran from the room.

"Come back here!" Martin yelled.

Gwen glared at him defiantly, then laughed.

"Damn it," Martin mumbled. He tossed his napkin on the table and stalked from the room.

Gwen waved her glass. "I guess I'll have to get my own wine." She wobbled away.

Adam stared at his plate. Haley couldn't tell if he was embarrassed or simply accustomed to their behavior.

She pressed her fingers to her lips, as if trying to recall something. "So, what did you tell me was the reason you moved into your own home?"

He looked up at her, and she gave him a smile. Adam relaxed marginally. "It was a tough decision." He tossed his napkin on the table. "Let's get out of here."

He clasped her elbow and they headed for the foyer, but commotion in the front of the house stopped them. The front door stood open, and two men were piling trunks in the foyer.

"Well, I'll be. It's Isabelle." A genuine smile parted Adam's lips, and he went into the parlor.

Haley followed and saw a tall, statuesque woman in traveling clothes standing in thc middle of the room. Gray streaked her black hair. Kip was at her elbow, looking mystified, while Gwen sipped another glass of wine. Shoulders hunched, Martin stood in the corner.

"Where have you been, Aunt Izzy?" Kip asked anxiously. "Lots of great places?"

"You dear, dear boy. The world—I've been around the world, I tell you. Wait until you see what I've brought for you." Isabelle gestured grandly with her hands.

Gwen raised her glass in a toast. "Here's hoping it's liquid."

"Adam!" Isabelle's gaze fell on him, and she threw out her arms. "Come here, you handsome thing."

"I missed you, Aunt Izzy." He crossed the room and reached for her hands.

"Wait!" Isabelle's eyes bulged, and she threw out her palm, stopping him. She pressed her thumb and forefinger to her temple. "Don't move."

Kip's eyes widened. "Are you getting a reading, Aunt Izzy?"

"Oh, for God's sake…" Martin groaned.

She squeezed her eyes shut. "I'm getting something." Isabelle rotated her outstretched palm in a circular motion. "Yes, yes, I'm picking up another aura."

"I know who it is," Kip exclaimed. "Adam got married."

Her eyes popped open. "Married!"

Adam smiled and gave her a hug.

"Martin finally goaded you into it, huh? What did he do, get you drunk and have the ceremony performed while you were unconscious?"

Adam caught Haley's gaze and saw the sharp intake of her breath. His chest tightened.

"Well, where is she? I've got to see this new blood. It's about time you and Amelia tied the knot."

Haley left her station in the doorway, then stopped dead in her tracks. An embarrassed silence fell over the room, and Adam shifted uncomfortably.

He took her arm. "Aunt Izzy, my wife, Haley. Haley, this is my aunt, Isabelle Gladmore."

Isabelle looked confused. "But what happened to—? Never mind, she had a strange aura, anyway." She gave Haley a solid hug. "Welcome to the family, my dear."

Despite her own heart's pounding, Haley liked Isabelle immediately.

"I got the letters you sent, Aunt Izzy." Kip's eyes were bright. "Did you get to go to England?"

She dismissed the idea with a wave of her hand. "England—boring, boring people there. No, dear, I sailed to Hawaii. Beautiful, pristine beaches and simple grass huts. I fell into a deep friendship with Queen Liliuokalani. She gave me my own island."

"Gosh."

"Can't you just go places like other people?" Martin complained. "Proper places?"

Isabelle pinched her lips distastefully. "Winter in New York, spring in Europe, summer in Newport. No, thank you."

"Where else did you go?" Kip asked anxiously.

"To the Far East, where I had an acquaintance with a Japanese baron. I visited Burma, and lived in the harem of an Indian maharaja—as an observer, of course."

"What's a harem?"

"Oh, for God's sake, Isabelle," Martin barked. "Not in front of the boy."

She turned to him. "And I didn't forget my only brother. Wait until you see what I brought you from China."

"Whatever it is, I don't want it."

"I've collected the most fabulous Oriental art." She whirled to face Haley again. "You've got to see them."

"I've got to," she agreed. "You must come over soon."

"You have your own home?" Isabelle eyed Adam. "So, one of you finally escaped this mausoleum. Good for you!"

"All right, all right, go get settled upstairs." Martin waded into the cluster of people in the center of the room, dispersing them. "I guess you're staying here."

"How long will you be with us, Aunt Izzy?" Kip asked.

She patted his slim shoulders. "Until the wind whips in from the east and whispers that it's time to go."

Martin rolled his eyes. "Christ..."

"I'm glad you're here, Aunt Izzy, because—"

"Wait!" She threw out her palm again and touched her temple. "I'm getting something."

Kip's eyes widened. "Another reading, Aunt Izzy?"

The room fell silent while Izzy closed her eyes, communing with some unknown force. After a moment, she shook it off. "Never mind. It was nothing. Stand aside, everyone. I have gifts to unpack."

As they all headed out the door, Isabelle caught

Adam's arm. "I must speak with you," she whispered.

Adam bent down. "What is it, Aunt Izzy?"

"It's your wife. I'm picking up a strange reading from her."

"From Haley?" Adam managed not to laugh at the concern that marked his aunt's brow. She was a dear, and he loved her, mostly because of her eccentric behavior. She'd claimed to get strange readings from Kip and Gwen for years, but it meant nothing.

"Watch over her, Adam."

"I will, Aunt Izzy."

She laid her hand on his arm and looked up solemnly at him. "Something is amiss with that young woman, I just can't pinpoint it. Watch over her closely. A life hangs in the balance."

Chapter Five

It was only a door.

Adam rolled the glass of bourbon between his palms and contemplated the carved wood and the brass knob before him. Not only was it merely a door, it was his door. He'd designed it, he'd selected the wood and hardware, he'd overseen its installation—he'd even paid for the damn thing. He could open it if he wanted to. Right?

Wrong.

He sagged against the door frame of his own bed-chamber, staring across the sitting room at Haley's door. She was in there. A crack of light shone on the carpet. It had been silent in there for a few minutes now. Chrissy had gone, surely. Haley was ready for bed.

His insides flamed; they'd been simmering all evening, even at his father's house. The woman was driving him crazy with want. Whatever she possessed that had caused him to marry her on the spur of the moment still plagued him. And unless he started doing something about it, he'd be in no condition to be seen in public ever again.

Adam set his glass aside and approached the door. He'd planned to give her a few more nights before he paid a call; he'd thought it the decent thing to do, given that they had skipped the courtship and gone straight to the honeymoon. And once he'd formulated a plan, he didn't change it. But now he had to deal with extenuating circumstances, which were pressing against his fly. That made a change in plans more than acceptable.

However, the problem of the closed door remained. Adam rubbed his hands together. He was setting a precedent here. If he knocked, he'd be obligated to knock every time. He didn't like asking permission for anything.

Adam opened the door slowly. "Haley?"

She sat on the bench in front of the vanity, studying her reflection in the large oval mirror as she brushed her hair. Turning, she looked surprised, but not shocked; it pleased him.

Adam gazed around. "All settled?"

She turned back to the mirror and ran the brush through her hair. "Yes, I think so."

"Good, good." He eased across the room and stood behind her where he could view both her back and her front reflected in the mirror. She wore a long-sleeved dressing gown that covered her ankles and buttoned up to a high collar. It was white, and made her look very pure and innocent.

Adam slid his hands in his pockets, jingling his coins. "Sorry about Aunt Izzy."

Haley stroked the brush through her hair and glimpsed his reflection in the mirror. He wore the same dark suit he'd worn to dinner, but his jacket was

off, the sleeves of his white shirt turned back, exposing his hairy wrists; his collar stood open.

"Don't be silly," she said. "I loved your aunt."

"She's a crazy old bird." He chuckled and ran his
hand through his hair. "Her and her...readings."

"I liked her."

"She travels extensively, knows people from one
end of the globe to the other. She's been married three
times that I know of. Martin claims more than that."

"So many husbands?" Haley's gaze met his in the
mirror. "How does she get rid of them all?"

The gleam in her eye unsettled him. "Never
mind."

A moment passed while Adam studied the vanity.
An assortment of delicate porcelain bottles, decanters
and jars sat there, pale blue, pink. There was a green
atomizer with a feather sticking out, and a huge powder puff. A jeweled hand mirror and comb lay to one
side. Mysterious woman things. It smelled good here.
He liked it.

"Who is Amelia?"

Adam's heart rose in his throat. His gaze dropped
to the carpet, and he studied the tips of his shoes for
a moment. "No one special," he finally said, and
lifted his gaze to meet Haley's in the mirror. "She
left a long time ago. Aunt Izzy is a bit out of touch."

Her woman's heart swelled, and Haley knew there
was more, but she let it go. "I thought I'd invite your
sister for luncheon this week."

Startled, he looked in the mirror and met her gaze.
"Gwen? You don't have to do that."

"It's the proper thing to do. That is one of the
reasons I'm here, isn't it? To insure you maintain the
proper social position?"

Yes, it was, but it sounded cold, hearing her say it. He shrugged. "No need to be proper with family."

"I'd like to get to know her better. I had no sisters of my own, you know. She must be only a few years younger than you."

He thought for a moment. "Thirty, this year."

"Married? Children?"

"Gwen never married."

"That's odd. Is she one of those career women?" Scandalous as it was, the idea of a job excited Haley, but she couldn't imagine Martin Harrington allowing it.

Adam frowned distastefully. "No, of course not."

Haley shrugged. "Then I wonder why she never married?"

Adam eased closer, drawn by the delicate scent wafting up from her. "Maybe she just never drank the punch at a wedding."

Haley froze as she felt his hand in the back of her hair. Soft, gentle, exploring fingers. Her body tingled, urging her to lean back, just enough to feel him against her. His hand plowed deeper, and she felt the warmth of his fingertips against her neck. Delightful. She wanted to melt against him. She wanted to encourage him. She wanted to—

Be anything but a lady?

Aunt Harriet flashed in her mind like a demon nightmare, cooling her runaway desire. Well-bred gentlemen like Adam Harrington expected a lady for a wife, she'd said. And Haley must be a lady—at all times.

Surely this was one of those times Aunt Harriet had alluded to. Haley forced herself to lean away from him and lay her hairbrush on the vanity. She didn't dare look in the mirror, fearing she'd see wanton desire in her face. What would Adam think of her if he saw it, too?

She looked embarrassed, but he'd expected she'd need some coaxing. Since she wasn't out of her head with drink this time, it would be different. But did she have to look so damn virginal? It was bad enough she had on that white dressing gown; did she have to lower those long lashes of hers so demurely? And this room. He'd like to kick the decorator in the butt right now for convincing him to do it in powder blue and white. Why hadn't he insisted on red with black lace?

Adam touched her shoulders and squeezed them gently. "Well, good night." He bent and planted a kiss atop her hair, drinking in the sweet smell of her hair.

Haley cleared her throat. "Good night."

He left her room. Next time, he'd bring a punch bowl with him.

They ate breakfast facing each other from opposite ends of the long dining room table, but spoke little. Adam kept his nose buried in *Engineering News* and sipped his usual Bloody Mary. The fact that after he'd come to her bedchamber last night he still considered her a lady brought Haley little comfort.

In the foyer, he and Bernard went through their usual morning ritual, and he left.

"Bernard? Did you get Kip his birthday present?"

"It will be delivered today, madam, the thirteenth."

"What did you get him?"

"A poetry collection bound in Moroccan leather. Quite valuable."

Just what every thirteen-year-old boy wanted. Haley forced a smile. "Thank you, Bernard."

"Yes, madam."

The butler was halfway across the foyer before she realized he was gone. "Bernard? When Edward returns with the carriage, have him wait out front for me, please."

The instructions seemed to throw him. "But, madam—"

"It's all right, Bernard. I'm not part of Mr. Harrington's schedule."

"Yes, madam." He slipped silently from the foyer.

An hour later, Haley made sure to notice the driver when he jumped down from the carriage in front of the house. Chrissy seemed quite taken with the young man, and had even asked to come along today, just to see him again. Not particularly tall, but very muscular, Edward handed Haley up into the carriage with a confident air and a pleasant smile.

The house needed a woman's touch, Adam had said, and Haley agreed. She jotted down a few notes as the carriage made its way into the city—places she wanted to shop, things she intended to purchase. The pieces Adam had furnished the house with were all good, but it needed some things to warm it up. Haley couldn't bear the thought of her home looking as stark and cold as her father-in-law's house.

She made Edward wait in the carriage, refusing his offer to follow along and handle the packages for her. It was just as well, since she found little that pleased her in the shops. Shortly after noon, she had him drive her to I Street and told him to have his own lunch and come back in an hour or so. Reluctantly, he drove away, leaving her alone on the busy street.

Haley craned her neck and looked up at a building that had seen better times. Holding her parasol securely in her hand, she went inside and climbed the stairs to the second floor. Faded gold lettering on the plate-glass door read Sacramento Building Company. She let herself in.

Vague recollections came to her, memories of being here as a child. Her father and uncle staring at charts and diagrams, her and Jay playing in the stairwell and in the alley out back.

The reception area needed a good cleaning now, and decent furniture; books, papers, folders, were littered everywhere.

"Hello? Jay? Are you here?"

A chair scraped the floor in one of the adjoining offices, and her cousin stuck his head out the door. His collar was open and his shirtsleeves were turned back.

"Haley? What on earth—" He waved a half-eaten chicken leg at her.

"I was going to invite you out to lunch, but I see I'm too late."

"Come in." He waved the leg again.

Haley followed him into his office, a small, cluttered room with a view of the alley. "I have such fond memories of coming here as a child."

"Does it look the same as you remember?"

"Yes." Only now it needed a good dusting and a coat of paint.

"Mr. Terwiliger still works here."

"Dear old Mr. Terwiliger? He used to keep candy in his desk drawer and sneak it to us. Remember? I'm surprised he's still alive—he must have been eighty back then."

Jay nodded. "He's cut back. Comes in every so often now to keep the books. Lord knows what's happening to my money. He came in last week with his trousers on backwards. But I haven't got the heart to fire him."

Jay pushed a plate of chicken across the desk at her. "Help me eat this, will you? Elizabeth brought it by. You just missed her. She must have cooked two birds. I think she's trying to fatten me up, hoping to catch me more easily."

Haley settled into the threadbare chair across the desk. "Running from your matrimonial fate?"

"As fast as I can." Jay sat down and took a plate, fork and knife from the bottom drawer of his desk and passed it to her. "There's potato salad here, fruit, and an entire pecan pie. Good God, I don't know what the woman's thinking."

Haley had met Elizabeth when she first arrived in Sacramento a little over a week ago, now. Jay Caufield and Elizabeth Denning did not belong on the same social level as Aunt Harriet, but she'd allowed Haley to have them over to dinner once, just to please Haley. Elizabeth was a wonderful young woman, totally captivated with Jay.

Haley pulled off her gloves. "She's crazy about you."

"Just what I need," Jay grumbled. "A crazy woman chasing after me."

Haley frowned at her cousin as she helped herself to some of Elizabeth's lunch.

"So," Jay asked, "what brings you by?"

"Several things." She tasted the chicken. "First of all, do you remember your thirteenth birthday?"

His brows drew together as he chewed. "Very clearly."

"What did you want most?"

"At thirteen, the thing I wanted most was to look up Mary Joe Patterson's dress."

"Jay!"

"What can I say? She was a goddess." He sighed. "Still is, too. I see her occasionally, and still wonder what's up there."

Haley fanned herself with her napkin. "Honestly, Jay, that's awful."

"Don't act so innocent. You have a husband now. You know we're all animals—and happy to be that way, too."

Haley shifted in her chair. If they were all animals and happy that way, why did they want wives who were perfect ladies *all* the time?

"Well, in lieu of a skirt to look up, what would a thirteen-year-old boy like for his birthday?"

"Something to keep his mind off looking up skirts."

"You're no help." Haley wiped her fingers. "Jay, we have to talk. You can't close Sacramento Building."

He sighed heavily. "It wasn't a decision I made lightly, Haley. But facts are facts. I simply don't have the capital to keep going."

"Then get more jobs."

"You need money to get jobs. Where do you think the materials, supplies and payroll come from? Thin air?" He waved the chicken leg. "There is a job pending I'd love to sink my teeth into. Johnny McKettrick wants housing built for the workers at his new factory."

"McKettrick?" Haley sat straighter. "Adam is working on those plans."

"I'm sure he is. And he'll get it, too."

"It's big, isn't it? A lot of prestige. Right?"

"You bet."

Haley sat forward. "Why don't we get that job?"

His eyes rounded. *"We?"*

She ignored his sarcasm. "Yes. You could do the plans as well as anyone. And if you got the job the Sacramento Building Company would be recognized as a strong, viable business. Everyone would come to us for work."

Slowly Jay wiped his mouth and sank back into his chair. "You know, it just might work. Truth is, the company is not exactly penniless, but I was saving what cash I have to start over somewhere else. If I budget right, maybe I could squeak by on this job."

"Jay, we have to try. After our fathers worked so hard to start this business. After all they sacrificed for it."

Jay sat back, rubbing his chin and thinking.

Haley held her breath. "I'll help you."

Finally he sat forward. "What the heck? It's only the very last cent I have in the world. I'll give it a try."

"Oh, Jay. Our fathers will be so proud of us." She reached across the desk and clasped his hands.

"People will sit up and take notice. The Mc-Kettrick job will be a turning point for the Sacramento Building Company. My future."

"Our future."

Jay chuckled and bit into another chicken leg. "As if you need the income from Sacramento Building."

"It's part my company, too, Jay. Our fathers

founded it together." She pushed her plate away. "I told you, I came to Sacramento to join you in the company."

"You got your architectural degree between tea parties?"

"I can help," she insisted, and looked around the office. "Haven't I already helped? I kept you from closing the company, didn't I? I want to see Sacramento Building succeed."

"Maybe it could, were it not for the likes of one Harrington Construction. But truthfully, Haley, I don't know why they're spending their time on jobs like McKettrick's. Harrington's is capable of much more. If I had their resources, I wouldn't be wasting my talents on tired, boring projects like McKettrick's."

"What would you do?"

He pointed toward the ceiling. "Straight up. That's the future of building."

"You mean those skyscrapers being built back east?"

"Exactly. Eventually we'll run out of room on the ground. There's nowhere to go but up." Jay shrugged. "But that's Martin Harrington for you."

"What does that mean?"

"Old man. Old ideas. If he wasn't such a pompous old so-and-so, he'd step aside and let the company grow into the next century, instead of wasting time with traditional projects like McKettrick's."

Haley dabbed at her mouth with a napkin. "Speaking of traditional projects, I'm here to arrange for some work. I need a window seat and some shelves built."

Jay swallowed hard. "What? You want Sacramento Building to go onto Harrington property and do a job?''

She batted her lashes. "I'm in charge of the Harrington household now."

He laughed. "Your husband is going to go straight through the roof when he finds out."

Haley shrugged. "I tried to discuss it with him, but he says to handle it myself. So I am."

"All right, if you're sure."

"I want the work done right away. Can you come by soon?"

"Sure." Jay sat back and patted his belly. "Sometime when your husband isn't there."

"I'll check Bernard's schedule." Haley rose and pulled on her gloves. "I'm off. I have a birthday present to buy. And get to work on the McKettrick plans. We haven't a moment to lose."

"Yes, boss. I'll get right on it...while you're off shopping." Jay turned to his desk. "If you see Elizabeth in town, tell her I've gone out and you don't know where."

"Jay, you're awful."

"I know."

She left him hunched over his desk, crunching an apple. Edward waited by the carriage when she got to the street looking as though he'd been there for a while. Haley made two stops in town before instructing him to take her to the senior Harrington's house.

Their aging butler greeted her. "Is anyone home?"

A stillness hung over the house. Somewhere, a clock ticked off the minutes; the sound echoed in the silence.

"Mrs. Gladmore is out. Miss Gwen is—" he cleared his throat "—indisposed."

ened in here?'' He stopped when he saw Haley,
ed at the window, then at Kip.

aley forced a smile and a silly little laugh. ''I
ss my pitch went a little wild. Sorry.''

Martin's brows drew together.

''I'll see that the window is repaired right away.
rry about the mess.''

He grunted, then riveted Kip with his gaze.

''I'm keeping it!'' Kip hugged the mitt to his chest.
'Haley gave it to me. I'm not giving it back—no
matter what!'' He bolted from the room.

''Get back here!'' Martin shouted after him, but he
didn't stop.

A long moment dragged and then Martin turned
and glared at Haley. ''Never mind about the window.
I'll take care of it.'' With that, he stalked from the
room.

Haley left, feeling she'd bungled Kip's birthday
badly. Now he would probably be afraid to speak to
her again, and she couldn't really blame him.

In the foyer, she took her parasol from the umbrella
stand, but stopped when she heard footsteps on the
stairs. Turning, she saw Gwen.

She looked horrible. She wore a faded dressing
gown and her hair hung uncombed around her shoulders. Wrinkles Haley hadn't noticed before cut deep
into her face. Her eyes were red, as if she'd been
sobbing for hours.

Haley pressed herself against the wall, feeling like
an intruder witnessing something that was none of her
business. Today was Kip's birthday, the day Gwen's
mother had died. Gwen must have been a young girl
at the time, probably fifteen or sixteen. Haley's heart
ached as she thought of her own mother; despite their

Aunt Izzy being out on the town already didn't
surprise Haley. But she wondered about Gwen, and
why she'd be indisposed at this hour of the afternoon.

''I brought these by for Kip.'' Haley held out the
two packages she'd brought in with her. ''Would you
see he gets them?''

''Master Kip is home. He's just arrived from
school.''

''So early in the day?''

''Classes dismissed early today, ma'am. Something
to do with a faculty meeting, I believe he said.''

Haley followed the butler to the sitting room off
the parlor. Rustling trees outside muted the light in
the already dim room. Kip sat in the window seat, his
knees drawn up to his chest, staring outside. He wore
gray knee trousers with suspenders and a white shirt;
a navy blazer with the Lamont Academy crest on the
pocket lay on the floor. Around him on the seat were
two ripped-open packages—a shirt and the books
Bernard had selected—both pushed aside.

Kip turned his head to look at her. His face was
almost unreadable, but she saw a hint of sadness behind those big blue eyes of his, eyes so different from
Adam's and Gwen's. And then she felt sad, too, for
the child opening his presents alone in the big, empty
house on his birthday.

Haley managed a smile. ''Having a good birthday?''

He looked out the window again. ''Sure. Like always.''

''Thirteen today, I understand. Thirteen on the thirteenth. That makes it a special birthday.''

Kip lifted his slim shoulders, but didn't answer.

''Can you stand more excitement?''

He uttered a short, bitter laugh. "Yeah. I think so."

Kip kicked the books and shirt onto the floor, and Haley sat down, holding the two packages on her lap. He sat cross-legged, facing her.

"This one you'd better share with me." Haley passed him the package and wagged her finger at him. "I was tempted to keep it for myself."

He looked mildly interested as he pulled loose the string and opened the bakery box, then smiled. "Cookies. What kinds?"

"All kinds." She'd wanted to buy him a real birthday cake, but settled for decorated cookies instead.

Kip's shoulders sagged. "I'm not supposed to eat anything good before supper. Father says so."

Haley glanced around the room, then leaned closer and whispered, "Then we'd better eat them quickly, before anyone catches us."

Kip's face lit up, and they shared a conspiratorial grin before digging into the sweets.

"What's that?" Kip asked around a mouthful of cookie.

She passed him the box wrapped in blue-and-silver paper. "I never had a brother, so I wasn't sure what to get. But I did consult with an expert." Despite Jay's recollections of his designs on Mary Joe Patterson at age thirteen, he had given her an idea of what to buy for the boy.

Kip popped another cookie in his mouth and ripped open the gift. His eyes lit up as he pulled a baseball and a leather mitt from the tissue paper. "Wow..."

"Do you like it?" Haley asked, though obviously he was thrilled.

"Yeah." Kip pulled on the glove and tossed the ball into it. "I never had a real one o... Father wouldn't let me have one."

"Oh? Why?"

Kip bounded off the window seat a... ball straight up. It tagged the ceiling; down as he caught it in the glove.

Haley rose. "Maybe you'd better go that."

"No, this is fun." He threw the ball barely missing the crystal light fixture in th...

"I really think you should—"

"Catch!"

"No!" She threw up both hands. "Don't—

The ball whizzed past her and crashed throu... glass window. Both their mouths flew open. K... to Haley's side, and they stared at the shattered... dow and the shards of glass glistening in the sunl...

The color drained from Kip's face. "Fath... gonna kill me."

Haley gulped hard. "No, we'll get it fixed befo... he gets home. He'll—"

"He's home now."

"What?" A childish knot of panic coiled in Haley's stomach as she recalled Martin Harrington's scowling face at the dinner table. She forced it down and drew in a deep breath. "Don't worry—"

"What the devil's going on?"

From somewhere in the back of the house, Martin bellowed, and his heavy footsteps sounded in the hallway.

Kip pulled off the mitt, his jaw set. "He won't make me give it back—he won't!"

Martin stomped into the room. "What the devil

differences, she didn't know what she'd do without her. And here was Gwen, whose mother had been taken from her at such a young age. Apparently it still weighed heavily on her mind, and the family's, too, since Kip's birthday wasn't celebrated.

At the bottom of the staircase, Gwen pulled a silver flask from her pocket and drank heavily. A bit unsteadily, she crossed the foyer and disappeared down the hall.

A chill ran down Haley's back. She hurried outside.

Edward opened the door to the carriage as she approached, and she was glad to be leaving the big, silent house, with its lonely little boy and heartbroken woman. Small wonder Adam had moved out.

Haley was turning to climb inside when a movement at the second-story window caught her eye. She saw Kip. He waved the mitt at her and smiled faintly, then disappeared. Her spirits lifted, and she climbed into the carriage.

"I guess we'd better get home, Edward. I know you can't be late picking up Mr. Harrington."

He closed the door. "No, ma'am. Five o'clock. Not a minute later."

She had Edward drive her straight home. Bernard met her in the foyer and took the few items she'd purchased in town.

"Has Cook begun dinner preparations?" Haley asked as she unpinned her hat.

"Yes, madam. Service will be promptly at seven, unless madam would care to eat sooner."

"And change Adam's schedule?"

"Mr. Harrington has departed on business. He is expected home in ten days."

The breath went out of her. "Ten days? He won't be home for ten days?"

"No, madam."

"Why wasn't I informed?"

"Begging your pardon, madam, but it was on Mr. Harrington's schedule."

"Thank you, Bernard," Haley said crisply.

"This arrived for madam." He retrieved a small white box from the table in the foyer and passed it to her. "From Mr. Harrington."

She headed up the stairs. So, Adam wasn't coming home tonight, or for the next ten nights. He'd left for more than a week, and he hadn't told her. A sharp pain stabbed her chest.

In her bedchamber, Haley opened the box. A plain gold wedding band nestled in the black velvet. Annoyed, she tossed it on the vanity.

The next morning, Haley summoned Bernard to the dining room as she sat alone at the long table. "Tell Edward to bring the carriage around. And don't expect me for supper this evening. I won't be back."

Chapter Six

Aunt Harriet had been quite pleased to see Haley in her parlor with the news that she wanted to spend the week getting to know the ladies of Sacramento. Thrilled with this newfound connection to the prestigious Harrington family, she sponsored Haley at club meetings and introduced her to everyone at luncheons and dinners.

By the end of the week, Haley found herself a member of several organizations, including the Current Events Club, and had been surprised to see Adam's aunt, Isabelle Gladmore, addressing the ladies on the living habits of the Indian maharaja she'd visited on her travels. The ladies of Sacramento had left the room stunned and pale, but remained cordial and friendly to Isabelle, as polite society demanded.

Haley had managed to fill every possible moment of every day. Now she was seated in Aunt Harriet's sitting room again as a polite round of applause sounded from the Sacramento Ladies Music Club as the final selection concluded. Dresses rustled and women murmured their appreciation as the gathering made its way into Harriet's dining room for refreshments.

Haley hung back until Elizabeth Denning had folded her sheet music and spoken to the musicians in her ensemble.

"Jay never mentioned you were so accomplished," Haley told her as they stood beside the piano. She was a soft-spoken young woman with dark hair and beautiful brown eyes.

Elizabeth smiled modestly. "I'm glad you enjoyed it. I appreciate your aunt asking us to play for the club. Have you joined?"

"Yes, I have."

With Adam away, she'd shopped, visited, dined— anything to stay out of the big, empty house that was now her home. She'd enjoyed her activities and her new friends, but at night, lying alone in bed, looking at the gold band on her finger, she found herself wondering where her husband was and what he was doing; she'd heard nothing from him since he left.

They eased their way toward the dining room. "I'd like to have you and Jay over for supper."

"Jay and I aren't seeing each other anymore." Elizabeth lowered her lashes. "It was Jay's idea. He felt we were limiting ourselves. He said we should see other people for a while."

"How do you feel about it?"

Elizabeth smiled. "I'm in love with your cousin. Seeing other men for a day, a week or a year won't change how I feel."

Haley fumed silently. She intended to give Jay a big piece of her mind when she saw him again. "I'm certain he'll come to his senses. You two are perfect together."

Elizabeth gave her a hopeful smile as they moved around the table.

After selecting a few items from Aunt Harriet's buffet and declining the punch—she never intended to drink punch again—Haley chatted with the other women. Being married to a Harrington and having come from the Hasting family of San Francisco, Haley found herself readily accepted by the women in Sacramento's society. Everyone was eager to make her welcome in their ranks.

"We're so pleased to have you with us," Mildred Price said. "I remember years ago, when your mother lived here in the city. Such a gracious hostess."

"Oh, she was. She certainly was." Freda Roland sipped her punch and bobbed her head. "I'd expected we'd have another former member here today. Amelia Archer. I heard she was—"

Mildred Price elbowed Freda, nearly upsetting her punch. "What a lovely dress you're wearing." She smiled broadly at Haley. "Was it done in San Francisco?"

Haley touched the skirt of her lavender dress; the significance of the name Amelia Archer did not elude her. She managed a smile. "Yes, it was."

Freda Roland's eyes bulged; she had plainly realized her misstep. "Oh, dear... Oh, dear."

"Evelyn Wyndham?" Mildred asked, determined to keep the conversation moving.

The Wyndham designs were well-known in San Francisco and beyond. "Actually, this one was done by Miss Wyndham's apprentice, Constance Porter."

Both women raised their eyebrows into their wrinkling foreheads appreciatively.

"When Miss Porter is ready to move out of the

great Wyndham shadow, have her come to Sacramento," Mildred said. "It will be well worth her while."

Freda smiled proudly. "If she were here now, I'd pay her a call myself. Howard is taking me back east for an extended trip."

"No!" Mildred declared. "How did you ever get your husband to leave his business for that long?"

Haley's ears perked up. "Yes, how?"

Freda smiled triumphantly. "He's leaving the business to his nephew. I suppose the boy can't do much damage in a few months' time. Just in case, if you need lumber, order now."

The ladies laughed, and Freda went on elaborating about the dresses she'd order, the packing, closing down the house.

After most of the ladies left, Haley stayed behind for a meeting of the special projects committee of the Ladies for the Beautification of Sacramento Club. Harriet had gotten her a coveted spot on the committee vacated by a lady who had just left town on the heels of a breathtaking scandal. Seated in the parlor, they sipped tea and finalized plans for the upcoming spring gala, the club's annual fund-raising event, dinner and dancing at the Madison Hotel.

Finally, with nothing left to do, Haley went home. Upstairs in her room, she pushed open the window and let the afternoon breeze in. A moment later, Chrissy joined her.

"There's a young man downstairs to see you."

"Who?" She wasn't expecting anyone.

"The mister's little brother."

He must have come straight from school, since the afternoon was early. Haley wondered if anyone at home would worry when he didn't arrive as expected, or if anyone would even notice.

"He's a sad-looking little thing, that's for sure." Chrissy busied herself cleaning the already spotless room. "Too bad about his mother, and all."

"How do you know about his mother?"

"Them servants downstairs chatter like a bunch of caged magpies in a windstorm. Some of them came from old Mr. Harrington's house. And all of them got their own theories."

"Theories on what? She died in childbirth. I don't—"

"Huh-uh." Chrissy looked up from the vanity. "She burned up."

"What?" Haley sank onto the bed.

"Died in a fire just after bringing that little fella into the world." Chrissy nodded sadly. "'Course, he wasn't born here in town—that's what everybody's wondering about. Seems his mama was off somewhere else when he came. Some kinda hotel fire, I guess."

"Oh, dear..."

"I reckon that's why don't nobody do nothing at his birthday, 'cause it's just a bad memory and all. Leastwise, that's what everybody downstairs says."

No wonder Kip's birthday was ignored. No wonder Gwen had been so distraught the day she saw her on the stairs. No wonder she had never married. Sadness clutched Haley's heart. "Does Kip know? Does he know how his mother died?"

Chrissy shrugged. "I don't know, since nobody is allowed to talk about it. Anyway, that's what I heard. Either way, it don't matter much. She died 'cause of him."

Haley drew in a deep breath, and suddenly she wanted very much to be with Kip. She found him downstairs in the sitting room, dressed in his school uniform, staring out the window. He turned when she walked in.

"What's all this junk for?"

She joined him at the window and gazed out onto the rear lawn. The landscaping wasn't completed yet, but set in the yard was a pile of lumber and the wooden framework of a small house. It looked as though it hadn't been touched in a while.

"I don't know."

He looked back at her. "Ask Adam. He knows. Adam knows everything."

If he was home where he belonged, she would. "I'll do that, when he returns."

"Where'd he go?"

"Away on business. He'll be back tomorrow." Or so Bernard's schedule indicated.

Kip left the window and wandered through the room, touching things. Finally he looked up at Haley. "I got the ball back. I found it under the bushes beside the fence."

"Your father didn't take it away from you, did he?"

"I snuck out and got it when he wasn't looking. Can I eat supper here?"

"Certainly. But aren't they expecting you at home?"

He shook his head. "I want to go outside and look at that stuff in the yard."

"I'll go out with you."

"It's probably something Adam's building. He

used to build a lot of stuff himself. He let me come over when he was building this house. I helped him.''

Haley smiled. ''Let's go have a look.''

On the way out, she instructed Bernard to send word to the Harrington home that Kip was with her and would dine there this evening. She wondered if he always wandered wherever he wanted to go, if no one watched over him.

Neither of them could do more than speculate on what Adam was building in the backyard, so they ate dinner together early and played checkers in the sitting room. Kip said he'd walk home, but Haley had Edward drive him. When he left, she admitted to herself that she'd enjoyed his visit. She climbed the steps to her room, thinking how glad she was that this was her last night alone in the house. Tomorrow, Adam would be home. Though she hadn't wanted a husband, she'd been lonely. Lonely for Adam. A warmth flashed through her. Maybe Adam had been lonely, too, lonely for her.

Tomorrow night, maybe he'd show it.

''I brought lunch for you, since no one else is going to.'' Haley dropped the sack on Jay's desk.

He pushed it off the blueprints spread out in front of him. ''How gracious of you.''

She frowned at him. ''What is wrong with you? Have you lost your mind completely?''

Jay sat back and pulled on his suspenders. ''I get the feeling, cousin, that you have something on your mind.''

''I most certainly do.'' Haley plopped into the chair across the desk from him.

''If it's about Elizabeth, I don't want to hear it.''

"Well, you're going to." Haley drew in a deep breath. "How could you let her go like that? She's perfect for you."

"I was smothering, choking—I couldn't breathe. Besides, all I suggested to her was that we see other people for a while. I didn't say I never wanted to see her again."

Haley's jaw tightened. "So, all this posturing was to allow you to see someone else. Is that it?"

"No." Jay opened the sack and looked inside. "I'm not seeing anyone at all. I just wanted to distance myself from Elizabeth for a while."

"And are you breathing better without her?"

"I certainly am." He dumped the contents of the sack—ham, cheese and an apple—on the desk and frowned distastefully. "But apparently I'm not eating better."

"Serves you right," Haley told him.

Jay broke off a chunk of cheese. "What are you doing in town today?"

"Adam's coming home. I thought I would stop by the office and surprise him."

"So anxious to get home to his new bride that he stopped by the office first? Nice. Very nice."

She'd tried not to be hurt when she read his intentions on Bernard's schedule. Haley changed the subject. "How are you coming on the McKettrick plans?"

"Zipping right along. I met with Johnny McKettrick and found out exactly what he wants."

"Any other big jobs on the horizon?"

Jay pushed his lunch aside. "You're not still thinking of working here with me, are you?"

She sat up straighter. "Yes."

"Fine." He slid the blueprints toward her. "Finish these for me, will you? I'd like the afternoon off."

"Make fun if you want. But I happen to know something that will greatly impact the construction business in the near future that no one else knows."

He gave her an indulgent smile. "And what might that be?"

"Howard Roland is traveling back east for an extended trip with his wife. He's turning his lumber business over to his nephew while he's gone."

Jay sat bolt upright. "His nephew? He's leaving his business to that buffoon? The last time Roland left, orders were mixed up for months. It was a disaster. I've got to get my orders in now—today!"

Haley sat back and smiled smugly as Jay rifled his desk drawers, tossing papers, pitching ledger books. She reached across the desk and touched his arm. "Well?"

"All right." He sighed bitterly. "You knew something no one else knew. There, I've said it. Happy now?"

"Almost. Go on."

He glared at her, then shrugged helplessly. "And you have something to contribute to the business. Thank you."

"That's better." Haley rose. "Well, I'm off—"

"No!" Jay leaped from his chair. "Don't tell Harrington about this. Roland will fill his orders first, and mine will get left for that idiot nephew of his to muck up."

"But, Jay—"

"Please, Haley. Just give me a day or two. That's all I need. Please."

"Well..."

"I'm your own flesh and blood, Haley. I'm your business partner. And who is Harrington? A husband who cares more about seeing his office than his wife."

She couldn't argue with that. "I'll tell Adam later."

"Thank you." Jay circled the desk and took her arm. "Now, promise me you'll let me know if you hear anything else. I had no idea women talked about such things."

A soft knock sounded on the door, and Elizabeth stepped into the room. She smiled and lowered her lashes demurely. "Hello, Haley. Hello, Jay. I hope I'm not interrupting anything."

"Good to see you." Haley sensed Jay growing tense.

"I won't take a moment of your time, Jay. I know how busy you are." Her words were soft and gentle, almost whispered. "I just wanted to let you know that I'm going out for dinner this evening with Phillip Mayfield."

Jay's eyes widened. "You're—what?"

"Since we're seeing other people now, I didn't want you to walk in and find us together and be surprised." Elizabeth lowered her lashes. "I thought it courteous to tell you."

Jay shifted and cleared his throat. "Well, I— But—" He cleared his throat again and stood straighter. "Thank you for coming by, Elizabeth. It was very courteous of you."

"Well, goodbye."

"Wait," Haley said. "I'll go with you."

She flung Jay a taunting look and left with Elizabeth.

"I have to admit I didn't think you'd see anyone but Jay. Do you really want to go out with Phillip Mayfield?" Haley asked as they descended the steps together.

"No, not at all."

"Then why are you going? Just to make Jay jealous?"

Elizabeth shook her head. "You know men, Haley. You have a husband. You know they only want what they can't have."

Elizabeth smiled sweetly and left Haley standing alone on the street.

A half hour later, Haley opened the door to the reception area of Harrington Construction. Leather chairs and walnut tables sat to one side of the large room; the receptionist's desk was painfully neat and orderly, but unoccupied at the moment. A heavy silence hung over the entire building.

Across the room, Adam's name was stenciled in gold letters on a plate-glass door. Haley felt a twinge of pride at seeing her husband's name. Her father-in-law's office was similarly marked, and his door stood open a crack. She heard voices inside. Without Mr. Harrington's secretary to announce her, Haley took matters into her own hands. She peeped into the office. Her heart surged when she saw Adam sitting in front of his father's desk, facing Martin. She was about to walk inside when she heard her own name mentioned. Unable to stop herself, Haley leaned closer.

"Has she done anything improper?" Adam asked.

Martin sat forward in his chair and tapped his cigar in the ashtray. "No. Not improper, exactly."

"Are there rumors, gossip?" Adam sounded considerably less concerned over the matter than his father.

"Talk. Only talk."

Adam puffed on his cigar, sending a gray cloud across the desk. "If it's only talk, I don't see why you're making so much of it."

The leather chair creaked as Martin sat straighter. "That wife of yours is all over town these days, meeting people, having lunches and dinners. Every time I turn around, somebody is telling me they saw her. It's not decent, Adam. You ought to have better control over your wife than that."

Adam dragged his fingers through his hair. "It's probably just those ladies'-clubs luncheons and receptions. They're always on some fund-raising crusade."

"Well, I don't like it. A man's wife belongs at home. She needs a firm hand, I tell you."

"I've been away a long time, Martin. She was probably just lonely."

"Lonely?" Martin snorted distastefully. "If she's lonely, there's a hell of a better way to handle it than having your wife parading all over town."

Adam chewed on his cigar, but didn't respond.

"Hell, get her pregnant. You need a son. Don't tell me you haven't considered it."

"That is the next item on my list," he admitted.

Martin squinted across the desk. "What are you waiting for? She's agreeable enough, isn't she?"

Adam shifted in his chair.

"Well?" Martin asked, prompting him. "Is she?"

"I will handle my wife in my own way." Adam got to his feet.

"Good." Martin sat back in his chair and rapped

his knuckles on the desk. "There'll be no more talk of her gallivanting all over town. Keep her at home where she belongs. Just get her pregnant. And make it quick. I want a grandson. Soon."

Adam glared down at him through the haze of their cigar smoke. "I said, I'll take care of my wife myself."

Haley's blood boiled. How dare these two men discuss her so crudely! And how dare the two of them decide her fate!

But her anger turned to hurt when she heard them turn the conversation to the business of Harrington Construction, dismissing her as another problem dealt with.

Haley spun away from the door and left the office fighting back tears. By the time she reached the street, her head ached.

So, having a son was the next item on Adam's list. As if she and the child she would produce were pieces of a jigsaw puzzle he was assembling.

Haley pushed her way through the crowded sidewalk. No, she wouldn't live Adam's way. She wouldn't let herself be used. And to think she'd actually been looking forward to his coming home tonight.

Haley steeled her feelings. Somehow, she would find a way to keep Adam from her bedroom.

"Brandy?"

Surprised, Adam slid his hands into his pockets as he stepped into the parlor. He'd seen the disapproving looks Haley gave him when he drank his Bloody Marys at breakfast and had a bourbon or two in the evenings. So it surprised him now that she was offering him a drink herself.

"Sure."

Haley smiled and poured from the heavy crystal decanter. "I asked Cook to make all your favorites for supper, to welcome you home. I hope it was good."

"Oh, yes." Adam's insides flamed. The meal had been beyond good, but the food on his plate had lent little to his enjoyment. It had been his wife that made the meal so enticing. She wore a blue gown that allowed him to feast his eyes on her soft, round breasts, peeking over her bodice. She'd been full of conversation, too, so enthralled in her stories that her breasts had strained the fabric of her clothing. And, in turn, he'd done the same.

Haley passed him the glass. "Did you accomplish what you'd set out to accomplish on your trip?"

Their fingers brushed as he accepted the drink, and his insides heated up. "Yes, I think so."

"Good." She smiled demurely and lowered her lashes. "Are you very tired?"

Was it his imagination, or did he detect some lustful undertones in her voice, her gaze? Could she want him as badly as he wanted her? Adam sipped his bourbon. Impossible.

"No, I'm not tired at all," he said, then hurriedly added, "But that's not to say I couldn't go to bed early."

A little blush crossed her cheeks, and desire flamed deep within him. He'd thought of nothing but Haley while he was away. Tonight, he'd have her again. He'd made that decision days ago, sitting alone in his bedroom at his Quaker host's house, night after night.

Haley lowered herself onto the settee and gestured to the chair across the coffee table from her. "There's a matter I'd like to discuss with you. A...delicate matter. If it's agreeable with you."

Agreeable. Wasn't that the word his father had used this afternoon? While he resented the hell out of Martin's interference with his marriage, he'd been enthralled by the suggestion he'd made.

Haley pregnant. Her small, beautiful body swollen with child. His child. He'd hardly been able to sit still at his desk all afternoon for thinking about it.

And, yes, Haley was most agreeable. So much so, he wasn't confident he could wait until a respectable hour to take her upstairs. She was so innocent and inexperienced, he didn't want to frighten her.

Adam smiled, trying to take his mind off the ever-increasing demands of his body, and sat down in the chair.

"What did you need to discuss?" he asked, somewhat amused by the serious look on her pretty little face.

Haley folded her hands primly in her lap and batted her lashes at him. "I want to have a baby."

Chapter Seven

"You want to...what?"

"I want to have a baby."

Adam's insides flamed. He'd been panting after her all evening, wondering how he'd delicately get her into his bed tonight, and here she was asking for just that. He could hardly believe his luck.

"I will, of course, need your cooperation."

The fire burning in his belly cooled down a notch, and he suddenly felt uncomfortable under Haley's businesslike gaze. "I am aware of the procedure."

"And I can count on your full support until I've achieved my goal? I think you'll agree it wouldn't be quite fair for you to quit or become unavailable."

Adam shifted uncomfortably and set his glass aside. "No...I'll see it through."

She gave him an indulgent smile. "Good. After all, it is one of the reasons I'm here, isn't it?"

"I suppose, but—"

"Excellent." Haley stood and rubbed her palms together briskly. "I went to the doctor today, and he—"

"You went to the doctor? Today? But you're not even—"

"I wouldn't dream of beginning a new project without first consulting an expert in the field. Would you?"

This whole idea was rapidly losing its appeal. Adam rubbed his forehead. "No, I don't suppose I would."

Haley folded her hands in front of her and paced behind the coffee table. "The doctor stated that the chance of conception is in direct proportion to the number of times the male and female engage in intercourse."

His lips curled down. "Intercourse?"

She stopped and looked down at him. "Yes. That's the proper medical term."

Adam's stomach rolled. He could have gone his whole life without knowing that.

Haley began pacing again. "According to the latest scientific studies, the male must—"

Adam waved his hands, silencing her. This conversation had drained every ounce of desire from him. "Maybe this isn't the best time to start this... project."

She nodded her understanding. "I realize, Adam, that this isn't your only duty."

His back stiffened. "My duty?"

"Yes." She smiled sweetly and whipped a piece of paper from her skirt pocket. "I know you're busy, so I've worked out a schedule."

His jaw slackened. "A schedule?"

She held up the paper. "Yes. I've allotted both mornings and afternoons, so you'll have part of every day free. The timetable I've worked out allows for travel between your office and home, and, of course, time for the act itself. I wasn't sure how long that would take. But don't feel pressured. You can take whatever time you need. I can always adjust the schedule, if I find you're taking longer than the allotted time. I'll give this schedule to Bernard. I know how orderly you like things. Do you have any questions, Adam?''

He shot to his feet. ''What the hell do you think I am? A stud service?''

''It's not necessary to use so crude a term. But, realistically, I suppose it's accurate.''

He snatched the paper from her hands. ''Do you actually think I'm going to be put on a schedule...like a trolley car! That I'm going to make a stop here twice a day and...and...*service* you!''

Haley shrugged. ''You promised you'd cooperate.''

He ripped the paper and sent it flying like bits of confetti. ''I have no intentions of being used! I will not be manipulated to suit someone else's perverse desires!''

She looked at him pointedly. ''Is that what this sounds like?''

Adam stalked across the room and threw her a contemptuous look from the doorway. ''And I can assure you, madam, it will be a cold day in hell before I come to your bed!''

He strode away, only vaguely aware that his own conscience was smarting as much as his pride.

Haley watched him disappear, with a mixture of emotions swirling within her. This afternoon she'd vowed she wouldn't be used as Adam and Martin wanted. The plan she'd devised to make Adam want to stay away from her had worked perfectly.

She sagged onto the settee. But if it was so perfect, why did she feel so awful?

Adam shifted uncomfortably in the dining room chair and shoved a forkful of potatoes into his mouth. She was watching him. He could feel her leering at him. Determinedly he kept his eyes focused on his plate, ignoring his wife, at the other end of the table.

He'd already had one hell of a day, and being home brought no pleasure. After last night, and Haley's demands for a baby, he felt like a whore on a street corner in her presence. But if she thought she could have her way with him, she could just think again.

"I'll be in my study if you need anything." Adam dropped his napkin on the table, and his gaze came up sharply to meet Haley's. He wished he could suck the words back in; she'd made it clear last night what she needed him for.

She smiled demurely and ran her gaze the length of him as he rose from his chair. "I'll keep that in mind."

Heat flushed him from head to toe. He stalked from the room without looking back.

Haley dabbed at her mouth with the linen napkin and sighed heavily. He acted as prim as an old-maid schoolmarm, as if he expected her to force herself on him. Haley shrugged indifferently. She hardly wanted anything to do with him, after the way he and his father had discussed her.

Haley went upstairs to her room. She'd had lunch with the committee members today and discussed the plans for the spring gala. The ladies had worn on her nerves, and now she felt unaccountably tired. Not wanting to wait for Chrissy, Haley slipped into the bathroom and ran the tub full of hot water. She felt a headache coming on, so she turned down the gaslights, leaving the room in shadows as she returned to her own chamber to undress.

He was so damn sick and tired of these McKettrick plans he wanted to toss them right out the open window. Adam sat back in his leather chair and pushed the blueprints away; cigarette smoke coiled from the edge of the desk.

Houses—ugly, small houses. The very last thing he wanted to work on again. He'd been out to the site today with Martin and listened to his ravings about McKettrick, the legislature, vandalism at other work sites. His father had grated on his nerves all day.

Well, to hell with it all. Adam shoved himself up from the desk, crushed out his smoke and left the study. He hadn't slept a wink last night—thanks to his lovely bride—and he was still tired from his trip, so he headed up to his room. Grumbling to himself, Adam pulled off his clothes and went into the bathroom. He heard the drip of water and squinted in the dim light. The tub was full.

Bernard. The man was a saint. How had he known a long soak in a hot tub was just what he needed?

Adam opened the window a crack and eased himself into the bathtub. He exhaled heavily and slid lower, resting his head on the slick porcelain as the warm water rose around his chest. He closed his eyes and relaxed.

In her room next door, Haley whipped her hair into a loose topknot and slipped into the bathroom, deliberately pushing thoughts of her husband from her mind. A long bath and a good night's sleep were her only concerns now.

She tossed her dressing gown on the hamper beside the sink. A breeze from somewhere brought a chill into the room, tingling her bare skin. Anxious for the warmth of the water, she stepped into the tub.

Her ankle brushed against something. Odd, it didn't feel like a soap bar or a back brush, but what else could it be? Halcy looked back over her shoulder. Two white eyes appeared above the water's surface, and a face formed.

"Adam!" Heavens above—if his head was *there*, then her ankle was resting against—

A strangled cry escaped her lips as his dark, smoldering eyes scorched her skin. Desperate to escape his gaze, Halcy plopped into the water and pushed herself backward, away from him. Water crashed over Adam's face.

Coughing and sputtering, he pulled himself to a sitting position. Beads of water glistened in the dark hair of his chest. "What the hell do you think you're doing in here?"

"I might ask you the same!" She crossed her arms over her bare breasts.

Water lapped at her bosom, causing his chest to constrict and his desire to blossom. "Out!" He pointed a dripping finger at the door.

Her eyes widened. "I am certainly not going to parade myself for you!"

"Yet you slip into my bath with your—your female wiles. I told you last night I have no intentions of being used."

"Don't flatter yourself!" She struck the water with

her fist. "You're the one who sneaked into my bath, and—"

"It's my bath!"

"It's mine!"

God help him, she was all naked and wet and slippery. The tub was a boiling cauldron. He couldn't stand another second of this, yet if he got out first she'd see what she'd done to him.

Adam gripped the edges of the tub with his fists. "This is my house, my tub and my bath."

"You weren't on the schedule." She threw the words at him.

Damn that schedule. "Just go!"

He had to be the most irritating man on the face of the earth. "Fine! You can have your bath!"

Haley grabbed a washcloth floating near her and threw it at him. It slapped his face and spread across his eyes. She lunged for the towel.

Adam pulled the dripping cloth from his face and flung it across the room. Who the hell did she think she was? And he was about to ask her that very question when his words were choked off by the sight of her rising from the tub. Sheets of water, shining in the soft light, cascaded from her breasts and slid down her hips and thighs.

What nerve this man had, ogling her so blatantly! Hurrying to escape his view, Haley lost her footing on the slippery bottom and plunged forward. Her body struck Adam with full force, pushing him under the water beneath her. Her belly crashed against his head, and her legs tangled with his. Frantically she grabbed for the side of the tub.

Suddenly Adam rose beneath her, causing her to slide downward along his body. His head broke the surface, and he gasped for air as her breast passed over his face. He sucked in one tiny bud. Their eyes met in astonishment.

His strong, naked body struggling beneath her sent Haley's senses reeling. Desperate, she spread both hands across his face and shoved his head back under the water. She struggled to rise, but her legs entwined with his.

Good God—now she was trying to drown him! Trapped under water, beneath her flailing limbs, Adam couldn't hold his breath another second. He twisted sideways and hooked his arm around her waist as he pushed himself upward. Lighter than he'd anticipated, she rolled onto her back and went straight to the bottom of the tub.

Jesus, what had he done! Adam rose to his knees and yanked Haley out of the water. His arm circled her waist and pulled her hard against him. She grabbed his shoulder, coughing and gasping for air.

"Are you all right?" She was so small, so light. What if he'd hurt her?

No! She wasn't all right! Heat from his body melted her bones and charged her flesh with sensations that robbed her thoughts, stole her breath.

This couldn't be happening. Haley shoved him away and scrambled out of the tub. Grabbing a towel, she raced into her own room and slammed the door, ignoring his calls. She heard water sloshing in the tub and a moment later heard his bedroom door close.

Haley clutched the towel against her, stunned by the effect he'd had on her. She'd managed to keep him out of her bed.

But how was she going to keep herself out of his?

* * *

"What the devil? Bernard! Bernard!"

Adam tossed his valise on the marble-topped table in the foyer, nearly upsetting a vase of fresh flowers, and threw back his head again. "Bernard!"

He scurried through the arched hallway. "Mr. Harrington, you're home early. I'm most distressed—"

"What the devil is going on here?" Anger tightened his chest as he pointed through the open front door to the wagon in the driveway bearing the name Sacramento Building Company on the side.

"Mrs. Harrington, sir, she—"

"Haley?" Sounds of hammering and sawing drifted into the foyer, and Adam glared down the hallway. "Where is she?"

"In the parlor, sir." He stepped aside quickly.

Adam stalked into the parlor. Haley sat on the settee, her feet curled under her, leafing through a book of fabric samples. "What in the name of heaven is going on here?"

She looked up. He seemed odd, dry and dressed—nothing like last night. "I wasn't expecting you home early today. It wasn't on Bernard's schedule."

He cringed, wishing he'd never have to hear the word *schedule* again, and crossed the room to stand in front of her. "Answer my question. What is the Sacramento Building Company doing here?"

"Putting in a window seat." She turned the fabric book toward him. "What do you think of this pattern? It's called Indigo Star."

He glared down at him, furious enough to find a rival construction firm working in his own home, but doubly annoyed that his wife didn't seem to realize his distress. "Did you not hear my question?"

"Did you not hear my response? You asked why they were here, and I replied they were building a window seat." She laid the book aside. She wasn't sure how he'd act this evening. Their exchange in the parlor two nights ago had been difficult enough, but last night's fiasco, when they both ended up in the bathtub together, had been another matter altogether. "Is there something wrong?"

He plowed his fingers through his hair. "You're damn right there's something wrong. In case you'd forgotten, I own a huge construction company, capable of handling the job a hundred times over."

Adam turned and paced the room, looking up, raising his arms to encompass the entire house. "I designed every inch of this house. I oversaw the construction of every board—some of it I even did myself. I don't want strangers coming in here, working on it with inferior craftsmanship."

He looked as though he'd been violated. Haley rose from the settee, trying to hold down her own temper. "The Sacramento Building Company is not 'strangers,' and it's not inferior."

"The hell it isn't." Adam whipped around. "I know my competition, and Jay Caufield couldn't build a—" He glared at her. "Caufield. Is he—"

"My cousin. And he's quite capable, Adam. I had no idea you'd be so upset over this. Really, I don't understand. It's only a window seat and some shelves."

His face hardened. "Sacramento Building is my competition."

"They can't compare to your own business. They're a small company—Jay is the first to say so.

Why do you find him such a threat? How can you begrudge him this small job?''

"Because I control the work in this city and I don't let anybody stand in my way. Like the rest of my competition, if Jay Caufield ends up facedown in the mud with my foot in his back, then so be it.''

Haley shivered. She'd never seen such intensity on anyone's face before. Tension had been high between them for days, and her displeasure with him surfaced easily.

"Can't you at least give it a chance? If the work doesn't meet your standards, you can do it over yourself.''

"I don't want them here.''

Her back stiffened. "You put me in charge of the house. I made the decision.''

Her nostrils flared a little, and her cheeks pinkened with anger. The overwhelming desire to have her right here in the parlor weakened his knees. God, what was wrong with him?

Annoyed with himself now, on top of everything else, Adam flung his hand toward the mantel clock. "Did you get that fixed, as I asked?''

Haley looked at the clock, then back at him. "There's nothing wrong with the clock.''

"Nothing wrong?'' Adam stalked to the mantel. "It's running fast. Two minutes fast.''

"Two minutes? *Two minutes?*'' Haley rolled her eyes. "Why didn't you tell me it was an emergency? I'd have gotten right on it.''

Even her sarcasm made her desirable. Adam turned away before he gave in to the urgings of his body and ended up being the *stud service* she'd demanded he become.

Slowly he rounded the desk and stood in front of her. He'd dressed this way purposely today, to present a clear picture of his authority. Adam tugged on his waistcoat. He'd lain awake most of the night, planning how to handle this.

"I believe I was remiss in my responsibility when I brought you here to my home."

"Your home? You said it was our home."

Adam slid his hand into his pocket, jingling his coins. "Well, yes, I did say that—and it is our home, as I said. But I didn't explain your place here as I should have."

Haley shrugged. "On the contrary, I believe you explained it quite well. You said the house was my responsibility to run."

"Yes, but—"

"Are you saying now that you didn't mean it?"

"Well, no—"

"Do you want to take over the house again? Plan the menus, supervise the staff, oversee the household account?"

"Oh, God, no." Adam waved away the whole idea. "What I'm referring to is other matters, such as the window seat."

"And how am I to know which matters you wish to be consulted on?" Haley gazed up at him. "When you place a foreman in charge of, say, building a house, don't you give him the responsibility of getting the job done?"

"Yes, of course."

"Isn't that the most efficient method?"

"Well, yes, but—"

"You certainly don't have time to oversee every minute detail, do you?"

"You can keep the carpenters, but they'd better do one hell of a job." He crossed the parlor, knowing it was unwise to look at her any longer. "Send them home now, though. I've got work to do."

Haley reined in her runaway emotions. "Tonight?"

He stopped and turned back. "Martin was ranting and raving at the office all day about the vandalism at the Bailey site. I couldn't get any work done."

"But the Padgettes are coming for dinner."

His temper flared again. "Since when?"

"I put it on your schedule."

There was that word again. Annoyed with Haley, the workers in the next room, the Padgettes and, mostly, himself, Adam stalked away.

That night, Adam lay staring at the dark ceiling above his bed, trying to figure just where he'd gone wrong. Things were not turning out as he'd planned. The fact that here he lay entertaining lustful thoughts that couldn't be acted on, while his wife slept only a few feet away, was proof enough that he'd made a critical error somewhere.

He rolled over and punched his pillow with his fist. Having a wife was supposed to make things easier for him. But instead, just the opposite had happened. She occupied most of his thoughts, day and night. Just a whiff of her delicate scent caused him to lose his train of thought. And he wanted her so badly at times that he felt like a teenager again. And he didn't understand why.

He'd tackled this phase of his life just as he'd handled everything else he ever did. He'd made a plan, gathered the necessary materials, assembled them correctly. It was like constructing a building. Blueprints, materials, construction, and a finished product resulted. He'd needed a successful business, so he'd worked to get one. He'd needed a house, so he'd designed and built one. He'd need a wife, so he'd married one. Everything should be perfect. Why wasn't it working out the way he'd planned?

Adam flopped over again and kicked off the quilt, stretching out his legs, feeling confined in his flannel drawers. Night sounds and a gentle breeze wafted through the window, cooling his heated body. Something had to be done.

Maybe Martin had been right. Adam locked his fingers behind his head and stared at the ceiling. Maybe a firm hand was needed for his wife. Nearly twenty years of marital experience must speak for something.

Thoughts of his mother overwhelmed him for an instant, and Adam allowed himself to enjoy them. He seldom thought of her; Martin had allowed no one to speak of her after the memorial service. She'd been dead for a long time now, and her memory had faded. Only Kip's presence marked the passage of time.

Adam closed his eyes and tried to remember his parents together. He couldn't recall an occasion when Martin had controlled his mother with a firm hand, as he'd advised Adam should do with Haley, but they'd always seemed happy together so apparently it must work. Maybe that was what was needed. Maybe that would get his life back on the path he wanted.

Well, that would certainly be easy enough to handle. Adam drew in a deep breath and sighed heavily. He'd never actually told Haley how he wanted his life run, so first thing tomorrow he would sit her down and explain it to her. Tomorrow, things would be back on track. He was sure of it.

"Did you want something?"

Haley stopped in the doorway of the study her hands on her bibbed apron. At his desk, with his head bent, writing in a ledger book nored her.

"Adam? Bernard said—"

He held up his hand, silencing her, and co to work.

Haley tapped her toe on the hardwood fl noyed that he'd sent a servant to summon he study, immediately. It was Saturday morning, had the entire kitchen staff standing by, wai her for direction.

"Adam, if you need something—"

"Just a minute." A long moment dragged fore he finally looked up at her. Her hair was into a loose knot atop her head, and bene apron, he realized, she wore a simple day dre no bustle or corset, the skirt draped her hips alluding to her gentle curves.

Adam steeled his emotions and rose from his desk. He gestured to the chair in the cor down."

She'd had her breakfast early, to get to w kitchen, and she hadn't seen him yet today realized that he wore a navy pin-striped sui with starched shirt, cravat and waistcoat.

"You're going into the office today? Bernard's schedule."

Adam gestured to the chair again. "I' day. Please, sit down."

Haley crossed the room and flopped "What is it, Adam?" *And please* wanted to add.

"Of course not."

"The same as running the house here. Is that what you're saying?"

Adam rubbed his forehead. He wasn't sure now what he'd been trying to say.

"Good, then that's all settled."

Was it?

Haley rose from the chair. "I'll be in the kitchen."

"I'm not finished." Adam pointed at her, and she sat down again. He straightened his cravat. "Another thing I want to discuss is all these dinner engagements you've planned for us."

"I'd think you'd be glad. We've had a number of invitations from the city's best families. We have social obligations."

"Yes, I know that, but—"

"That is one of the reasons I'm here, isn't it? To ensure your social position?"

Adam plowed his fingers through his hair. "I want to be consulted before plans are made."

Haley's eyes softened. "I put them on your schedule."

Adam shifted. She was looking at him like that again. Every time the word *schedule* was mentioned she looked as though she were sizing him up. He cleared his throat. "All I'm saying is that in the future—"

"Do you prefer handling our social calendar yourself?"

"No."

"Shall I use some system other than Bernard's schedule?"

"Bernard's schedule is fine. I—"

Haley rose. "Good. Then we'll continue on as we are. Is there anything else?"

Adam drew himself up straighter. "The point I'm trying to make is that I intend to have some say in what goes on in my own home."

"Good. The grocer is delivering at the back door. You can pay him."

Haley left the room, her skirt swaying across her bottom. He felt as though he'd been buffeted by a small tornado. Adam poured himself a bourbon and slumped in his chair. Where in the hell had he gone wrong this time?

It wasn't supposed to be this way. Having a wife in his house shouldn't always leave him angry and befuddled, intrigued and confused. A wife should bring peace and comfort, as his mother had when he was small, and as Amelia had—

He tossed back the bourbon. Odd how she'd come into his mind at this moment. He hadn't thought of her in months.

Adam took another gulp of bourbon and made his way to the kitchen—one of the few times he'd been in the room since the house was completed. Big and airy, it held all the latest equipment—two stoves, worktables with dangling copper pots, storage units with sliding drawers and concealed cupboards. The back door stood open, filling the room with morning sunlight and fresh, clean air, affording him a view of the grocer's wagon just outside.

Haley stood in the center of everything, ledger in hand, checking off supplies as they were brought in, calmly directing the staff. She handled the house beautifully, and in that respect she'd had a soothing effect on his life. Then she bent over to retrieve the pencil she'd dropped, and his body reacted swiftly. Cursing himself, he hurried outside.

To his surprise, Kip sat on the tailgate of the wagon, swinging his legs and eating an apple. Adam sidestepped the delivery man.

"What are you doing out here?"

Even with the advantage of sitting on the wagon, Kip had to look up at him. "Haley said it was all right. I was here last week. She said I could come back whenever I wanted."

Adam gazed into the kitchen at Haley. His brother had been out here before? Why hadn't she mentioned it?

The line of Kip's mouth tightened. "I can stay if I want. Haley said so."

"I've got a lot of work to do today."

His face brightened. "Can I help?"

"I don't think so."

He shrugged, as if he hadn't expected any different. "Here. I got something for you."

Kip tossed his apple core into a crate of potatoes and opened the knapsack beside him. He pulled out a new baseball mitt. "It's for you."

Despite himself, Adam smiled as he took the glove. "Where'd you get this?"

"At the store."

"Where'd you get the money?"

Kip shrugged and pulled his own mitt and baseball from the knapsack. "See? I got one, too."

Adam laid his hand over the mitt. "I asked you where you got the money."

He pulled away. "I got it from Gwen, okay? Haley gave me this one. It's mine."

"Haley gave it to you?" Adam gazed into the kitchen.

Kip stood on the tailgate and waved the ball. "Haley! Look!"

She came out onto the porch. "Good morning, Kip. You brought your baseball things, I see."

"I got one for Adam, too. I wanted to play, but he says he can't."

Haley came down the steps and stood beside Adam. "Why not?"

"I'm working on the McKettrick plans all day."

She nodded. "Well then, Kip and I will entertain ourselves."

Kip picked up his knapsack and jumped to the ground.

"Don't you have some project in the kitchen you're doing today?" Adam asked.

"Nothing that can't wait."

"But you'd planned to do it today."

Obviously the concept of changing plans was foreign to Adam. Haley grinned. "You'll find I'm quite rebellious that way."

Adam just stared at her.

She draped her hand over Kip's shoulder. "Come on inside until I get the groceries put away. By the way, did your father get his window fixed?"

Kip laughed. "Boy, what a mess!"

"What's this?" Adam trailed along behind them.

Haley looked back over her shoulder. "Don't let us keep you from your work."

Grumbling, Adam went into the house and settled behind his desk in the study. He forced his attention on the ledger in front of him, trying to block out the beautiful morning just outside the window and his beautiful wife, loose in the house, wearing no corset or bustle. He lit a cigarette and grabbed his pencil.

"Sorry to bother you." Haley breezed into the room a short while later. She picked up the baseball mitt he'd left on the edge of his desk. "Can I borrow this?"

He eyed it, then her. "What for?"

"Kip wants to learn to play baseball, and since you haven't got time, I thought I'd help him."

"Do you know how?"

Haley turned the glove over in her hand, then squeezed her fingers into it. "How hard can it be?"

"You've got it on the wrong hand."

"Oh." She shrugged and waved away the cigarette smoke hanging in the air. "Well, don't give us another thought. Go ahead with your work."

She turned to leave, then went back and pulled open the window behind his desk. "I'm airing out the house today."

"Fine." He shifted in his chair and watched her swaying skirt disappear out the door.

In the backyard, Haley found Kip tossing the baseball in the air, trying to catch it in his glove. "Come over here. We'll play."

Kip followed her across the yard. "Isn't that where Adam's working? Won't we bother him?"

She eyed the open window of his study. "We'll play quietly. He'll never know we're here. Adam has his day scheduled, and he'll let nothing interfere with his plans."

Kip lifted his small shoulders. "Okay. If you're sure. He might get mad if we mess up his plans."

Haley smiled. "Believe me, the very last thing I intend to do is interfere with your brother's plans."

Chapter Eight

Damn it, how much was a man supposed to take?

Adam stomped through the kitchen and into the backyard. Since he sat down to work in his study, he'd heard nothing but Kip's laughter and Haley's giggles, squeals and horrendously bad advice on catching a baseball. How could he concentrate on his ledgers with all this fun going on?

At the corner of the house, he stopped. They were playing beneath the big oaks, the morning sunshine beaming through the leaves. Kip was doing pretty well throwing the ball, but Haley cringed and turned her head away each time. She missed it, of course. Adam watched her bend over to retrieve the ball until he couldn't stand it another second.

"Toss it here!" he called.

"Adam!" Kip bounced on his toes.

Haley brushed a stray lock of hair from her face, thankful to heaven that he'd finally come outside. He was dressed to play, too, wearing tan trousers and a plain shirt. The vertical line of his suspenders and Wellington boots added to his height.

Haley heaved the ball at him. It fell short. Adam

jogged forward and scooped it up, then threw it to Kip. The ball sailed effortlessly through the air.

He joined Haley under the oak. Her cheeks were pink and her breath was short; she looked marvelous. Suddenly it didn't matter that they had been at each other's throats for the past few days.

Adam grinned. "You throw like a girl."

"So I've discovered." She pressed her hand to her chest and gulped in two big breaths. "Thank goodness you're here. I don't understand how a boy so small can have so much energy."

"How about if I take over for a while?"

"Gladly."

She passed him the mitt and took a seat on the lumber stacked nearby. Early spring flowers had begun to bloom. Determinedly she studied the landscaping the gardeners worked on daily, then forced her gaze to the lane on the opposite side of the grounds that led to the carriage house, then curved around to a barn in the distance. Rolling green hills surrounded the house, giving it an isolated, peaceful feel. Yet Haley felt anything but peaceful.

Again and again her gaze strayed to Adam as he and Kip threw the ball back and forth. Tall and rugged, Adam looked even bigger beside Kip. His back was to her, and through his shirt she could see the play of his muscles as he threw the ball. She'd never noticed that on any other man before. Did they all look that way?

For a big man, he was incredibly agile as he corralled Kip's wild throws. She remembered his legs when she'd walked in on him at the bathroom sink. Long and tight with muscles, brushed with dark hair, a white towel barely concealing his thighs. At the time, she'd never imagined that such powerful legs could be almost graceful.

Nor had she imagined they could occupy so much of her thoughts. Stunned by her blatant ogling, Haley sprang to her feet and hurried into the kitchen.

She returned a short while later and strolled casually along the row of camellias planted beside the house. She stole glances at Adam. Surprisingly, he was patient with Kip, coaching his brother on improving his burgeoning skills. And Kip listened to every word he said, trying hard to turn the mitt properly, keep his eye on the ball. Finally, they stopped and walked over to her, Kip in front of Adam—walking backward—chattering nonstop.

Kip spun around. "Did you see me throw, Haley? I caught the ball ten times in a row. Did you see?"

Haley smiled. "Yes, I saw. You're doing great."

Adam ruffled his brother's hair. "You're doing pretty good."

Kip beamed with pride.

"Anybody hungry? I told Cook I have two hungry baseball players on my hands today." She gazed toward the house. "Here comes Mrs. Ardmore now."

Neat and tidy, the gray-haired cook made her way down the back steps, carrying a large wicker hamper.

"What's this?" Adam asked.

"I thought we'd have a picnic lunch today."

"Great!" Kip pulled on Adam's arm. "Can we go down by the creek?"

Adam frowned at Haley. "You mean eat outside?"

"That's what a picnic is." Haley smiled up at him. "But if you're too busy, you can work in your study all afternoon. I don't want to interfere with your day."

The thought of sitting indoors working on the McKettrick plans held no appeal at all, but he was behind schedule. Adam pulled at his neck. "I've got a lot to do."

"Ah, come on, Adam. Come with us."

"I understand. You have work to do. Kip and I will have a picnic ourselves." Haley took the heavy hamper from Mrs. Ardmore. "Did you pack the chocolate cake?"

Adam's eyes lit up. "Chocolate cake?"

"Yes ma'am." Mrs. Ardmore smiled proudly. "Baked fresh this morning."

Adam took the hamper from Haley. "I can catch up on McKettrick's plans tomorrow."

Kip let out a whoop. "I know the best place to go."

"Lead the way."

Kip ran ahead of them, bouncing, jumping, racing back to tell them something as they walked down the lane past the carriage house and barn. They crossed a meadow and settled on a grassy area at the edge of a shallow creek. Elms, oaks and willows shaded the spot and cooled the breeze that rustled through the leaves.

Haley spread out the red plaid blanket. Mrs. Ardmore had packed enough to feed an army—cold beef and ham, boiled eggs, cheeses, fruits, fresh bread— and Kip and Adam dived in as if they hadn't eaten in a week.

When Kip finished, he jumped to his feet. "I'm going to climb that tree." He nodded to the oak at the creek's edge.

Haley passed him a napkin. "Wipe your mouth."

He licked the chocolate from the corner of his

mouth, then swiped the napkin across for good measure and took off.

Haley curled her legs under her and smiled. "How does he go so hard all the time?"

Adam draped his arms over his drawn-up knees and shook his head. "I don't know."

"Hey, Haley! Look at me! No hands!"

Already Kip had climbed onto the oak's lowest limb, and he sat there waving his arms at her. Haley drew in a quick breath and clasped her hand over Adam's forearm. "Can he do that? I mean, he won't fall, will he?"

"Every kid gets his share of knocks."

"He thinks the world of you, Adam. He's very proud of his big brother."

Adam just shrugged.

"It's true. You should show him a little attention. I think it would help him a great deal."

"Help him?" Adam looked down at her. "What's wrong with him, besides being too smart-mouthed sometimes?"

"I think he does that to get attention, something I suspect he gets little of at home."

Adam grunted and gazed off at Kip in the tree again.

She scooted across the blanket to his side, where she could see Kip clearly. "He's so small. I'm afraid he'll get hurt."

"He won't be small forever. He'll grow."

"I suppose you're right. You and your father are both tall. Aunt Izzy is taller than average. That just leaves Gwen as the short one in the family. What about your mother?" She felt Adam tense beside her. "I'm sorry. I shouldn't have brought her up."

Adam shrugged. "It's all right. We don't ever talk about her. It's too hard on Gwen."

"Losing her mother so young. She must have been only what, seventeen?"

"Sixteen." Adam plucked a blade of grass from the edge of the blanket and studied it thoughtfully for a moment. "She was there."

"What?"

Adam looked down at her. "Gwen was with her when she died."

The breath left Haley in a huff. "How horrible."

"It was a miracle all of them weren't killed." Adam uttered a bitter laugh. "She'd gone there to have the baby, and died instead."

Since he seemed willing to discuss it, Haley asked, "Where were they?"

"Somewhere near San Bernardino. A sanitarium, or something. The climate was supposed to be better for her. Kip came along late in her life."

"I'm sure she felt fortunate to have Gwen with her. When I was sixteen, the last thing I would have wanted was to go away and miss all the parties and things."

Adam was silent for a long moment, then plowed his fingers through his hair. "Fire swept the place the night Kip was born. Gwen got out with him. After we heard the news, Martin went down there. He brought Kip home, along with an army of nurses. Gwen didn't come home for a long time."

"Where was she?"

"I don't know. Recuperating somewhere from shock, I guess. I was nineteen at the time, and matters of childbearing weren't discussed with me. I remember hearing Kip crying up in the nursery. He was sick and needed constant care. Dr. Mather was always rushing in at all hours of the day and night. And Martin...'' Adam shook his head slowly. ''Martin was like a stone pillar through it all.''

Haley laid one hand on his forearm and touched the other to his shoulder. ''You must have been very frightened.''

His gaze came up quickly and locked with hers. ''I had to be strong, like Martin.''

''That was a lot to ask of yourself, at so young an age.''

He shrugged and looked away. ''Nothing was ever the same after that.''

''Hey, Haley! Look! Look at me!''

She gasped when she looked up and saw Kip standing on the thin outer limbs of the tree. Just then, a branch broke under his foot and left him dangling.

''Adam—''

But he was already on his feet and running. He closed his arms around Kip's knees and held him securely as he let go of the limb. Instead of putting him down, Adam turned him over his shoulder and swatted his bottom playfully.

''You be more careful, you little monkey.''

Kip laughed and wiggled until Adam set him down. Then off he went again, this time playing along the edge of the creek. Adam returned to the blanket and stretched out beside Haley, propping himself up on one elbow.

Haley drew in a deep breath and let it out slowly. ''It's beautiful here.''

''Yes, very beautiful.''

She felt his gaze upon her and wondered if they were both referring to the landscape. He'd been so different today, mellow and calm. It was a relief that the tension between them was gone now. Haley considered adding picnic time to Adam's schedule from now on, since he didn't seem to relax on his own. She wondered if he even knew how.

Haley touched her fingertip to her lips. "Adam, what does the word *spontaneous* mean?"

His brows bobbed as he looked up at her. "Well, it means doing something on the spur of the moment, with no previous plan. Why?"

Haley shrugged, and a little grin tugged at her lips. "I just didn't think you knew what it meant."

She had him, he admitted, and chuckled softly. Adam pushed himself higher on his elbow. "How's this for an example of spontaneity?"

He slid his hand behind her neck and pulled her down, covering her mouth with his. Gently he plied her lips, caressing them softly, kneading them together with exquisite care. He heard her moan softly, and his gut tightened, urging him to press further. With extreme willpower, he resisted temptation and released her slowly, lingering for a moment with their lips close but not touching, feeling her warm, sweet breath against him.

Haley sat straighter, her head whirling. She felt her cheeks redden and her breath shorten to tiny puffs. For a moment, she dared not look at Adam, too uncomfortable with her own feelings to confront his. Then she looked at him; his beautiful green eyes were heavy with desire, the arrogant jut of his jaw was softened by need and vulnerability. Images of him flashed in her mind, vague recollections of the wedding and reception where she'd first seen that look.

Adam favored her with a teasing smile. "If there

are other words you need definitions to, don't hesitate to ask.''

Haley laughed. She felt gloriously alive, here in this beautiful spot, with the sun and breeze, and Adam beside her.

They spent the rest of the afternoon there, talking, watching Kip exploring, eating again. Finally, as the sun dipped toward the horizon, they gathered the last of their picnic and walked back to the house.

Kip arrived in the backyard first and jumped onto the stack of lumber. ''Hey, Adam, what're you building?''

He eyed the wooden skeleton nearby. ''A gazebo.''

''Can I help?''

''Sure.''

''When it's finished,'' Haley said, ''we can have supper out here.''

Adam frowned at her. ''You mean eat in the gazebo?''

''We can watch the sunset. It will be fun.''

Adam just shook his head, dismissing the whole idea.

Kip jumped down from the lumber. ''I'm hungry.''

Haley waved him inside. ''Supper will be ready shortly. Go wash your hands and face.''

She started up the steps behind him, but Adam caught her elbow. His grip felt warm and sure.

''It's nice of you to let him stay.''

Haley looked at him in the fading light, his normally meticulous hair now falling over his forehead. ''I didn't have a large family, so I intend to make the most of yours.''

Adam shifted uncomfortably. ''I don't know that mine is the best example of a family.''

That was certainly true. But Haley smiled and touched her fingers to his cheek. "They made you what you are—even with all your quirky habits—so that makes them all right with me."

Adam's brows drew together. "Quirky habits? I don't—"

"Let's go have supper." Haley smiled softly and headed up the steps.

He stared after her for a moment. "Do I have quirky habits?" When he didn't get an answer, he followed her inside.

They had supper in the dining room, then settled into Adam's study, since the sitting room was under construction. Kip and Adam played checkers. Then Haley searched the leather-bound books on the shelves behind Adam's desk and read aloud Arthur Conan Doyle's short stories on the adventures of the detective Sherlock Holmes. After only a few pages, she realized she'd put her audience to sleep.

Kip was curled on the end of the settee, snoring softly, and Adam sat resting his head on the wing-backed chair, his eyes closed. She rose and touched him gently on the shoulder. He roused and dug his knuckles into his eyes. The vision of waking beside him at the Madison flashed in Haley's mind, and she felt herself flush. She turned away quickly.

"Kip is asleep."

Adam stood and stretched. "No sense sending him home tonight. Some of those rooms upstairs ought to get used."

Haley nodded. "You should have Edward take a note to your father and have him send Kip's clothes for church tomorrow. I'll get him upstairs."

Haley shook Kip's shoulder gently, but he didn't

rouse. She called to him and jostled him several times, to no avail. Finally, she looked back at Adam, who was writing the note to Martin. "I can't wake him."

Adam slipped the note into an envelope and passed it to her, then simply scooped Kip off the settee and carried him out of the room.

Haley's stomach warmed. Adam was so big, so strong, and after seeing him with Kip today, she sensed much more of him than she'd first imagined. The bond between Adam and his brother was fragile, but it was there. And it comforted Haley to know that her husband was capable of such emotion.

Haley took a lantern from the pantry and walked through the darkened yard to the carriage house. The door creaked as she stepped inside. It was pitch-black. She was relieved to see a halo of light in the open doorway to the tack room at the back of the building. Cautiously she made her way around the carriage, her footsteps silent on the earth floor, and peered inside. Haley gasped.

Amid dangling harnesses and shelves of tools and liniments, Chrissy and Edward giggled, rolled and groped each other atop a stack of horse blankets. Haley froze, both horrified and mesmerized by the sheer joy her maid and driver displayed in each other's arms.

Suddenly, Edward looked up. His eyes bulged, and he shot to his feet, dumping Chrissy on the floor.

"Mrs. Harrington— I— We— Excuse me, ma'am." Edward turned sideways and fastened his trousers.

Chrissy sat up and pulled her blouse closed with one hand and yanked her skirt down with the other. Her eyes shone like saucers. "Miss Haley—"

"Take this note to Mr. Harrington's father, Edward, and wait for a reply." Haley dropped the envelope on the nearest shelf and hurried away.

Gulping in deep breaths of cool night air, Haley crossed the yard, the image of Edward and Chrissy burning in her mind. She couldn't be sure what she felt, shock...or envy.

Chapter Nine

The following morning, Haley woke to find Chrissy laying out her clothes for church. As soon as she rose from the bed, Chrissy hurried over.

"Morning, Miss Haley. I mended your stocking this morning. See? Looks better than new." She twisted her fingers into the delicate fabric. "When it comes to sewing, I'm faster than a cowboy on Saturday night—everybody says so. You got anything else you want mended? Anything at all?"

Haley reached for her dressing gown. "No, thank you."

"Oh, Miss Haley, I've just got to talk to you." Chrissy moaned. "I couldn't sleep a wink last night, wide awake as a hickory full of hooty owls. You're not going to send me back to your aunt's place, are you? 'Cause of me and Edward?"

Haley pushed her hair off her shoulders. "It's early in the day for such a discussion, but I suppose we may as well get it over with."

Chrissy wrung her hands. "Oh, Lordy me, you're going to fire me, aren't you? Just don't go blaming Edward. He didn't have nothing to do with it."

Haley's eyes widened. "He certainly seemed involved last night."

She waved her hands. "He couldn't help himself. Yeah, I know he was sniffing around like a dog on point, but I'm the one who went tracking after him, so to speak."

"Do you mean you initiated it?" Haley was stunned.

"Sure." Chrissy shrugged and grinned. "You know how it is, what with your new mister, and all."

"That's different. A well-bred gentleman would never want a woman to be so...demonstrative."

Chrissy rolled her eyes. "Where did you get a dang-fool notion like that?"

"A gentleman expects his wife to be a lady."

Chrissy laughed. "I tell you, Miss Haley, any man—gentleman or not—who finds himself with a wife as cold as a gravedigger's backside will be looking for warmer comforts someplace else."

"But—" Haley turned away.

"You're not going to fire me, are you?"

Haley sat down at her vanity. "No, Chrissy, I'm not."

"Or Edward, either?"

She studied Chrissy's reflection in the mirror. "You know, your conduct was hardly appropriate, no matter what you say. When is the wedding?"

Her eyes widened. "Wedding? I don't know about no wedding. We were just doing it for fun."

"Fun?" Startled, Haley sat straighter on the vanity bench.

Chrissy shrugged. "Sure. Fun. You know, like when you and the mister do it just for fun."

Haley's cheeks flamed. "Never mind about me.

No, I won't fire either of you. But, Chrissy, I think we should discuss this further some other time.''

"Well, okay, if you want." Chrissy turned away. "But, no kidding, I really can sew a blue streak, so if you need anything done, just say so."

After church services, Haley invited everyone home for lunch, including a friend of Isabelle's, Virginia Mason. Virginia was an attractive widow whom Haley had met at several club meetings and liked very much. Martin grudgingly accepted the invitation, frowning at Isabelle and grumbling. Kip came, too, and Haley encouraged him to invite a friend. The whole concept seemed foreign to him, and she figured the child seldom brought friends home. He asked a towheaded young boy from his Sunday school class, who also went to Lamont Academy. No one mentioned Gwen's absence from church, but when Haley quietly suggested to Adam that they drop by the house and invite her to join them, he gave her a quiet but emphatic no, and she left it at that.

At the dining room table the mood was light, Haley careful not to let the conversation stray to the workings of Harrington Construction. At her left, Kip and his friend Teddy ate quietly, but both were steeped in anticipation of something, their eyes darting around the room, then toward each other; Haley had no idea what they were up to. Virginia Mason, seated on Adam's left, had recently returned from a trip to New York and shared her experiences.

"Quite spectacular," Virginia said, "but I admit I missed my home here."

Beside her, Martin grumbled. "There's nothing anywhere worth leaving California to see."

"Really, Martin, how shortsighted of you." Isabelle pursed her lips. "The world is out there to be appreciated. My third husband, Ralph, always said that to—"

"He was your second husband, Isabelle," Martin said, interrupting.

Her brows drew together. "No, I'm quite certain Ralph was my third. Dewey was my second."

Martin let out an exasperated huff. "Dewey was your third husband." He turned to Adam. "You remember Dewey—tall, rangy man with a limp."

Adam shrugged. "I thought Dewey was fourth."

"Third," Martin insisted.

"He liked to travel?" Virginia asked.

Isabelle gestured with her hand. "Ralph—not Dewey."

"Neither of them fit for an honest day's work," Martin complained.

Virginia turned to Martin. "And why is that?"

"Gallivanting all over the country, looking at this and that, not accomplishing one darn thing."

"Seeing the world is an education." Isabelle turned to Adam. "You were in Chicago only a year ago. Didn't you find it enjoyable?"

Adam glanced at his father. "I was there on business."

Suddenly something Jay had told her bounced into Haley's mind. "Skyscrapers."

Adam's gaze collided with hers along the table; he seemed stunned, as if she'd glimpsed his soul. "Yes... How did you know?"

Everyone turned to her, Martin scowling. "It's the future of building. Of course Adam would be there."

Martin snorted and turned back to his plate.

"I'm going to Egypt," Isabelle announced. "Adam, you should come with me. The pyramids— now there's a monument to construction."

Martin snorted again.

"Egypt?" Kip's eyes widened. "Can I go, Aunt Izzy?"

"No, you're not going anywhere," Martin muttered.

The line of Kip's mouth hardened, and he turned back to his lunch.

"Well, how about it? Egypt in the fall?" Isabelle asked Adam. "Better still, take Haley, and you two enjoy a long honeymoon."

Haley's stomach quivered as she looked down the table at Adam, who shifted uncomfortably in his chair.

"He's got too much work to do." Martin spoke first, keeping Adam from replying. "There's no time to go traipsing around the world with no good reason."

"Good gracious, Martin." Virginia spoke softly but forcefully. "You sound like an old man."

He jerked as if he'd been poked in the ribs, and turned to Virginia, beside him. "I don't think—"

"Wait!"

Startled, everyone jumped, then looked toward Isabelle. She pressed her thumb and forefinger to her temple and squeezed her eyes shut.

"I'm getting something."

"See!" Kip elbowed Teddy. "I told you she'd do it."

Teddy's mouth fell open, and his eyes widened. "Wow…"

Isabelle stretched out her other hand and rotated it slowly. "Yes...yes, I'm getting a reading."

Kip bounced in his chair. "What is it, Aunt Izzy?"

Teddy stared at her. "Gosh..."

"Good God, Isabelle, cut out this nonsense," Martin complained.

Beside him, Virginia laid a palm on his forearm. "I'm surprised a man with the vision to build a successful business would be so scornful of new things."

Stunned, Martin just stared at her.

"I'm getting something." Isabelle closed her eyes tighter and rotated her hand in bigger circles. "A new aura. Yes, that's it. I'm seeing a new aura."

Kip's eyes bulged. "Is it Teddy?"

Teddy gasped and sank back in his chair.

Everyone else at the table leaned forward, gazes locked on Isabelle as she swayed momentarily, then dropped her hands, the spell broken. A collective sigh of relief slipped from everyone's lips.

"It's gone," Isabelle reported. "I've lost it."

Kip turned to Teddy. "See? I told you."

"Gee...you're lucky."

After lunch, the boys went outside, arguing over which of them could burp the alphabet the loudest, and everyone else headed for the parlor. Martin hung back, and Isabelle hooked her arm through his.

"Come along. You can sit by Virginia."

He pulled his arm away. "I'm not sitting by her. I don't like her."

Isabelle gave him a scornful look. "Virginia was right. You do sound like an old man."

Martin walked on, and Isabelle turned to Adam. "I felt it again," she whispered.

Adam pressed his lips together to keep from smiling and leaned his head down. "Felt what, Aunt Izzy?"

"There's a strange aura present."

"Maybe it's Kip. You're always getting readings about him."

"No, no." Isabelle shook her head frantically. "I only get readings about him when Gwen is present. This is something different, very different. This time I saw the aura around...you."

Adam patted his aunt's shoulder. "I'll be careful," he promised, and shepherded her into the parlor.

Later, when everyone was gone and the house quiet, Haley left the kitchen after discussing the week's menu with the cook and went in search of Adam. As she expected, she found him in his study, poring over blueprints.

Yellow light from the gas jets bathed him as he sat with his sleeves turned back, working. His hands looked big and strong, dwarfing the finely crafted drafting tools in his fingers. He was so absorbed in his work, he jumped when Haley approached.

"Sorry, I didn't mean to startle you."

He looked up at her and splayed his hands over the blueprints. "It's all right. I was just..." He cleared his throat. "Did you want something?"

Haley stopped in front of his desk and looked down at the blueprints. "I guess you'll be glad when the McKettrick plans are completed. Wait, these aren't McKettrick's plans."

"No." Adam cleared his throat again. "It's nothing."

She rounded the desk and peered over his shoulder. "It's awfully big for a nothing."

He looked up at her and worked his bottom lip for

a moment, then sat back. "It's just something I've been thinking about."

"A skyscraper." Her gaze left the blueprints and met with Adam's. "That's what you're designing, isn't it?"

"Yes," he admitted.

She touched his shoulder and gestured to the drawing in front of them. "Explain them to me."

Surprised by her interest, Adam briefly described his designs. "I was in Chicago a year ago, Haley, and you should have seen what they were doing there. The first true skyscraper was the Home Insurance Building, built about ten years ago. Since then, the Montgomery Ward store and the Unity Building have gone up using steel and iron frames. That's the trick, you see, building a frame to support the structure. The Garrick Theatre Building there is seventeen stories— seventeen—with an office tower and a thirteen-story rear wing extending over a theater."

"And New York? They're building skyscrapers there, too, aren't they?"

Adam scooted to the edge of his chair. "Right now, they're working a braced and riveted steel skeleton for the American Surety Building. Twenty stories, Haley. I tell you, we'll hit thirty before the turn of the century."

She'd never seen such elation in him before, such excitement over his work. It made her excited, too. "Imagine…a thirty-story building. You could design that, Adam. You could build it."

"Damn right I could."

He stopped then and sat back, tossing his pencil aside. "However, I'll be here in Sacramento, designing a ceaseless number of McKettrick houses."

She understood his disappointment. Adam might disagree with his father, but because of loyalty and respect, he let Martin run the company as he saw fit. Jay had been right. Old man, old ideas.

"Have you talked to your father about your designs?"

Adam surged to his feet and quickly rolled up the blueprints. "I've got real work to do. I've got to get McKettrick's plans finished."

Sadness knotted her stomach as she saw him put away his skyscraper designs and pull out the McKettrick blueprints. "I appreciate the respect you have for your father, but the construction business is for young men. You're doing him—and yourself—a disservice by not speaking up."

He didn't respond, just kept working, and Haley wondered if she'd have been wiser to keep her mouth shut. Sighing inwardly, she turned to leave.

"Haley?"

She looked back at him.

"Thanks for having my family over."

Haley nodded. "I'm concerned about Kip, Adam. He seems to be holding in a lot of anger."

He shrugged. "He's just a kid. Anyway, thanks. The last couple of days have been...nice."

She smiled faintly. "Yes, they have been."

Could they all be that way? Haley left the room thinking that, yes, they possibly could.

But the next morning, it was business as usual. Adam at the breakfast table behind *Engineering News,* sipping his Bloody Mary, then conferring with Bernard in the foyer as they went over the day's schedule. From her customary station beside the front door, Haley waved as he crossed the porch. He climbed into the carriage without looking back.

At midmorning, Haley had Edward drive her into town. She met Jay coming out of Sacramento Building. He looked dapper in his navy suit, the sunlight reflecting off his blond hair as he settled his bowler into place.

"Haley, what are you doing out and about on this fine Monday morning?"

She smiled and unfurled her pink parasol, the gentle breeze ruffling the lace trim. "Running a few errands. How is Elizabeth?"

He frowned as he fell in step beside her. "I wouldn't know."

"Spending your days in the company of other women?"

"No."

"Good."

Jay glanced down at her. "I would think you have enough problems with your own husband that you wouldn't concern yourself with other love lives."

She tossed her head. "As a matter of fact, I'm on my way to have lunch with Adam now. I'm going to surprise him. He'll be at the Oak Tree Café at noon. I heard him tell Bernard this morning."

"He told Bernard? Not you?" Jay grunted. "Yes, I can certainly see that you have time to concern yourself with me and Elizabeth."

Haley ignored his remark, not wanting to face the truth of it, after two such wonderful days spent with Adam. She changed the subject. "Have we experienced any vandalism at our construction sites?"

"No, *we* haven't."

She knew he still had problems accepting the tiny

role she played in Sacramento Building. "By the way, you can expect the price of masonry work to increase."

Jay stopped suddenly and looked down at her, his playful expression gone, his businessman's face in its place. "Why? What have you heard?"

"Mary Carlin is putting a wing on the house and redecorating. Her husband will have to pay for it somehow."

"Haley, you're a jewel." Jay kissed her cheek with a loud smack. "I can't believe you get all this information from talking with those old hens at your ladies' clubs."

"I spoke with her at church yesterday. You should get over there right away with some ideas for a new dining room."

Jay nodded. "I'll make an appointment with her husband this afternoon."

Haley shook her head. "Abner Carlin dotes on her completely. He'll do whatever Mary wants. Talk to her."

"A jewel—you're a perfect jewel." Jay's expression darkened. "You didn't tell Harrington about this, did you?"

"I hardly think Harrington Construction will be interested in a job this size."

Jay uttered a cynical laugh as they resumed walking. "Martin Harrington doesn't want a shovelful of dirt turned in this town without one of his men on the other end. He'll want the job, believe me."

"Well, you have a head start."

They turned the corner onto Second Street and ran right into Elizabeth Denning, a man at her side. A stunned, awkward moment passed while she and Jay gazed at each other.

Finally, Jay spoke. "Good day, Elizabeth." His stance stiffened, his grim expression demanding an explanation of the man beside her.

Elizabeth lowered her lashes and smiled. "Jay. Good to see you, Haley. I'd like you to meet Charles Potter. Charles is taking me to lunch."

"He is, huh?" Jay looked the man up and down.

"Yes. Well, we must go." Charles's hand cupping her elbow, they disappeared down the street.

Jay watched them go, his gaze boring into their backs.

"He seemed like a nice man," Haley commented.

"Nice? Nice!"

"You wanted Elizabeth to see other men."

Jay's mouth fell open, then snapped shut. "Yes. And I'm very happy for her."

They stood outside the Oak Tree Café, the bright green-and-white awning shading them from the sun. Haley gestured through the plate-glass window behind her. "Would you like to have lunch with Adam and me?"

Jay rolled his eyes. "No, thank you."

She touched his arm. "You might enjoy it. Adam is not as bad as you think."

Jay turned toward the street. "I'm sure he's lovely—"

He looked as if he'd seen a ghost. "What's wrong, Jay?"

"Nothing, nothing." He captured her elbow and hurried her down the street. "Look, Haley, maybe you and I should eat somewhere else. Alone."

"What's going on?" Haley dug in her heels. "What did you see?"

"No, Haley—"

He reached for her arm, but she pulled away. Across the street, at the entrance of the Madison Hotel, stood Adam. Beside him was a woman.

Beneath the brim of her large hat, Haley saw enough of the woman to know she was very pretty. Dark hair. An elegant dark gown, matching parasol, kid gloves and shoes. Haley pressed her fingers to her throat, and a lump of emotion rose in her breast.

The woman gazed up at Adam, and he looked into her face. They talked. A familiarity bound them together, radiated from them. A hansom cab pulled up, blocking them from Haley's view. A moment later, it pulled away, leaving Adam on the curb. He stood there watching as the seconds crawled by unnoticed. Finally, he turned and walked away.

Jay shuffled beside her. "It's probably nothing, Haley. Just because they spoke on the street doesn't mean anything is going on."

Outside the Madison. Waiting for a hansom. She'd stood there herself, a few weeks ago, with Adam by her side. The knot wound harder and tighter in Haley's stomach, until it circled her heart and yanked it nearly to a stop.

"Who is she?" Her voice was low and measured.

"Really, Haley, you don't know—"

"Who is she?" Haley turned on Jay, her eyes burning.

Jay drew in a deep breath. "Amelia Archer. I'd heard she was back in town, her mother's ill or something. She and Adam were involved for about a year. But that was long ago, Haley."

Her heart pounded in her ears as she watched Adam walk back up the street, away from the Madison. Amelia. Isabelle had mentioned her name when she arrived in town, thought it was she Adam had married. And the ladies at the club meeting—they, too, had known about the relationship between Adam and Amelia Archer, though they tried hard to cover it.

"What happened?"

"Rumor at the time had it they would marry. Then Amelia left town."

Dread welled in Haley stomach. "And?"

"The next thing anyone knew, she'd married. She never came back."

"Until now."

Jay nodded. "Until now."

Chapter Ten

Jay rose from his desk chair when she walked in, concern creasing his brow. "Where have you been?"

She knew she must look as grim and tense as she felt, judging from the expression on Jay's face. "Walking."

"Haley, seeing your husband with Amelia on the street today means nothing. They could have simply run into each other."

Jay, always the diplomat, always concerned for her feelings. She drew in a deep breath and sat down across the desk from him. "And it was simply coincidence we saw them outside the Madison? I won't be my mother. I won't live in a marriage with two people conducting separate lives."

"You're getting way ahead of yourself, Haley."

"You saw the look on Adam's face. It spoke volumes."

"It didn't say a word to me," Jay insisted, and sat down.

Haley shook her head. "He loved her, and she married someone else. He didn't even have a chance to talk her out of it. Adam must have been devastated."

"If you're that concerned about an encounter on a public street, in broad daylight, then go home and talk to him." Jay cleared his throat. "Things are all right between the two of you at home, aren't they?"

Haley's breath caught. Things couldn't have been worse between them. Thanks to Martin, thanks to Adam…and thanks to her own plan. Now more than ever, Haley knew something had to be done.

She rose. "You're right. I'll talk to him."

"Good."

"How are the McKettrick plans coming?"

"Almost done." Jay rose from the chair. "Now quit stalling and get out of here. Go do something nice for your husband."

A tiny smile crept over her face as Jay kissed her cheek, and she left the Sacramento Building Company with his instructions in mind. She walked to the Harrington Building.

Mr. Trembler greeted her as she stepped into the reception area. "Good day, Mrs. Harrington. Mr. Harrington is in conference with Mr. Harrington."

"Good. I'd like to see them both." Haley ignored his protests and let herself into Martin's office.

Adam stood gazing out the window. He turned when she walked in. "Haley, I didn't know you'd be in town today."

Martin gave him an I-told-you-so look and clamped down on his cigar.

Adam's brows furrowed. "Is something wrong?"

Yes, everything was wrong. Haley's heart pounded. How long had he been with Amelia Archer today? Was he thinking of her now?

She forced herself to remain calm. "I'm glad I found you both together. Martin, I'd like you to come to supper with us. I've invited the McKettricks to join us."

"The McKettricks?" He chomped his cigar.

"I know how important this project is to the business. I thought some socializing with them might give you an edge."

Martin grunted and sat back in his chair. He eyed Adam, and for an instant Haley thought she saw a flicker of pride in her husband's eyes.

"Sounds like a good idea," Adam said.

"Tomorrow night."

The words hung in the room for an instant. Haley's gaze remained on Adam. Did he flinch? Did he shift uncomfortably? Would he refuse and go to Amelia instead?

He did none of those things, at least not that she could detect.

"Seven o'clock?" Adam asked.

"Yes." Haley smiled faintly. "Adam, could I speak with you privately for a moment?"

"Sure."

Martin glared at them as they left his office.

They crossed the reception area to Adam's office. It looked like his house—deep blue carpet, heavy masculine furniture. It smelled like him, too. Haley's heart squeezed tighter.

He eased himself onto the corner of his desk, rested his hands on his thigh and swung his leg. "Is something wrong?"

Haley gripped the handle of her parasol. She should have planned what to say, she should have thought it over.

"At a club meeting...a few days ago, someone mentioned that an old acquaintance of yours was in town." Haley lifted her gaze to his face. "Amelia Archer."

He flinched. It was instantaneous, but she saw it. Haley willed her emotions to calm.

Adam leaned forward slightly. "And?"

"And I..." Haley fidgeted with her handbag. Inside her gloves, her palms dampened. "And I wondered if you'd like to invite her for supper."

He stared at her for a long moment, while her heart pounded and her thoughts ran wild. Finally, he drew in a quick breath.

"Amelia Archer and I were involved. She left town to visit relatives, and married someone else." Adam rose and slid his hand into his pocket, jingling his coins. "That was nearly a year ago. It's all over with and forgotten."

"And you haven't seen her since?"

He pressed his lips together. "No."

"I see." Haley swallowed the lump of emotion in her throat. "Well, I'd better let you get your work done."

She felt Adam behind her, but didn't look back as she hurried from the office.

Iris McKettrick had been introduced to Haley at a meeting of the Ladies for the Beautification of Sacramento Club and she had liked her well enough. She had dark eyes that flashed with a quiet intelligence. She and Johnny, her husband, were young, not yet thirty, but Johnny had already put over ten years into his business. Only in the past two years, though, had it flourished, and the speculation was that his marriage to Iris had helped him immeasurably, though no one would admit aloud that she was the brains behind the operation.

Haley rang the brass bell at the McKettrick home, a fashionable place set amid a finely manicured lawn. Acceptable calling hours ended at five o'clock, and it was nearly that late now, but Iris was congenial when she received Haley in the parlor. They chatted for a few minutes, and Haley invited her to supper. She knew Iris would accept. The fact that they had money now hadn't ensured their place in polite society. An invitation to the Harrington house wouldn't be rejected. Haley left a few minutes later, mulling over the next step in her plan.

Supper that evening was a strained affair for Haley, but Adam didn't seem to notice. He ate, talked little, sipped wine. Was the McKettrick job on his mind? Or was it Amelia Archer?

Haley tossed and turned in bed while Adam worked downstairs in his study. She heard him in the bathroom sometime after midnight, then lay awake for hours, staring into the darkness, trying to think of some other possible reason Adam had lied about seeing Amelia, apart from the obvious.

Martin arrived early for supper the next evening and monopolized Adam's time in the study until the McKettricks arrived. Keeping conversation at the table light and flowing wasn't easy with Martin there. Finally, the meal was concluded, and Haley and Iris retired to the parlor while the men went into Adam's study for brandy and cigars. By then, Haley had a headache.

"I'm sure they're discussing the plans for your

houses Adam has been working on." Haley smiled. "They'll probably be in there all night."

Iris settled on the settee. "I imagine so."

Haley could tell Iris wanted to be in the study with the men, beside her husband, analyzing the plans, but such a breach of decorum was unthinkable.

"To be honest with you, Haley, I'm not in favor of this project. It's Johnny's idea."

Haley sank into the club chair across from her. "Providing housing for your factory employees sounds like a progressive idea to me."

Iris shook her head. "All those tiny, nondescript houses near the factory will look good when they're new. But after a few years? It will look worse than the West End. I hardly want the McKettrick name associated with dismal bars, flophouses and drunks."

"I see your point. Have you discussed it with Johnny?"

"Of course. Several times. The factory is a long way from town. He thinks he's doing the employees a good turn by providing housing. But I won't have the McKettrick name associated with a slum."

Haley's headache began to pound worse as she thought of all the work both Jay and Adam were putting into the plans, plans that might never come to fruition, if Iris McKettrick got her way. Still, she couldn't disagree with her concerns.

Finally, she heard the men coming from the study, and they met them in the foyer. Bernard appeared with cloaks and hats, and goodbyes and thank-yous were exchanged. Martin lingered a moment after the McKettricks left.

"He liked them." Martin winked slyly at Adam. "He liked the plans."

Adam slid his hand into his pocket and jingled his coins. "I think so."

"One problem." Martin's expression darkened. "He heard about the vandalism out at the Bailey work site. I don't like it. It could lose us the whole project."

"We could post guards for a while, until the culprit is caught," Adam suggested.

"Damn good idea. Just what I was thinking." Martin's eyes narrowed. "But I want them armed."

"Armed?" Adam shook his head. "That's a big step, Martin. We don't know who's responsible. I don't want somebody getting hurt—or killed—over some spilled paint and overturned nail kegs."

"It's not about paint or nail kegs. It's about integrity. The integrity of Harrington Construction. I'm not losing this project because a client can't trust us." Martin pursed his lips and nodded. "I'm hiring armed guards first thing tomorrow morning."

Adam shook his head in dismay as Martin left.

"I talked with Iris about the project," Haley said from across the foyer. "She doesn't like it. She'll talk her husband out of doing it."

"Great." Adam plowed his fingers through his hair. "That's just goddamn great." He turned and stalked back down the hall.

"I need a lawyer. Does the Sacramento Building Company retain one?" Haley said as she breezed into Jay's office the next morning, pulling off her kid gloves.

He looked up from the pot of coffee warming on the stove in the corner. "Certainly."

"Is he any good?"

"Best I can afford. But—"

"Then hire the best—and keep my name out of it."

"Haley, what in the world has gotten into you?"

She'd awakened this morning filled with purpose and energy. She didn't want an ounce of it to be wasted. "I'm investing. I need a lawyer to handle the transaction— confidentially, of course. We'll put it in the company name."

"Investing? In what?"

Haley turned in a circle. "We need this place painted, inside and out. New furniture, too."

"Has this got something to do with seeing your husband's old girlfriend the other day?"

"Maybe."

"Did you talk to Harrington?"

"Yes, and he told me about their previous relationship. Then he lied about seeing her."

Jay shook his head. "That's hardly the end of the world. He's just married you. He certainly isn't going to be spouting off about seeing an old girlfriend, no matter how innocent the circumstances."

"Or how guilty."

"Stop thinking the worst."

Haley drew in a deep breath. "I suppose you're right. How I can't sit at home day after day letting these thoughts and worries consume me. I have to do something with myself. I came to Sacramento to join you in the business, Jay, and that's what I'm going to do."

"I never realized you felt so strongly about the Sacramento Building Company."

Haley smiled. "My memories of this place are all so wonderful. My father, your father. You. Even when I was in San Francisco, a little part of me was always here. And now that I have the chance, I want to help make sure the Sacramento Building Company succeeds, for our fathers' sakes as well as our own.''

"Certainly, there's nothing wrong with that.'' Jay turned back to the stove. "So Harrington has nothing to do with this?''

"Well…''

He turned to her again and frowned. "Haley?''

Since supper on Sunday when Aunt Izzy talked about seeing the pyramids in Egypt, and Adam showed Haley his skyscraper designs, the picture of Adam's face had stayed in her mind. He wanted those things. They were his dream, his secret dream. If she helped Jay, maybe it would give Adam the nudge he needed to pursue them.

But this wasn't something she should tell Jay. It was too personal.

Haley straightened her shoulders and looked directly at Jay. "We're going to make the Sacramento Building Company a force to be reckoned with in this city. How quickly can you get the painters up here?''

"Hold on there. That costs money, and I need every cent I have in case the McKettrick deal comes through.''

"I have money.''

Jay laughed. "You're spending Harrington money fixing the Sacramento Building Company?''

"Dear Grandfather Hasting, remember? He set up a fund for me. It's all the money I need to get this place going.''

Jay grinned broadly. "Won't he be surprised when he gets back from Europe and sees what his money has bought?''

"It's my money. I can spend it as I choose.''

Jay sighed. "I'll get somebody up here right away."

"But keep my name out of it, out of everything."

"It certainly wouldn't do for the Harringtons to get wind of this," Jay agreed.

"Oh, and one more thing. These McKettrick plans?" Haley lifted the blueprints from Jay's desk and tore them in half.

"Haley! What are you doing?" He dived for the plans as she ripped them again.

"They're no good."

Jay sprawled across the desk, grasped for the shreds. "I've worked like a dog on them!"

"Iris McKettrick is stopping the project. She doesn't like it."

Jay gulped as Haley tossed the blueprints in the air. "I just finished them last night...."

"I know what Iris wants." A little grin crept across Haley's face. "I know exactly what she wants."

"Oh, God, please tell me you haven't already told Harrington."

"No one knows. No one but me."

Chapter Eleven

The ladies of the Current Events Club were avoiding her. Nothing overt, just skirting around her at the refreshment table, stealing glances at her, bending their heads together to whisper. For the first time since her arrival in Sacramento, Haley felt uncomfortable in a social setting.

Aunt Harriet moved alongside her, the lines of her mouth tight with a forced smile. She leaned in slightly. "Remember yourself, Haley. You mustn't make a scene."

"What are you talking about?"

Her lips pinched tighter. "I certainly would have warned you, had I know she'd be here today."

"Who?"

"Amelia Archer."

Haley's heart skipped a beat. No wonder everyone in the room was on edge and Aunt Harriet looked as if she might pop a stay at any moment.

"I have no intention of making a scene."

Aunt Harriet pressed her palm to her chest. "Everyone is watching for your reaction."

Though she'd been reared in this web of social correctness, it grated on Haley's nerves sometimes. She couldn't bear the tension in the room, everyone waiting for the worst to happen.

"Introduce me to her, Aunt Harriet."

She gasped. "We mustn't fall from favor with the Harringtons, Haley. I don't think your husband would approve."

"Then I'll find her and introduce myself."

Aunt Harriet blanched. "No, no, don't do that. I'll make a proper introduction, if you insist. But, Haley, please remember yourself."

She followed Aunt Harriet to the far side of Mildred Price's parlor, keeping a smile in place as she felt the heat of the gazes upon them as introductions were made. When she was standing face-to-face with Amelia Archer, it struck Haley how much the woman looked like her. Same build, nearly identical hair color. Had Adam not married her in a drunken haze, she'd have wondered at the coincidence.

Amelia took her hand, and a genuine smile parted her lips. "I'm so pleased to meet you, Haley."

Her warmth was overwhelming. Haley had expected to feel uncomfortable, even a bit jealous or confrontational, but instead she was touched by Amelia's sincerity.

"I'm very glad you could join us today. I understand you're in town visiting."

Amelia's smile dimmed. "My mother is ill. Not seriously, I don't think, but I wanted to see for myself. Besides, I've been away for nearly a year, and it was such a good excuse to come back and visit."

A quiet moment passed, and the ladies looking on lost interest and moved away.

Amelia grinned. "I think they're disappointed."

Haley glanced around and saw that they were alone. "I'm sure they'll find someone else to talk about."

"I want you to know I'm genuinely glad Adam married. I hope you're very happy together. I'm sure it hurt him when I left for a simple visit to my cousin's, then married so suddenly."

"He told me you two had been seeing each other for quite a while."

Amelia nodded. "We had a very pleasant relationship. Very comfortable. That's probably what went wrong. When I met my future husband at my cousin's home and felt the sparks and fireworks, I knew Adam and I could never have that together. Our marriage would have withered and died, taking us along with it."

"Did Adam agree with you?"

"I don't think so. I wrote to him, tried to explain, but I never heard back." Amelia smiled again. "That's why I'm so glad he has you now."

Haley smiled, but wondered if Adam really felt the same way.

She stayed at the club meeting until everyone had gone, sure that an early departure would prompt speculation as to the reason why. Aunt Harriet was visibly relieved that nothing untoward had transpired between her and Amelia, while Mildred Price looked disappointed.

Alone in the carriage, Haley replayed in her mind the look on Adam's face when he explained his relationship with Amelia—impassive, stoic. Yet he must have been hurt. He hadn't responded to Amelia's letter explaining her feelings.

She sighed and looked out the window at the shops

rolling past. Great displays of emotion were hardly the hallmark of the Harrington family.

Haley alit from the carriage and told Edward she'd return shortly. She had an important errand to complete that couldn't wait, and hurried into the Sacramento Building Company.

"We'll need to contact our attorney immediately," she announced as she buzzed into Jay's office.

He sat back and slid his thumbs down his suspenders. "Is that all you've got to say? Look around. See what dear Grandfather Hasting's money bought."

A faint smell of fresh paint stung her nose. Haley turned a critical eye on the new interior of the Sacramento Building Company—sparkling white walls, drapes of deep green floral picking up the rich hue of the new carpet, mahogany desks and leather chairs, brass accents. Masculine, businesslike, but relaxed and friendly.

She smiled in earnest. "I love it."

Jay scurried to the door. "A bit showy, I know, but I couldn't resist." He gestured grandly toward his name, stenciled in gold letters across his office door.

"The new sign will be installed outside as soon as the painters are finished. The reception area looks so good, Mr. Terwiliger might actually start coming to work more often. And Haley, I really think I can afford to hire a real secretary if the work keeps coming in like this. Who knows? Maybe even an assistant."

The place looked grand, and Jay was positively beaming with pride. Haley smiled broadly. "We got the Carlin job? How about the Wrights' new house? Did you talk to them?"

"Yes!" Jay clenched his fist. "We got them both!"

Haley squealed with delight and gave Jay a quick hug. "This is wonderful, Jay. How are the new McKettrick plans coming?"

"I took your suggestions and expanded on them. Look, let me show you." Jay opened the new storage cabinet behind his desk and made a grand show of taking out the blueprints. "If I get this job, Haley, the Sacramento Building Company will be on top. I hope you're right about what Iris McKettrick wants."

"Don't worry. She'll love it, and she'll convince her husband to love it, too." Haley nodded emphatically, but said a silent prayer that she hadn't misread Iris McKettrick's concerns.

They looked over the blueprints together, Jay carefully explaining everything, pointing out Haley's ideas, then his own embellishments.

"It's perfect, Jay. You're brilliant."

"Thank you." Beaming, he rolled up the plans, then paused. "You're sure you've got the funds to cover this?"

She waved away his concern. "Thanks to Grandfather, I have more than enough."

The McKettrick job had been on her mind all week. Adam had worked diligently on the plans. They'd hardly spoken in the evenings. Sometimes she'd wondered if Amelia occupied his thoughts, as well.

Haley sighed. "Now, to other matters. Did you get a new attorney?"

"The Sacramento Building Company has one of the best new attorneys in the city." Jay locked the blueprints safely inside the cabinet and turned to Haley. "And, best of all, Mr. Bolger has no connections with Harrington Construction, so you needn't worry."

"Good. You need to see him immediately. The

Sacramento Building Company is buying land. I spoke with a Mrs. Lucy Myers, at the meeting of the Current Events Club, who's here with her husband on business. He's buying a tract of land in the fruit-growing area just east of town for twenty-five dollars an acre. His Chicago firm plans to lure easterners here with a pitch about our healthy climate, then sell the land for up to one hundred and twenty dollars per acre. I want the acreage adjacent to that tract.''

Jay's eyes widened. ''We'll make a killing on the land, then build the newcomers' houses to put on the lots.''

''Exactly. Have Mr. Bolger get right on it.'' Haley tucked her parasol under her arm. ''And, Jay, Sacramento Building can afford to give you a regular salary now. Something generous. You deserve it.''

''Is this courtesy of dear Grandfather Hasting?''

''A successful businessman should look like one. I'm sure Grandfather would agree.''

Jay grinned. ''I should have taken you on as a partner years ago.''

Adam stepped into his father's office and closed the door behind him, shutting out the relentless peck of Mr. Trembler's typewriter. From the way Martin's teeth were digging into his cigar, Adam knew something was wrong.

Martin grumbled and pushed papers across his desk. ''Two jobs right under our noses, and we lost them. Lost them!''

Adam pushed back his jacket and slid his hand into his pocket to jingle his coins. ''What happened?''

''Buckner Wright's having a new house built outside of town, and Abner Carlin's adding a whole wing on his place—and his masonry prices are going up to pay for it.'' Martin shoved himself back into his leather chair. "We should have known about this. We should have gotten our order in long ago.''

Adam walked to the desk. "Who got the work?''

"The Sacramento Building Company." Martin jerked his chin in disgust. "Both of them, Carlin's and Wright's.''

"Sacramento Building? How would they get word of this before we did?''

"That's what I'd like to know.''

Adam shrugged. "Two jobs. It won't hurt us.''

"We should have had them!" He glared at Adam.

His back stiffened. "Are you saying this is my fault?''

Martin chomped down on his cigar.

"If I wasn't spending every free minute of my life on those damn McKettrick plans, maybe I'd have known about them!''

Martin's temper eased marginally. "Just get them finished. We're losing too much business because of them.''

"They're a waste of time, anyway. I told you what Haley said. Iris McKettrick doesn't want the project in the first place.''

Martin surged to his feet. "Women talking—it's nothing, I tell you. Johnny McKettrick runs the business. I don't know why the hell he lets his wife stick her nose in.''

Adam clamped his mouth shut, holding in his anger. He'd told Martin over and over that he didn't like the project, and he'd told him what Haley had said. Whether Martin chose to accept it or not, McKettrick's project could be lost.

"Get those plans finished and close the deal." Martin walked to the window and looked down at the city below, his face grim.

Adam had seen that look before. "There's something else. What is it?"

"The headmaster of Lamont Academy was here this morning. What's his name—Snyder? Ryder?"

"Binder. What's happened? Is Kip all right?"

"Nothing a belt across the seat of his pants won't fix." Martin turned to face Adam. "Seems the boy's been missing school, leaving early, not turning in his lessons. It's been going on for some time now."

"And Mr. Binder just told you about the problems today?"

Martin shrugged. "No. He's been over here two or three times. I just let it go, figuring the boy would straighten himself out. But this morning Binder said Kip started a fight with some other kid."

"That's not like Kip." But even as he said it, Adam realized Kip had changed over the past several months; he was testy and sullen much of the time. What had Haley said just the other day? Kip had a lot of pent-up anger. "Maybe you should get a governess again."

Martin snorted and waved away the idea. "They were all a pain in the ass. All of them wanting a job, then bellyaching when it wasn't perfect. Since the last one left after Christmas, my life's been a hell of a lot easier."

"Obviously, Kip needs the supervision."

Martin turned back to the window. "It's just his age. He'll straighten out."

"You're not going to take a belt to him, are you?"

He stared outside for a long time. "No."

"I'll go by the house tonight and talk to him. Maybe he'll tell me what's wrong."

Martin looked back over his shoulder. "Stay out of it. Nothing's wrong with him."

Adam debated a moment, then left the office. When he was Kip's age, if he did the things his father had just described, he'd have certainly felt the sting of Martin's belt. But Adam couldn't find it in himself to envy Martin's leniency. Often Adam had wondered if Martin remembered he had a second son.

As Adam stepped into the reception area, Isabelle rose from the leather couch. She was a welcome sight, holding out her arms for a hug; Virginia Mason was beside her.

"What brings you down, Aunt Izzy?" Adam kissed her pink cheek; she smelled the way old women always smelled, sweet and musty. He nodded a greeting at Virginia.

"We're taking your father to lunch."

Adam cringed inwardly. "Is he expecting you?"

"Of course not." Isabelle laughed heartily, then leaned closer. "I think it would be good for Martin to spend some time with Virginia."

Adam grinned. "Are you picking up an aura between them, Aunt Izzy?"

She gave him a sly wink, then headed for the office. "Martin! Guess who's come with me to take you to lunch!"

Through the open doorway, Adam saw his father's face contort at the mention of Virginia Mason's name, but, surprisingly, he didn't scowl.

Haley shoved her arms into her dressing gown and opened the bathroom door with no thought that her husband may not appreciate her intrusion at this delicate moment. She only knew that she'd heard him retching and that he was sick and that she should go to him.

The cold tile floor stung her bare feet as she saw Adam close the lid on the water closet and pull the chain on the overhead tank. He braced his arms heavily on the sink, his head sagging into his shoulders, his flannel drawers dropping on his hips, his bare chest heaving.

She touched his shoulder; his skin felt clammy. Mild surprise registered on his pale face as she drew a glass of water. "Here. Rinse your mouth."

He groaned and did as she said, then frowned as she dampened a washcloth and wiped his face.

"Gracious, you look terrible. Let's get you back to bed." She expected him to resist, but he didn't. She took his arm and guided him into his room, as if she might actually hold him up if he fell. He eased his big frame onto the bed, and she fluffed his pillow, then pulled the sheet over him.

Early-morning rays of sunlight slanted through the drapes, lighting the clock at his bedside. Haley knew his schedule; it wasn't time for him to be up yet. She eased onto the bed beside him.

"What happened?"

"I don't know...."

He looked absolutely miserable. Haley laid her palm across his forehead. He was cool to the touch. "You don't seem to be feverish. Doesn't anything else hurt?"

He dragged his hand over his mouth. "No."

Her shoulders straightened. "Were you drinking last night?"

The very idea made his stomach roll. "Oh, God, no."

"It couldn't be something you ate, since we both had the same thing for supper last night, and I feel fine." Gently she laid her hand on his belly. "It must be a simple tummyache."

A tummyache. Adam flopped his arm across his forehead. She made it sound so benign—almost pleasant—when his belly actually felt six times its normal size, knotted and gnarled and ready to explode again. But her hand felt good against his skin, stroking his belly gently, soothing him. He dropped his hand loosely on the bed and relaxed.

The bedroom door opened, and Bernard entered, crisply dressed in his usual waistcoat and cravat. Seeing Haley perched on the bed, he dropped his gaze. "Begging your pardon, sir..."

Haley rose and pulled her dressing gown together. "Mr. Harrington is ill."

Bernard's impassive expression remained steady. "Shall I summon the doctor?"

She glanced at Adam. "That won't be necessary at this point. It doesn't appear to be serious. Have Cook prepare warm tea and plain bread. And send word that Adam won't be at work this morning, possibly all day."

"Yes, ma'am." Bernard left, closing the door behind him.

"Got to go to work... Got to finish McKettrick's plans." Adam pushed himself up, bracing his arms behind him. Then his stomach knotted, and he groaned.

Haley eased him down on the pillow again and smiled. "Don't worry about the McKettrick plans.

Besides, I already told you they're going to cancel the whole project."

He exhaled heavily and looked up at her. "You have a terrific bedside manner, Nurse."

She laughed softly. "Well, get used to it, because you're staying home today and I'm taking care of you."

Adam muttered something under his breath and sank back into the pillow.

When Bernard left the breakfast tray a few minutes later, Adam grumbled and complained as Haley stuffed pillows at his back, and grimaced at the sight of the tiny teacup and crusts of bread on the tray across his lap.

"I don't want any." He turned his head away.

Haley pushed her hair back from her shoulder and spread the linen napkin over his chest. "Take a sip or two. It will settle your stomach."

"Tea?" The whole idea seemed preposterous.

"Just try it."

Calmly she lifted the teacup to his lips. He glared at her, then relented and tasted it. He took another, longer drink.

"See? It's not so bad."

He gave her a scathing look, not willing to admit that she was right, but drained the cup and ate most of the bread.

Haley set the tray on the bedside table. "Feeling any better?"

"No." Adam pulled the extra pillow from behind his head and yanked the sheet up over his chest.

"Try to sleep some."

"I slept all night. I don't know how you think I can sleep now."

Anyone as grumpy and cranky as he needed some rest, Haley almost told him. But instead she smoothed down his sheet and smiled. "Then lie quietly. I'll be here if you need anything."

He grumbled again and stared at the ceiling for a few minutes before his eyes fell shut and he drifted off.

Sometime later, he awoke. The drapes were partially drawn, leaving the room dim and cool. He blinked, and Haley came into focus.

She was seated at his bedside in the rocker she'd pulled from the corner, a narrow golden ray of sunlight slanting through the drapes, bathing her. She wore a pale blue gown, and her hair was done up loosely atop her head. Her sooty lashes fluttered against her cheeks. She seemed to glow.

She was resting her head against the back of the chair, as if she'd been sitting there for some time. Her hands lay in the folds of her skirt. Her legs were crossed, and Adam could see the kid slippers on her feet and glimpse her ankles, encased in white silk stockings.

The morning at the Madison. As now, she'd been the first thing he saw. Beautiful then, beautiful now. Maybe more so this morning.

A familiar stirring low in his belly caused him to shift on the bed. Haley roused and rose from the chair.

She laid her palm on his forehead. A delicate fragrance wafted over him, winding desire tighter in him. Adam laid perfectly still, soaking up the feel and smell of her.

"Are you feeling better?"

He'd been sick? Adam's brows pulled together. Yes, nausea, the dash to the water closet at dawn, tea and bread, Haley in her dressing gown with her hair loose on her shoulders.

"You're not feverish." Haley withdrew her hand from his forehead.

Adam closed his hands over the edge of the sheet. Had he really been grumpy with her this morning? What the hell had he been thinking?

He coughed softly. "I feel better...a little better."

"Good." She sat on the edge of the bed. "Do you think you can eat lunch?"

Her hip grazed his thigh and, even with the layers of fabric separating them, his flesh tingled, sending fingers of fire racing through him.

"I'll try."

She left, then returned a few minutes later with a bowl of chicken soup, some bread and a cup of tea.

"This is an old family recipe. I think you'll like it." Haley settled the tray across his lap and wedged pillows at his back.

Adam breathed deeply of her sweet fragrance. If she knew what was happening beneath that tray, she'd likely dump the old family recipe over his head.

He ate slowly, savoring the sight of Haley in the rocker, the melody of her voice as she spoke. Haley always had something to talk about—the house, friends, a news article in the *Sacramento Union*. Adam scraped every drop of soup from the bowl, devoured every crumb of bread, even drank all the tea, just to prolong the moment.

She took the tray away and set it aside. "You're looking much better."

He felt much better, good enough to pull her into bed with him and spend the afternoon rolling around with her under the covers.

Adam captured her hand as she stood beside the bed. A woman's hand, soft and pliant. He ran his thumb across her gold wedding band.

"I should have gotten you an engagement ring."

His big fingers felt powerful, entwined with hers. Haley shrugged. "No, thanks."

"A lady refusing diamonds?" Adam leaned back against the pillow and tucked his other hand behind his neck. "Can I tempt you with a very large ring? Something almost vulgar, perhaps?"

She slid her hand from his and smiled faintly. "I never had an engagement—why should I have an engagement ring?"

Bustle swaying gently, Adam watched as she took his lunch tray and left the room. The nausea was gone, but now a different lump settled in his stomach. Maybe he'd been selfish. Maybe he should have given her a proper engagement and wedding, with all that went with it, all the things women liked so much.

Adam settled back and stared at the ceiling. Maybe he'd done a few other things wrong in his life, too.

The next morning, Adam woke again, sick as a dog. He made it to the water closet, and afterward found Haley at his elbow, giving him a sip of water and toweling off his face.

"I think we should call for the doctor."

Adam pulled the washcloth from her hand and tossed it into the sink. He'd spent all day yesterday at home, letting his work go, ignoring his responsibilities. He couldn't do it again.

"No. Absolutely not."

Pale and drawn, he arrived at the breakfast table, and almost retched again at the sight of the Bloody

Mary waiting for him. Haley sent it away and brought in tea and warm bread. He ate most of it and left for work. There, Martin bellowed at him as soon as he walked past Mr. Trembler's desk.

"We got hit again last night." Martin came up from his desk chair as Adam stepped inside his office.

Heavy gray cigar smoke hung like a haze in the room. Adam's stomach pitched.

"Jesus…" He waved the smoke away and yanked the window open wide.

Martin clamped down on his cigar and squinted one eye at him. "What's wrong with you?"

"Do you have to smoke that thing? It's nasty." He braced his arms against the sill, thinking he might retch out the window at any minute.

Martin eyed the glowing tip of his cigar, then crushed it out. "You're not sick, are you?"

"No." He pulled at his neck. "What happened last night?"

"Bailey site again. Damn-fool guards." Martin sat back in his chair and folded his arms over his chest. "I gave them instructions to shoot. They didn't do it, so I fired every damn one of them. Believe me, whoever this culprit is will be feeling some hot lead next time."

"That's just great," Adam muttered. He turned away from the window. "Did you talk to Kip?"

"Hell, no. That's just what the boy wants. Behavior like this has to be ignored. Like a tantrum. You cater to a kid when he's throwing a tantrum and he'll keep doing it."

Adam's chest tightened, knotting like his belly. "You're wrong."

"What?" Martin looked up quickly, stunned.

"Haley's commented a few times that Kip is holding in a lot of anger."

Martin jerked his chin. "When that wife of yours has produced a son, then she can tell me what to do with mine."

Anger coiled Adam's stomach into a tighter knot. "Something is bothering Kip, and you'd better find out what it is."

Martin threw himself back in the chair and waved away his concern.

Adam stalked halfway across the office, then turned back. "And another thing. I'm sick and tired of working on plans for every henhouse, doghouse and outhouse in Sacramento."

Martin's hands curled into fists, but he remained in his chair. "I built this firm on that kind of business. It's our bread and butter."

Butter. Adam nearly gagged. "I'm not doing it anymore. I'll finish McKettrick's plans, then I'm making some changes around here."

He stalked out of his father's office, slamming the door and rattling its plate-glass window.

Adam greeted the next dawn on his knees again, but Haley didn't come in to help this time. He forced himself to dress and went downstairs.

Two trunks sat in the foyer. The front door stood open, and the carriage was waiting in the drive. Edward, Chrissy and Bernard were scurrying like mice. Amid it all stood Haley, dressed in a pale gray traveling suit.

"What the hell is going on here?"

Haley peered at him from beneath the wide brim of her hat. "I'm leaving."

Chapter Twelve

"Leaving? What the hell do you mean, you're leaving?"

"I'm visiting my mother."

"Oh." The knot in his churning stomach lessened. "I put it on Bernard's schedule."

Damn that schedule. Adam rubbed his hand over his belly. He'd hardly felt like moving these past few days, let alone reading the schedule.

"Is your mother ill, or something?"

"No." Haley shook her head. She pointed at her trunks. "Edward, load those now, please."

"Then why are you going?"

The trip had less to do with seeing her mother than with taking care of some other, more pressing matters. Besides, if she was lucky, her mother wouldn't yet be back from the trip she'd taken to escape the gossip of the Reginald Farnsworth incident.

Haley pulled on her gloves. "I'll be back day after tomorrow. Don't worry, the servants all have their instructions. Your aunt Izzy is coming for supper tonight, and tomorrow night she is taking you, your father and Virginia Mason out."

"Christ..." Adam rubbed his forehead. "I don't want you gallivanting off to San Francisco alone. It's not safe."

"I'm not going alone." Haley tucked her parasol under her arm. "Elizabeth Denning is going with me."

"Who is Elizabeth Denning?"

"Chrissy, did you pack my cloak?"

"Yes, ma'am."

"Who the hell is Elizabeth Denning?" Adam followed her across the foyer.

"A friend." Haley paused in the doorway. "Well, goodbye, Adam."

"But..." Adam stood on the porch until the carriage disappeared from view.

The house felt unaccountably empty, and he didn't go to the office. In his study, he dutifully pulled out the McKettrick plans. Adam sat at his desk and reared back in his chair. From the corner of his eye he caught sight of the bourbon decanter on the table beside the window, and his stomach rolled again. He bellowed for Bernard.

"Take that thing out of here. Get them all out, out of every room. I don't want another drop of liquor in this house. And take these things too." He shoved the silver cigarette case across the desk at him. "Throw them out. Take them behind the carriage house and burn them—right now."

"Yes, sir." Bernard scurried away.

Grumbling, Adam turned back to his work, only to be interrupted by the peal of the door chimes. It sounded a second time, then a third. Realizing he'd sent Bernard away, Adam got up and went to the foyer himself.

He jerked open the door. A slender man with delicate features and blond hair stood on the porch. Stunned, he looked up at Adam, pressing his bowler against the front of his respectable, though far-from-expensive, suit.

Adam's hand tightened on the door knob. "Are you selling something?"

His chin went up a notch, and he gave Adam a once-over. "I'm here to see Haley. I am—"

"Caufield. Jay Caufield." Adam knew him by reputation only, a small-time operator eking out what business he could in Sacramento, taking Harrington Construction's leftovers. But now he recognized the resemblance to Haley.

An awkward silence passed between them. Finally Adam said, "She's not home."

Jay shifted uncomfortably. "When will she return?"

"Not until Saturday. She's out of town."

His brows drew together. "She didn't tell me she was leaving town. Where did she go?"

Jay's familiarity with Haley rankled Adam. "Visiting her mother."

Jay chuckled. "That's rich." He laughed harder. "That's really rich."

Annoyed further now, because Jay knew something about his wife that he himself didn't know, Adam shifted his weight, drawing himself to his greatest height, towering over Jay. "What's so funny about that?"

Jay swallowed his laughter, but smiled broadly. "Visiting her mother on the heels of the Farnsworth fiasco? She's got guts, I'll say that. But of course you already knew that about her."

Damn right he did. Adam hitched up his trousers. "Do you want to leave a message for her, or something?"

Jay sobered and cleared his throat. "Actually, I'm here to inspect the work in your sitting room. I didn't expect to find you here."

And he wished he wasn't here, facing the man who knew his own wife so much better than he, the man who owned the construction company that had invaded the house he'd built with his own two hands, practically.

Jay leaned closer. "Is it all right if I come in? It won't take but a minute."

A long moment dragged by. Finally Adam stepped back from the door. "Yeah, I guess so."

In the foyer, Jay dropped his bowler on the marble-topped table, his gaze roaming the ceiling, the staircase, the floor. He followed Adam through the arched hallway to the sitting room, eyeing the fine details of the home that only a craftsman would notice.

Adam motioned him inside. He hadn't been in the sitting room himself since Haley ordered the work begun. Now he followed Jay, taking in the window seat and shelves the Sacramento Building Company had added to the room.

Grudgingly Adam admitted to himself that the work was good. An intricate design of cabinets built beneath the window seat, carved with twining vines, matched the room's woodwork. A shelf unit now stood along the wall.

After completing his inspection of the cabinets, Jay rose and stood beside Adam. They both stared at the window seat for a long, awkward moment.

"It's an interesting design," Adam said at long last. "It's good."

Jay nodded slowly. "Too bad I've got to rip it out. Haley's changed her mind. She wants something different."

They shared an isn't-that-just-like-a-woman look. The tension between them dissipated. "I was about to have—" Bourbon? He couldn't stomach the thought. "Tea. Join me?"

Jay drew in a deep breath, feeling lost for a moment, then shrugged. "Sure. Why not?"

They spent the afternoon in Adam's study, talking about the construction business, comparing stories, looking over *Engineering News,* discussing the future of building.

"No doubt about it, skyscrapers will crowd the landscape in the years to come." Jay sat back on the settee. "But give me a home to design, any day."

Adam settled deeper into his chair. "You like the residential work?"

"Something about planning a home for a family appeals to me." Envy saddened his features as he gazed around Adam's study. "Compensation for the cubbyhole I occupy over the butcher shop, I guess."

Adam toyed with the pencil on his desk. "So, I guess you know Haley's mother pretty well?"

Jay gave an exaggerated shiver. "As well as anybody knows the woman, I suppose. Warmth and compassion are not her best qualities. All in all, I'd say you're lucky to have your mother-in-law so far away."

He grinned. "Sounds like it."

"We used to call her the ice queen—behind her back, of course." Jay chuckled at the memory. "The only feelings she ever showed were for Haley, but after the Farnsworth thing, even that's in question.''

Adam sat up straighter. Farnsworth. That name had come up in the report Oscar did for him on the day he found himself married to Haley. The scandal in San Francisco, the one the private investigator hadn't been able to find details on. Now his interest was piqued.

"Her mother took it pretty hard, I understand." He was only fishing, hoping Jay wouldn't notice.

Jay laughed and slapped his knee. "I only wish I could have been close enough to see the look on that woman's face, when right there, amid all the pomp and pageantry, in front of some three hundred guests, when Haley turned to ol' Farnsworth and said—"

He stopped suddenly and swallowed his laugh. "Well, you know the rest. It's not right for me to talk about it behind Haley's back. You know how women are.''

Adam could have throttled him. What had she said? he wanted to shout. Instead, he nodded wisely, as if he already knew.

"Luckily, old man Hasting was in Europe. Her mother nearly disowned her. But Haley wouldn't budge. And after what Farnsworth had done, who could blame her?''

Adam drummed his fingers on the desk. "Of course.''

Their conversation turned back to architecture, and Adam settled back in his chair again, convinced it was time he found out exactly what this Farnsworth business was all about.

And he intended to hear it from Haley.

* * *

This place stank.

Adam, in his drawers and undershirt, squirmed on the hard examination table as the cold disk of Dr. Mather's stethoscope pressed against his back. He hadn't been here in years—his mother had brought him the last time he visited the doctor—but it still looked the same. Strange, intimidating devices used for things he didn't even want to imagine, glass and steel, puffs of cotton and rolls of gauze, shelves of bottles with thick, odd-colored syrups. And the smell. He was nauseated enough, without that horrid odor permeating everything.

"How is your father doing?" the doctor asked. "Take a deep breath."

Adam complied and felt the doctor lift his undershirt higher as he moved the stethoscope across his back. "Grouchy as ever."

"Sounds like Martin hasn't changed a bit. You've had this for how long?"

"A week." A long, miserable week.

"Hits you every morning. Is that right? Then gets better as the day goes on? How is Gwen doing?"

He wished the doctor would stand where he could see him. "She's fine."

"Take a deep breath, and hold it. I only saw Kip once over the winter. I told Martin he'd outgrow most of his problems. He's turning into an ornery thing, though."

Adam exhaled. "Martin says it's his age."

"Maybe. Heard you got married. Congratulations."

He jumped as the doctor poked his kidneys. Haley

would be back from her mother's late this afternoon, according to Bernard's schedule.

"Is the new missus feeling poorly?"

He hadn't thought to ask her. "No, I don't think so."

"Anything different with her?"

Different? Adam shrugged his shoulders. "Not that I know of."

"Huh."

Adam couldn't begin to interrupt that diagnosis, but by the scowl on Dr. Mather's face as he rounded the examination table, it didn't look good. "What is it, Doc?"

The chair at his desk creaked as he lowered his round frame into it. "Can't find anything wrong."

"I've been puking my guts out for days. What do you mean, there's nothing wrong?"

He swiveled the chair to face him. "I didn't say you weren't sick. I said I couldn't find anything causing it."

Adam's heart sank. Bad enough he'd come to this torture chamber, endured the poking and prodding—but to have it come to nothing?

"You must have some idea what's wrong."

Dr. Mather chuckled. "Well, if you were a woman I'd say you were pregnant."

Adam vaulted from the table. "This is absurd."

Dr. Mather rocked back in the chair. "No, not really. I recall your father getting the sickness when you and your sister were on the way. He knew before your mother."

"Ridiculous." Adam shoved into his trousers.

The doctor shrugged. "It happens."

"Nobody was sick when Kip came along. I know. I remember."

Dr. Mather chuckled. "Maybe the third time will be the charm for you, too."

Adam yanked his shirt on. "If I'd have wanted a bunch of hocus-pocus, I'd have asked Aunt Izzy for a reading."

"Scientific fact. Rare, but well documented." Dr. Mather threaded his fingers together across his full belly. "One way to tell, though. Have your wife come in to see me."

Shadows stretched across the front lawn as the growing twilight engulfed the house. On the porch, Adam flipped open his pocket watch and scowled at the hands, which were seemingly frozen in place. She was late. She should have been home two hours ago. He stuffed the timepiece into his pocket again and resumed pacing.

Funny how he'd lived in this house for months and it had never seemed so silent before. Until Haley had been here, then left. It hadn't seemed like home, either, as it did now that Haley had added her touch to it. Adam wasn't certain exactly what she'd done, but the rooms looked warmer, more cheerful. The house smelled good too. Occasionally he'd whiff the fresh flowers she kept in all the rooms, but mostly, the house smelled like her.

Adam paced faster. He should have gone to the station with Edward to pick her up. What if the carriage had broken down? Or the train had been wrecked? Adam gulped in a breath of the cool evening air. What if she decided not to come back home? He slid his hand into his pocket, jingling his coins.

Just when he was about to have a horse saddled and ride into town himself, the creaking of the carriage came up the driveway. Edward pulled the team to a stop in front of the house. Adam heaved a sign of relief. The top was loaded with trunks.

He bounded down the steps and yanked open the carriage door. Deep in the shadows, beneath a hat he hadn't seen before, Haley smiled at him. His heart lurched.

"Where have you been? You're two hours late." The words came out in an angry huff, the anger born of worry and fear.

"The train was delayed." She ignored his outstretched hand and got down from the carriage herself.

That annoyed him further. "I waited supper for you. I haven't eaten yet."

She smiled faintly and headed up the walkway. "You're feeling well enough to eat?"

No, he wasn't. But that wasn't the point. He followed along behind the swish and sway of her skirt, the fragrance of her pulling him along. "No, but—"

She stopped on the first step and looked back at him. Her face softened. He could see that she was tired, but her smile was...hopeful?

"Then what's wrong?"

He shifted his shoulders, feeling guilty for snapping at her. "Nothing...really. I just—"

She took a step closer. A warmth that surrounded her urged him nearer.

"You just what? Missed me?"

Adam stepped back and shoved his hands into his pockets. "No, I, ah..." He cleared his throat. "I was hungry."

The lines of her face hardened. She gathered her skirt and marched into the house without looking back.

Adam cringed and hurried in after her. "Your cousin came by while you were gone."

She ignored him as Chrissy came down the stairs, taking her coat and parasol.

"Why, Miss Haley! Lordy, how we missed you! You're as welcome as the clang of the dinner bell."

At least somebody cared. "Thank you, Chrissy."

Edward came in with the trunks, and Bernard materialized from nowhere, asking about supper service. Haley could hardly think, while her mind churned up every foul name she could imagine for that man who called himself her husband, standing in the corner eyeing her every move.

She'd actually missed him. Actually lain awake in her grandfather's house these past two nights, thinking of Adam. Now she was sorry she'd wasted the mental energy on him.

"Bernard, you may serve supper in a half hour. Mr. Harrington is hungry. And Chrissy, take care unpacking—"

"Wait!"

Startled, everyone turned to find Isabelle standing in the doorway, a hansom cab waiting in the drive. Its arrival had gone unnoticed in the confusion.

"I'm getting something!" Isabelle rotated her palm over the foyer and squeezed her eyes tight. "Yes...I knew it!"

The servants drew back.

Her eyes popped open, and everyone jumped again. Like a luxury liner steaming into harbor, Isabelle crossed the foyer and headed up the stairs. "I'm moving in. Have the driver bring up my things."

Haley and Adam stared at each other, then shrugged helplessly as Isabelle proceeded up the staircase.

Supper was a tedious affair. Anyone not having a stomachache beforehand had one at the meal's conclusion.

"I simply could not abide another moment in your father's house." Isabelle waved her fork.

"Did something happen?" Haley asked.

"Auras. The auras were all dark and dank." Her expression hardened. "Martin is nearly intolerable. But he always is. It was your brother and sister again."

Adam gave up all pretense of eating and dropped his fork. "Kip and Gwen? What's wrong with them?"

"I get strange readings from them."

"Aunt Izzy, you always do. What's so different now?"

"I don't know." She turned back to her meal.

Adam and Haley exchanged a look of quiet surrender across the long table.

Afterward, Haley went upstairs with Isabelle to help her get settled.

"I want to show you my Oriental art collection. I know it's here somewhere." Isabelle sorted through the dozens of packing boxes stacked in the corner.

Haley settled on the edge of the bed, tired from her trip and wanting to retire to her own room. "That's all right, Aunt Izzy, I can see it tomorrow."

"Oh, no, no. You must see it. Here. Look through this box while I keep searching."

Haley opened the lid of the box Isabelle had passed to her and found it full of old family photographs. She smiled as she lifted a grainy photo and turned it toward the light.

Years old, it was a young Martin, with a woman beside him who must have been his wife. Tall and straight-shouldered, she was a pretty woman, with a quiet intelligence the camera hadn't missed. Beside them stood Adam, in knickerbockers, and Gwen, with her hair in long braids.

Haley grinned as she looked at the four of them, clustered together, Martin's commanding presence dominating the photograph. Then her smile faded. The family...before. Before Kip was born. Before their mother died. Before Gwen sought solace in drink.

"Quite a group, wouldn't you say?"

Haley looked up to find Isabelle peering at the photograph over her shoulder. "I hadn't seen a picture of Adam's mother before."

"Gloria. A pretty woman, a good mother and wife. Weak, though. I told her she ought to stand up to Martin. He was a headstrong man back then, even more so than now." Isabelle shook her head. "When she was lost, the family hardly went on. I came as soon as I got word about the fire, tried to help, but Martin was absolutely unmanageable. It was almost as if he refused to believe it had even happened."

"I understand no one was allowed to speak of his wife after the memorial service."

"I told him to bring Gwen home, that months in that sanitarium, away from everyone, wasn't good for her, but no, he wouldn't listen. Seemed determined to keep her there. I don't think Adam really understood what was happening. And little Kip, so sick. A tragedy, just a tragedy.''

"Did anyone ever know what caused the fire?''

"I don't think so. The newspaper reports are in that box. Some well-intentioned acquaintance sent them to me, as if I'd want to learn the details.'' Isabelle crossed the room, searching for her Oriental artifacts again. "Go ahead and read them, if you'd like. They're in there somewhere.''

With some trepidation, Haley dug through the photographs and found a yellowed newspaper clipping at the bottom of the box. A cold, fact-filled account of the fire of unknown origin that had swept the Del Vista Boardinghouse in the late afternoon hours, it told of the loss of life, the injuries, the property loss. It did not foretell the catastrophic events that had befallen the Harrington family.

Haley's chest tightened as she finished the piece. Something was amiss. What was it? She read it again, and the realization caused her to spring from the bed.

"Isabelle, can this account be right?''

She looked back over her shoulder. "Certainly. It's from the newspaper in the area of the fire. Why?''

"The date. Did you notice the date of the fire?'' Haley studied the clipping, making sure it was clear in her mind, then looked up at Isabelle.

"How could Kip have been born two days after his mother died?''

Chapter Thirteen

A seat on the steering committee of the spring gala was to be coveted, but at the moment, Haley wished she'd never heard of the event. Exhausted, she entered the foyer and handed her parasol to Bernard.

"I trust madam's day was pleasant," he intoned.

Far from pleasant. With the spring gala upon them, and Mildred Price suddenly proposing a complete change in the gala's theme and taking it upon herself to cancel the musicians, today's meeting had nearly erupted in chair-throwing and hair-pulling.

Haley smiled evenly. "Quite pleasant, thank you. Please let me know when Mr. Harrington arrives home."

"Mr. Harrington is home, madam."

She stopped halfway to the staircase. "He came home early? Is he ill again?"

"He didn't say, but I think not."

"Working on the McKettrick plans again," Haley concluded, and headed toward his study.

"Begging your pardon, madam, but Mr. Harrington and his guests are on the lawn."

Guests? She'd seen no one's name on Bernard's

schedule this morning. Haley went into Adam's study and leaned out the window. The late-afternoon breeze cooled her face and tugged at a wisp of hair at her temple.

Pounding nails and male voices drew her attention to the gazebo skeleton under the trees. She recognized Adam immediately—or was her eye just naturally drawn to him?—in his suit trousers and white starched shirt, sleeves turned back, chest hair curling through his open collar. Beside him, Kip was driving a nail while Adam held the board in place.

Another moment passed before Haley recognized the other man with them. It took a longer moment for her to believe what her eyes saw. Jay. Her cousin Jay was working alongside Adam, pointing, talking and assisting in the construction of the gazebo. He was dressed much the same way Adam was, and they both looked as if they'd gotten up from a business meeting and gone to work.

Haley leaned against the windowsill. Kip seemed thrilled to be there and anxious to please. Adam and Jay talked steadily. They moved like a well-practiced unit, hammering, sawing. The setting sun slanted golden rays of light across the yard, while the cooling breath of wind ruffled their hair and tugged at their shirts.

Tempted to go outside and join them, Haley decided to let the men have their moment and went upstairs to ready herself for supper.

While she was conferring with the cook in the kitchen sometime later, Adam, Jay and Kip finally came inside. They were deep in conversation, and Kip was the first to notice her beside the worktable.

"Hey, Haley, you should see what we did!" Grinning broadly, Kip hurried to her side.

Beads of perspiration dotted his nose. She hugged his shoulder. "I saw you through the window. You're all quite industrious this afternoon."

Jay crossed the room and gave her a quick peck on the cheek. "You don't know the half of it, cousin. I've been hard at work most of the day, thanks to you."

"Jay took out your window seat," Kip explained. "He was here when I got here from school, and Adam came home early."

Her gaze met Adam's. His brow was damp and his cheeks were flushed; he looked healthier than she'd seen him in days. But, she noted, of the three of them, her husband was the only one who hadn't welcomed her with a kiss or a hug.

"Home early to work on your plans?" Haley asked.

He nodded. "Didn't get very far, though."

"My fault." Jay held up both hands. "I noticed what appeared to be an outhouse under construction in the middle of your backyard—"

"And, of course, he couldn't keep his mouth shut about it," Adam added, as both he and Jay grinned.

Kip lifted his slim shoulders. "So, we all went out and worked on it."

The three of them took over the kitchen, washing at the sink, dripping on the floor, wadding up the linen towels and tossing them aside, all of which left Haley at a loss. Adam had mentioned that Jay had been out to inspect the window seat while she was in San Francisco, but she had had no idea they'd become friends. It was the last thing she would have imagined.

They moved into the dining room for supper. The casual atmosphere, the men in their shirts, with no cravats, waistcoats or jackets, brought an odd pleasure to Haley. Adam always looked rugged and masculine, but tonight even slender Jay looked heartier, and Kip seemed to have grown taller.

Adam looked up at Haley. "How did your meeting go today? You ladies all ready for the spring whatever-it-is?"

Haley rolled her eyes. "No thanks to Mildred Price, the gala is all set. By the way, Jay, I have tickets for you."

"For me?" He laid down his fork. "Me?"

Not used to traveling in Sacramento's exclusive social circles, he'd never been to the spring gala before. This year, Haley had several reasons for her cousin to attend. "Yes. And be sure to bring a guest."

Pleased, Jay sat a little straighter. "Perhaps this would be a good time to approach Elizabeth."

"I don't think so. I gave her two tickets, also. I think she's inviting someone else."

"Oh." Jay's shoulders slumped a little.

"Would that be the same Elizabeth you went to San Francisco with?" Adam asked.

"Yes, and wait until you see the beautiful gowns Elizabeth and I commissioned while we were there."

"I'm sure I'll enjoy seeing Elizabeth in a beautiful gown on some other man's arm, thank you very much, Haley." Jay gave her a sour smile. "But that's fine with me. We're both free to see whomever we choose."

"Where is Aunt Izzy?" Adam looked around the table, having just now noticed her absence. After announcing she intended to take up permanent residence

Kip pulled his arm away and clamped his mouth shut as he glared up at Adam.

"Did you get into a fight again? Some bigger boys picking on you?"

His lips lost color from being held together so tightly, but Kip still didn't answer, just stared defiantly at him.

"You're not leaving here until you tell me." Adam folded his arms over his chest and leaned against the door casing. "I can wait as long as you."

Several long minutes passed before Kip finally dropped his gaze and drew in a deep breath. "It's those girls...."

He'd whispered so softly, Adam wasn't sure he'd heard correctly. He leaned closer. "Girls?"

"Yeah, girls!" Kip glared at him again. "A bunch of dumb girls came to school again today from Balmore Academy, and we were supposed to *dance* with them."

He made it sound as if it were the most dreadful, horrifying experience possible in life. Adam thought back to when he'd been Kip's age. Somewhere around that time, girls had gone from being the most useless nuisances under the sun to being the sun itself. Kip, apparently, hadn't yet experienced that moment, when nothing in life would ever be the same again.

Adam shook his head slowly. "Dancing with girls, uh? That's bad."

Kip's chest puffed out, and his cheeks pinkened. "Yeah. The last time they came, I didn't dance with em—I didn't care what Mr. Binder said. So this e, he said—"

Obviously, to Kip, Mr. Binder's decree had a fate

with them, she was as likely to be gone as to be present.

"She's with Father. And that lady."

Adam and Haley gazed at each other, then turned to Kip.

"Do you mean Virginia Mason?" Haley asked.

He shrugged and stared at his plate. "I guess."

Jay left shortly after supper, with a hearty handshake from Adam and an invitation to come back and continue work on the gazebo. Haley walked with him to the foyer. Bernard passed Jay his bowler and jacket, then left them alone.

"You never cease to amaze me, Jay. I never expected to find you here socializing."

"In a Harrington house?" Jay's gaze swept the crystal chandelier overhead and the staircase sweeping up to the second floor. He plopped his bowler on his head. "See what you've done to me?"

Haley smiled. "You and Adam seem to hit it off nicely."

He huffed a resolute sigh. "Yes, I admit it. I'm beginning to understand what you see in him—Harrington or not."

"Oh, that reminds me." Haley hooked Jay's elbow and drew him out to the front porch; golden halos circled the white globes beside the door, casting pools of light into the darkness. "Do you remember the Montgomery home?"

"Of course. The Sacramento Building Company built the place. It was the first summer I was old enough to work for the company. You remember, your father brought you over every now and again."

"Have you seen it lately?"

Jay strolled across the porch beside Haley. "It's

terribly run-down. Leonora Montgomery hasn't kept it up since her husband died.''

''Would you say it's structurally sound?''

''Absolutely. That house was built to stand a hundred years.''

''I heard this morning that Mrs. Montgomery is moving to her daughter's in Los Angeles. I think we can buy the property, fix it up and sell it at a handsome profit.''

Jay shook his head. ''I don't know, Haley. We've got a lot on us, especially if the McKettrick job comes through.''

''I know, but I've always loved that house. And I know you have, too.''

''Oh, yes. Seeing that house go up made me decide to follow along in the family business. Remember, you and I talked about it one dreadfully hot afternoon, when I was working like a dog and you were standing under your lace parasol in the shade of the carriage.''

Haley smiled at the memory. They'd both been so young then, and Jay had looked so capable that day, working alongside the other carpenters. ''So, we're in agreement?''

''Leonora Montgomery is a tough old bird, nearly sixty and still going strong. What makes you think she'll sell?''

''She'll sell if we approach her in the right way. Her husband loved that house. They were very happy there. Assure her we'll restore it to its old grandeur and be choosy about the new owner.''

''How? By looking twice at the color of their money?''

''No, by selling it to someone who will appreciate the place. I have someone in mind already.'' Haley

smiled. ''Charm her, Jay. You have a quality abou[you that older women can't resist.''

Jay uttered a cynical laugh. ''Just what I need. Bu[who knows? Maybe Leonora Montgomery will go t[the spring gala with me.''

The front door stood open, and Adam could see[Haley talking with Jay on the porch. They seemed[deep in conversation, which suited him fine. He fol[lowed Kip into the study.

''Want to play checkers?'' Kip reached for the[game on the shelves.

''In a minute.'' Adam folded his arms across hi[chest. ''First, I want you to tell me how you got he[so early today.''

Kip froze in midstretch, then turned to him. ''I to[you, school let out early.''

''I know you're driven back and forth to scho[every day. Why didn't the driver come for you?''

The line of Kip's mouth hardened. ''He just did[that's all. I don't want to play checkers. I'm g[home.''

Adam caught his arm as he stormed past. [until you answer my question.''

''Let go of me!''

Kip pulled against him, but Adam held him [with a gentle but firm grip on his upper ar[you leave school today without permiss[asked in an even tone.

His cheeks blanched, but his anger didn'[''What do you care, anyway?''

Adam loosened his grip. ''What happe[why you left.''

worse than death. Adam draped his hand over Kip's shoulder. "What did Mr. Binder say?"

Kip gulped hard. "He said I'd have to dance with one of them, all by myself—in front of everybody."

At that instant, Adam hated his father. Simple, everyday problems such as this one had been eating away at Kip for months now, it seemed, and despite Kip's poor behavior and the personal visits from Lamont Academy's headmaster, his father hadn't lifted one finger to get to the bottom of the problem. Again Adam wondered if Martin even remembered Kip existed—or if he simply wanted to ignore him.

Adam squeezed Kip's shoulder. "Don't worry. I can fix this."

Kip's eyes rounded. "You can?"

It was hardly a serious matter; it was one that a little diplomacy—and a reminder of the Harrington's long-standing contributions to Lamont Academy—could take care of.

"I'll go have a talk to Mr. Binder on Monday morning."

Kip seemed stunned and overwhelmed, his blue eyes getting even rounder. "You will? You'll really go?"

"Sure." Adam didn't doubt that in another few months he'd be thinking of ways to get Kip's mind off girls. The transition from boy to young man was different for everyone, and Kip hadn't turned that corner yet. But given the limited feminine influence on his short life—no mother, a string of impersonal governesses and, of course, Gwen—it was hardly a surprise.

Adam patted Kip's shoulder. "I'll see to it Mr. Binder doesn't have you dancing in front of everyone.

But you will have to dance with the rest of your class."

"Only..." Kip's gaze fell to the floor again. "I don't know how. Last time Balmore girls came to school..."

"You left again?"

He shook his head glumly. "And I didn't learn how."

Adam blew out a heavy breath. "All right, I'll tell you what. How about if we get Aunt Izzy to help you learn?"

Kip shook his head frantically. "Father will find out."

"Okay then, how about Haley?"

His face brightened. "Sure. She's not a real girl, or anything."

Adam held in a chuckle. He hoped he'd be present the day girls suddenly became appealing to Kip. He wanted to see the look on his face.

"Let's go ask her."

Kip hurried toward the door, but Adam caught his arm once more. He pointed a stern finger at him. "This doesn't mean it's all right for you to leave school."

He nodded, then scooted out. Adam followed, glad this problem was solved, though he couldn't help wondering what else Kip held inside and hadn't told him—or anyone—about.

Kip met Haley crossing the foyer, and it took only one request before she agreed to help with the lessons. In the parlor, Adam pushed back the furniture and rolled up the rug.

"Who can play for us?" Haley nodded toward the upright piano in the corner. Nearly everyone played.

There were more households with pianos than with bathtubs.

Haley went through the simplest dance steps with Kip, while Adam searched out a pianist among the staff. She showed Kip over and over, counting, encouraging, keeping her own toes out of harm's way. Adam returned and leaned against the doorway, watching them, as Chrissy breezed in straightening her mobcap.

"Land sakes, I haven't sat down to a piano in a month of Sundays. My playing probably screeches like a hog scenting the butcher's block."

She riffled through the sheet music in the storage compartment under the piano seat, then sat down to play. Chrissy coaxed more than a few clinkers from the keyboard, but the beat was solid, and that was what they needed.

The music, however, made it even more difficult for Kip. Adam came from the corner and tapped his shoulder. "Maybe if I show you how it's supposed to look?"

Kip, who'd started to perspire, readily agreed and collapsed on the settee.

Adam offered his hand to Haley. "Shall we?"

She felt herself flush. "Certainly." She could hardly say no.

Adam swept her into his arms, and they glided around the room, looking into each other's faces, lost for a moment in the erratic melody Chrissy provided.

"I don't believe we've danced together before." Adam's gaze held hers.

"We have," Haley said. "At the wedding. Don't you remember?"

He grinned. "No, I don't remember...dancing."

Haley felt her cheeks pinken. She knew what he was remembering; she remembered it, too, and she dipped her lashes.

"I remember how pretty you looked that night." His gaze grew bolder. "I remember being quite taken with you the moment I laid eyes on you."

"So you asked me to dance." Haley recalled that moment with clarity, how her heart had lurched at his invitation, how overpowering he had seemed when she was locked in his arms.

"And then I asked you to marry me."

She smiled. "You remember?"

"Vaguely. How about you?"

The punch-induced fog clouded most of her memories of that night, but the thrill of reckless abandon that had gripped her when she said yes still caused her heart to beat faster. "I remember." And she remembered, too, that she had fallen in love with him that night on the dance floor.

The music stopped, and the spell between them was broken. Adam didn't release her from his arms.

"Kip, pay attention now."

He was lounging on the settee with his feet thrown over the armrest, fiddling with a loose button on his shirt, but he looked up when Adam spoke.

"It's important that you treat a lady with respect when dancing with her. First, don't hold her hand too tight."

Adam traced his fingers along Haley's hand and swirled his thumb against her palm. A delightful rush tingled up her arm.

"And keep your hand in the middle of her back. Not too low, like this."

Adam eased his hand lower, until the tips of his fingers pressed against the small of Haley's back.

"Never on the side, either."

He slid his hand to her side and splayed his fingers until his thumb rested inches below her breast. Haley's breath caught.

"And, Kip, always maintain a discreet distance from your partner. Never like this."

His arm tightened around Haley and pulled her full against him. Her breasts yielded to his chest and were pushed upward in her bodice. Their thighs met. Her tummy quivered at the feel of his hard belly. Every fiber of her body crackled to life. Heat pinkened her cheeks.

"Any questions, Kip?"

Adam asked it casually, as if their embrace meant nothing to him. Still, he held her tightly in his arms. Haley shifted to pull away, then froze as his own intense interest in their dance lesson pressed itself boldly into the folds of her skirt.

Haley drew in a quick breath and stepped away. "I think that's enough dancing for one night. Kip, we'll continue this another time."

Kip rolled to his feet. "Want to play checkers, Adam?"

What he wanted to do was about to drive him completely out of his mind. "I've got work, and you'd better get home. It's late."

"Edward is back with the carriage." Chrissy shuffled her feet. "I just happened to notice it coming up the drive. Come along, dearie, I'll see you safely to the carriage house."

"I can get there by myself."

"We can't take any chances, now can we?" Chrissy hurried after Kip as he waved goodbye.

Now that she was alone with Adam in the parlor, the walls seemed to close in on Haley, and Adam's presence grew tenfold. At once she was aware of every stitch of clothing where it touched her skin, and of the heat radiating from Adam like a cookstove.

She cleared her throat, willing herself to look at his face, not lower. "It was good of you to help Kip."

Adam's emerald eyes darkened, and he took a step closer. "I couldn't stop myself."

A lump of emotion rose in Haley's throat. She backed away, putting more distance between them. His gaze felt hot against her skin, and she was thankful when he went to work putting the parlor back in order.

There was no reason to stay, but she couldn't make herself leave, either. She racked her brain for a shred of conversation.

"Adam, are you sure about the date of Kip's birthday?"

He looked at her as though she'd taken leave of her senses, and rolled the rug back into place. "Sure. It's the thirteenth."

"Yes, I know that when it's celebrated, but are you certain it's the day he was actually born?" The discrepancy in the dates revealed in the newspaper account of the fire had nagged at her for days.

"Since I wasn't there, I wouldn't know for sure. What difference does it make?"

"Your aunt had an old report of the fire that stated it occurred on the eleventh, two days before Kip was born. How can that be?"

He shrugged as he moved the wing-backed chair back into place. "Probably just a misprint."

"Hmm..." Haley nodded. "That's what Aunt Izzy said."

Even the exertion of moving furniture did nothing to relieve the tautness in his body. Adam stole glances at her; her lips were pouting slightly, and her brows were drawn together in concentration. Even that made him want her more.

Heat flushed Haley at Adam's gaze, all thought of the inconsistency in the newspaper report gone. Alarmed, she backed away.

"Well, good night." Haley scurried from the room.

Watching her go only caused his desire to wind tighter within him. After being ill for so long, he'd awakened yesterday morning feeling like his old self again. Now he was fully recovered, and his body felt strong again. Strong and restless. Anxious and needy. His gaze followed Haley across the foyer and up the staircase. He swallowed hard. Very needy, indeed.

He wanted her. He'd wanted her every day since she came into his house. Though he hated himself for his weakness, he even wanted her since she demanded he provide her with a baby. Since that time, he'd considered that being a stud service would have its advantages, but his pride wouldn't let him give in. Adam cursed aloud and headed off to his study.

There he flung open the window and collapsed into his chair. Cool night air drifted in, bringing the chirp of crickets with it. He swiveled sideways and stared at the table where the decanter of bourbon used to sit. Though he felt better, his desire for an evening drink, a Bloody Mary at breakfast, a sip of liquor to bolster his spirits during the day, had not returned. And just as well, Adam decided as he pulled his drafting tools from the desk drawer. Better to keep a clear head.

He forced himself to work, concentrating on the blueprints, trying not to notice the tub running upstairs, in the bathroom directly over his head. Or to imagine Haley undressing. Lowering her delicate, soft body into the water. Warm liquid gliding over her limbs, turning her skin pink.

"Jesus..." Adam dug his knuckles into his eyes and shifted in the chair as the demands of his body intensified. Determinedly he ignored his instincts and continued to work. He'd told her it would be a cold day in hell before he went to her bedroom again, and he'd meant it. He wouldn't give in.

Adam settled down to work, and he'd almost gotten himself under control when a whiff of perfume tantalized his nose. The scent swirled within him, setting him aflame again. Haley. He knew it was Haley.

She stepped into his study a moment later, and all hope of continuing his work evaporated. Dumbly he sat staring at her. Her thick hair was caught at her nape in a single blue ribbon. She wore a light blue dressing gown—silk, clingy, covering her from ankle to wrist to chin. The pencil clasped between his hands snapped in two.

"I didn't mean to disturb you. I think I left my book in here."

His throat was closed off, so he gestured with his broken pencil. "I haven't seen it."

"Don't let me keep you from your work." Haley smiled lightly as she stepped inside. He looked intense in the glow of the gas jets, and she guessed he was working on something intriguing.

He made no pretense of continuing on the blueprints as Haley walked through the room. Methodically she stretched to look at the top bookshelves, bent to peer at the lower ones, her silk dressing gown shifting and sliding over her hips, across her bottom, revealing the fine flesh of her calves and ankles. Smoldering want and need grew like a firestorm in Adam, each of her movements stoking the flames. Mesmerized by her actions, he couldn't drag his gaze away. Finally, when she leaned over the settee, he shot to his feet.

"What's so important about that goddamn book?" He couldn't restrain himself another second, and his churning emotions erupted in anger.

She straightened and rounded on him, her face set in indignant lines. "Why are you shouting at me?"

Her stance caused her breasts to strain against the dressing gown. Adam flung down the remains of his pencil. "I'm not shouting at you!"

Emotions had churned deep within her all night. She slipped easily into anger, too. "If you continue *not* shouting at me, you can expect to *not* get shouted at in return!"

Adam choked back his anger and waved her toward the door. "Just leave. I've got a lot of work to do tonight."

"I certainly don't want an outpouring of emotion to interfere with the McKettrick plans!" Sarcasm tinged her angry words. "The earth might crack open and swallow the entire city if one of the Harringtons actually displayed their true feelings!"

His jaw tightened. "What is that supposed to mean?"

"I'll tell you exactly what it means." Haley advanced on him, pointing her finger. "You and your entire family go to great lengths to pretend nothing is wrong—ever! You bottle everything up, except for some occasional grumbling and complaining, and refuse to face the fact that you have problems.''

His eyes rounded. ''You're crazy. Nobody in my family has any problems.''

''That's exactly what I mean! Look at your father. He's never faced the fact that his wife died, never allowed his children to mourn her—just shoved it under the rug, as if it never happened. And Gwen. She stays locked away in that house, drinking entirely too much. There's a reason for that, Adam. She's very troubled.''

''She has good reason to be.''

''Exactly! And someone should have helped her long ago. Kip is going to turn out just like her. He's crying out for help, but no one is listening.''

Adam flung out both hands. ''This is absurd! Just because we don't go around airing our family laundry doesn't mean there's anything wrong!''

Haley gripped the edge of the desk, leaning forward until her nose stretched up to his chin. ''You're the worst one, Adam Harrington. I know why you married me, and it had little to do with being drunk. It was because of Amelia.''

He reeled back. ''That's a lie.''

''She was the one emotional chance you took, and she left you. But marrying me made it easy, didn't it? You didn't have to put your feelings out there again, and take a chance they'd get stepped on. You could pretend I was another item on your mental checklist with no emotional involvement. You could have a wife and not have to love her!''

''You don't know what the hell you're talking

about!'' Adam waved his hands around the room. ''I gave you free rein on a beautiful new house, I offered to buy you all the jewelry you wanted, I even promised not to interfere with your life—and this is what I get in return!''

''Stop lying to yourself, Adam!''

''I have feelings for you!''

''You have lust. There's a big difference.''

''I never made demands on you!'' Adam curled his hands into fists. ''Not like you did, with that—that trolley schedule you worked out for me. I never asked you to do anything, except fix the mantel clock, which, I might add, you've never done!''

''You and your schedules and clock-watching. And while we're on the subject, maybe if you'd relax your standards a bit and do some things that make you happy, you'd be designing skyscrapers and touring pyramids in Egypt, instead of working yourself into the ground pleasing your father!'' Haley leaned closer, her eyes narrow. ''You want that mantel clock fixed? I'll fix it myself, and you won't ever have to worry about it running fast again.''

She whipped around and stormed out of the study.

''You get back here!'' Infuriated by the sight of her back, Adam ran after her.

In the parlor Haley yanked the heavy clock from the mantel. Defiantly she glared at Adam as he ran across the room and stopped a few feet from her.

''Put that down.'' He pointed at the empty space on the mantel, then at her. ''Don't you dare break it!''

She raised it high over her head.

''I'm warning you.'' Adam stepped closer, his jaw set. ''If you—''

Haley smashed the clock on the floor between them. The crystal face shattered, the cabinet broke open, a spring shot up, coiling in and out.

"There! Now it's no longer two minutes fast!"

For a stunned second, Adam stared at the remains of the clock. His jaw sagged open, then clamped shut as he lifted his gaze to Haley. Her chin went up triumphantly. Absolute fury roiled through him. He lunged at her.

She didn't budge as he jumped over the remains of the clock, seemingly welcoming the confrontation as much as he. He grasped her upper arms, seeing the emotion churning through her, feeling the same in himself, building to a fever pitch.

Haley jerked away. He circled her waist and pulled her hard against him.

Then he kissed her. His mouth devoured hers in a demanding kiss, and he bent her backward until he felt her body pressed against the length of him. She struggled, intensifying his desire. He plowed one hand into the thickness of her hair, tearing away the ribbon, releasing its fullness. Tense and struggling in his arms, Adam couldn't stop himself as he slid his tongue deep into the sweetness of her mouth.

Haley moaned softly as this torrent of emotions assailed her. She wanted to hit him, to smash him on the floor along with the mantel clock, but, like quicksilver, her anger took a turn and she was overwhelmed by the feel of him against her. Deep within her, a knot coiled, urging her on. She threw her arms around his neck, grabbing a handful of hair. Opening her mouth fully, she met his tongue with hers, boldly matching his movements.

He wanted her. All of her. Adam slid one hand

around her to the mound of her breast and cupped it in his palm. The silk of her dressing gown, the softness beneath it, pumped his blood hotter. She moaned and arched into his palm. His heart swelled. He pressed himself against her, rocking back and forth, and heard her sigh deep in her throat. Adam kissed her hungrily as he eased his leg between her knees. He'd never wanted another woman in his whole life the way he wanted Haley now. He would have her.

Amid the sighs, the heavy breathing and his own heart pounding in his ears, another sound seeped into Adam's consciousness. A movement caught his attention from the corner of his eye. Adam lifted his head.

Bernard, Mrs. Ardmore and Chrissy, holding a broom, stood gaping at them.

"Begging your pardon, sir, we heard the crash and thought a crisis had arisen."

Something had arisen, all right. Adam bit off a string of curses and straightened, bringing Haley up with him. She wobbled in his arms, lost in the haze of passion, then let go of his hair. He felt her grow tense as she recognized the servants staring at them. Color flooded her cheeks. She looked up at Adam, horrified and embarrassed.

"Oh, dear..." Haley pushed away from him and ran from the room.

"Damn it," Adam swore under his breath. He started to go after her, but didn't. Given the humiliating moment, it seemed unlikely she'd welcome the sight of him again tonight.

The servants gave him a wide berth as he stalked from the room.

Haley lay awake for hours, staring at the ceiling. The room was hot, or maybe she was still angry. She wasn't sure. She hiked her nightgown up to her thighs.

Vaguely it occurred to her that something else might be responsible for the heat that clung to her like the morning mist. Adam. A tiny tear slipped from the corner of her eye and splashed onto the linen pillowcase.

She'd said some harsh things to him downstairs this evening, but they were all true. And harsher still was the realization that the two of them could never have a marriage—a real marriage—unless Adam acknowledged those things. She wouldn't live as her mother did, married to a stranger.

Haley curled on her side and buried her tears deep in the pillow. If she and Adam were to survive together, he'd have to love her, fully and completely.

Because that was how she loved him.

Chapter Fourteen

It was worse than she'd imagined.

From the doorway, Haley glumly stared at the empty chair at the head of the table. Adam hadn't had breakfast. After last night, she'd thought he'd be angry about the way she'd talked to him, outraged that she'd smashed his clock, and at least a little contrite over the way he'd kissed her, but she'd never expected he'd do the unthinkable.

Adam had changed his schedule.

Feet dragging on the floor, Haley made her way down the hallway. She hadn't really expected to find him at her door this morning, thanking her for solving not only his but his whole family's problems, pouring out his love, sweeping her away on the wings of love and commitment. But she'd thought he'd at least be in the house, that at least they might talk about it. No, now that wouldn't happen. Adam's absence this morning was like the last shovelful of dirt being thrown on the coffin of her dead marriage.

"Does madam require anything?"

She turned to find Bernard behind her, looking lost;

Adam's abrupt change in the morning schedule had evidently confounded the butler as much as anyone.

"When Edward returns with the carriage, would you let him know I'll need him today?" A number of items for the spring gala required her attention. "And could I see Adam's schedule?"

She reviewed the paper Bernard passed to her, detailing his meeting this morning with Ralph Myers, the businessman from Chicago in town to buy the land adjacent to the tract the Sacramento Building Company had already purchased; it gave her small satisfaction that she had known of that deal before him. After that, lunch with his father and Abner Carlin, then the afternoon at his desk. A notation squeezed between leaving the office and working at home this evening indicated an appointment with a party identified by the initial *A*. It stuck out because Adam always spelled out the names of people on his daily schedule. How odd.

Haley's heart lurched suddenly, suspicion taking away her breath. No, it couldn't be true.

She passed the schedule back to Bernard and hurried up to her room, sick and afraid. If her suspicions were correct, tonight, after work, Adam was meeting with Amelia.

Chrissy's soft humming faded as Haley entered her bedroom; the maid was fawning over the gown hanging from the door of the armoire. She turned and smiled broadly.

"I tell you what, Miss Haley, you're gonna look pretty as a speckled pony in a daisy pasture in this new gown of yours. The lady in San Francisco that made it for you, she can sure turn a needle."

Constance Porter had done an exquisite job on her

gown, personally selecting the deep sapphire fabric to match Haley's eyes. "Thank you, Chrissy."

"'Course, it looks a bit binding, if you get my meaning."

"It's conservative," Haley said. "A married woman needn't expose her bosoms so freely."

"I don't know. I think your mister might enjoy looking at them." Chrissy laughed. "Anyway, I'll have all your things down to that Madison Hotel tomorrow morning first thing. You can take your time and get all done up pretty as you please once you get all your business finished with."

She'd rented a room at the Madison, knowing there'd be no time to get back home to change after a full day of overseeing the last-minute details of the spring gala.

"Good. It will be one important item I won't have to worry about."

Haley left the house a short while later, a schedule of her own inside her handbag. As the day wore on and the list dwindled, Haley's spirits sagged. Her imagined future played out in her mind. Pictures of years passing with her and Adam ensconced in separate bedrooms, separate lives. No children. Endless spring galas to mark the years, until finally she'd move back to San Francisco with her own family. And be her mother.

The prospect sickened Haley. She rested her head against the window of the carriage as Edward drove her toward Mildred Price's house, her final stop in the long day. She might as well have married Reginald Farnsworth.

That thought drove her straight up on the leather

seat. Farnsworth—the unthinkable. No, she couldn't face a future like that. She wouldn't.

Haley breezed in and out of Mildred's parlor, refusing refreshments, brusquely reminding her of her duties tomorrow night at the gala. Then she left Mildred openmouthed, and instructed Edward to make one additional stop.

Amelia Archer's mother had a lovely home set amid elms and oaks. Haley braced herself as she stepped onto the porch; she'd sent Edward away two blocks over, not wanting him to report back to Adam where he'd dropped her this evening. She wasn't sure what kind of reception she'd get from Amelia.

The butler let Haley into the parlor, a spacious room dimmed by heavy floral drapes and the trees outside. She perched on the edge of a wing-back chair, facing the cold hearth and waited. Finally, she heard footsteps behind her.

Haley held her breath and rose from the chair. From the distance she couldn't see Amelia's expression clearly, but as she drew nearer, she knew she wasn't looking into the face of an adulteress.

"How nice of you to call, Haley." Amelia squeezed her hand warmly.

Feeling guilty now for her suspicions, Haley drew in a deep breath. "I believe I've done you a disservice. I thought Adam was planning to be here tonight. To see you."

"But he was."

Haley's spine stiffened. "What?"

"I received a note from him this morning asking if he could come by. I responded immediately and told him that no, under no uncertain terms could he come here." Amelia folded her hands in front of her. "I am a married woman. I would not receive an unescorted gentleman so late in the day, especially him, given the circumstances."

"I see." Haley pressed her lips together. "Did he say why he wanted to see you? Some business matter, perhaps?"

"Oh, dear." Amelia touched her arm compassionately. "You're thinking he wants to rekindle our relationship?"

"I don't know what to think."

"I'm sure it's nothing a good cup of tea can't get us through." Amelia gave her a bolstering pat on the arm. "The servants are all upstairs with Mother. She had one of her episodes today. I'll fix us something myself."

Left alone in the parlor, Haley sagged into the wing-backed chair again, grateful Amelia hadn't lit the gas jets. The dim, gloomy room suited her mood.

Vaguely, she heard the doorbell chime, then footsteps behind her on the parquet floor of the foyer, the door opening, and finally coins jingling. Haley's heart squeezed nearly to a stop. Adam. He always jingled his coins when he was nervous. He'd come to see Amelia after all.

Haley rose from the chair and crept to the arched parlor doorway where she saw Amelia in the foyer and Adam standing on the porch.

Amelia stiffened. "Adam, your—"

"Don't be mad at me, Amelia," he said. "I know you told me not to come, but I had to."

Haley held her breath. Was it true? Had she been right all along?

"A lot of things have happened lately, most of

which I don't understand." Adam stood in the doorway, still jingling his coins. "When I ran into you on the street outside the Madison the other day, I saw how happy you were, Amelia. Last year when you left me, I didn't understand why. I was hurt. And bitter."

"I'm sorry for that, Adam," Amelia said. "I wrote you and tried to explain."

"It's all right." He waved away her concern. "I didn't know that all we were to each other was friends. Until..."

"Until what, Adam?"

He drew in a quick breath. "Until I fell in love with my wife."

"She's lovely."

"You've met Haley?" Adam rubbed his hand over his forehead. "Yes, she is lovely. She's also irritating, outspoken and entirely too independent for a woman. But I can't get her out of my mind. Something about her compels me to keep coming back for more. I figured out this morning that I'm in love with her."

"Just this morning? Really, Adam, you men...." Amelia laughed softly. "Do you plan to share this news with your wife?"

He jingled his coins in his pocket again. "I'd like to but I've got a problem. You see, I shot off my big mouth and painted myself into a corner—one I want desperately to get out of, but my pride keeps getting in the way."

"I'm sure you'll figure something out."

He nodded. "Anyway, that's why I wanted to see you, so I could tell you I understand why you left. You did the right thing, for both of us. Goodbye,

Amelia. I wish you and your husband all the happiness in the world.''

Amelia closed the door and Adam's footsteps faded away. Haley covered her face with her hands and cried.

Amelia stopped in the doorway. "You heard?"

Haley sniffled and slumped onto the settee. "Yes."

"There, then. You see? Nothing is wrong with your marriage."

"Oh, but there is." Haley sobbed harder. "I was angry at Adam and said some things that at the time he deserved. But we haven't been…close…since."

Amelia nodded wisely. "I see."

"I don't know what to do. Adam is so prideful and stubborn." Haley dabbed at her eyes.

"Yes, all men are." Amelia rose and folded her hands primly together. "But there's something else all men are."

Haley sniffed and looked up at her. "What?"

"Do I need to say the word?"

"Oh. That."

"If intimacy is all that's needed to get your marriage back on track, that can be arranged easily enough. Simply provide your husband with proper motivation, and nature will take its course."

Haley sniffed, and her tears stopped. "Do you think so?"

Amelia smiled. "I'm sure of it."

"But that's hardly proper conduct for a lady."

"Which do you want to be? A lady, or a wife?"

Haley rose from the chair. "Thank you, Amelia."

She hugged her. "I'm sure you'll figure out what to do."

Haley left Amelia's house, her mind already spinning a plan. She hailed a hansom cab and went to the express office. They were closing for the night, but she rapped on the door until the agent finally opened it.

"I must send a telegram immediately. It's an emergency."

The balding agent stepped back. "Priest? Doctor?"

"Dressmaker."

"Huh?"

Later, Haley arrived home charged with energy and excitement. Adam wasn't there, but she'd expected that; he was having supper this evening with his father and Johnny McKettrick, and presenting the plans he'd spent weeks working on. It suited Haley that he was gone. She needed time to put the finishing touches on her plan.

In her room, she found Chrissy sitting under the gaslights, humming softly, a mountain of fabric on her lap.

"Evening, Miss Haley. I'm just tightening up some of these buttons. Everything is gonna be right as the town clock for you tomorrow night."

Haley tossed her hat on the bed. "There's a change in plans. You were right, Chrissy—that gown is too conservative. I've sent a telegram to Constance Porter in San Francisco. I've instructed her to meet me at the Madison tomorrow and make a few changes."

"Well, good for you, Miss Haley. You're a pretty woman, you ought to show yourself off. It don't matter what them old hens will be cackling about. They're just jealous because you'll be catching every eye in the place."

The only eye she wanted to catch was Adam's. It

was the first step in getting him into her bed tomorrow night.

"Bernard!" Adam threw back his head to bellow again, bringing the servant into the dining room.

"Yes, sir?"

He pointed an accusing finger at the table set for only one. "Where is my wife this morning?"

"The spring gala, sir. Mrs. Harrington left early. She will be at the Madison all day. She's indicated that you are to meet her there this evening. It's on your schedule, sir."

Adam grumbled under his breath and plopped into his chair. Mrs. Ardmore brought in his breakfast, but he just stared at the bowl of hot cereal, the fruit and the warm muffin. He'd wanted to see Haley this morning. He had so much to tell her.

The meeting last night had gone well. He and Martin had taken Johnny McKettrick out for supper, then gone back to the Harrington Building and unveiled the final plans he'd prepared. McKettrick had loved the squat, ugly cracker-tin houses. The concept was exactly what he wanted. Martin had pushed to close the deal on the spot, but McKettrick wasn't ready; he had two other builders' plans to look at.

Though he didn't relish the idea of overseeing the project, Adam felt good about the presentation, and wanted to tell Haley about it this morning. Only she wasn't here.

He stared down the table at her empty chair. Last night when he came home, he'd wanted badly to go into her room. It had taken a lot, but he'd managed to swallow most of his pride. After leaving Amelia's, he'd convinced himself that being in love with his wife, wanting to share himself with her, didn't really mean he was nothing more than a stud service. That problem dispensed with, he'd moved on to the next natural step. But after what they'd been through, working his way into Haley's bed might not be easy.

So, he'd made a schedule. Adam ate slowly, mentally reviewing his plan. Haley was very innocent, very inexperienced, though he remembered how willing she'd been at the Madison the night they married. For a moment, he considered plying her with punch at the spring gala tonight, but then he disregarded the notion. He wanted her to remember their lovemaking this time, to wake up and be glad she was in his arms. And that meant moving slowly. He must not rush her or seem anxious. The last thing he wanted was to scare her.

A week. Adam drank down the last of his tea. He'd give it a week. Carefully, over the next seven days, he would court his wife, gain her confidence and trust, and by next Saturday night he'd have her in his bed.

Adam rose from the table. A week. Damn. He just hoped he could hold out that long.

"Is she here yet? Have you heard from her?"

Haley swept into her room at the Madison, frantic.

"Not a peep." Chrissy gestured at the sapphire gown with the scissors in her hand. "I was just trimming off a few loose threads. What do you suppose is keeping that Miss Porter? You think the train is late, or something?"

"She should have been here hours ago. The gala is starting soon. If she doesn't get here before—"

Haley touched her hand to her forehead. She was counting on the daring alterations to spur her husband's interest in her. Short of coming straight out and asking him to hop into bed with her, she didn't know how else to broach a subject so delicate.

Chrissy eyed the gown. "Wouldn't take much to fix it."

"If only Constance would get here." Haley collapsed in the chair. She'd had a trying day, overseeing the last-minute details of the gala, the flowers, the food, the musicians, who'd only just arrived.

"This is real important to you, isn't it, Miss Haley?" Chrissy tapped the scissors against her palm.

It was the only way she could think of to get her marriage going again. "Oh, Chrissy, you have no idea."

Chrissy nodded briskly. "Well, then, I say we just take matters into our own hands."

"What do you mean?"

"I say we fix this gown ourselves."

"But, Chrissy— No! Wait!"

Chrissy yanked up the gown and whacked a chunk of fabric out of the bodice.

Chapter Fifteen

The last time she walked down the corridor of the Madison Hotel, she'd had a hangover and a new husband, and been frantic to get rid of both. This evening, excitement knotted Haley's stomach with anticipation of the night ahead, and the man beside her was anything but intimidating.

"You look stunning." Jay eyed her appreciatively.

Haley closed the door to her room, catching a glimpse of Chrissy's smile. Though her maid had nearly given her heart failure, wielding the scissors like a madwoman, the gown had turned out perfectly. Haley slid her arm through Jay's.

"Thank you. Constance Porter is the designer, but my maid did a few alterations." Alterations that barely left her bosoms covered and exposed her shoulders completely. The sapphire-and-diamond tear-drop pendant originally meant to brighten the gown now hung between her breasts, focusing attention on her cleavage. The skirt, cut in the new slimmer style, called attention to her thighs and small waist, then blossomed into a high, ruffled bustle in back.

Jay's eyebrow crept upward. "Very daring. You'll turn more than a few heads tonight."

The only head she wanted to turn sat atop her husband's shoulders.

"Wait until you see Elizabeth's gown."

Jay stopped short. "Elizabeth got a gown like— like yours?"

"Would it bother you if she did?"

His face reddened. "I won't have other men ogling her as if she's a peach ready to be plucked."

She shrugged. "I don't know what you can do about it, given your relationship right now."

Jay clamped his mouth shut and tugged on his sleeve. "Elizabeth, of course, is free to do as she chooses."

"And it doesn't bother you?"

"Of course not."

"You look quite dapper yourself, this evening," Haley said as they continued down the long corridor.

He preened, showing off his black tuxedo. "It seems I'm coming up in the world. And I like it."

Jay looked handsome, and she felt beautiful. Haley smiled sadly. "What would our fathers say if they saw us now? Their years of hard work, with so little to show for it. Their sweat and toil to bring the Sacramento Building Company to life, and their struggle to keep it going despite the competition from Harrington Construction."

Jay hooked Haley's arm over his and patted her hand. "I think our fathers would be proud they produced you and I, regardless of where the business went."

"Maybe you're right."

They descended the grand staircase together. Below them, the double doors of the entrance stood open and the cream of Sacramento society flowed in. Brightly colored gowns shone amid stunning black tuxedos, diamonds and gems sparkled in the crowd, as couples made their way across the lobby and into the ballroom.

"I hope you've planned a large buffet. I'm starved."

Despite his slender stature, Jay could eat his weight at any meal. "Don't worry. I've seen to it that you won't go hungry tonight."

"And plenty to drink tonight?" He cast her a sidelong glance. "Punch, maybe?"

"Unless you want to wake tomorrow morning married to someone, I suggest you steer clear of the punch." Haley grinned. "Oh, look. There's Elizabeth."

Jay stopped short on the stairs. Dressed in an emerald gown, Elizabeth crossed the lobby below them. Though not as daring as Haley's, her gown dipped below her shoulders, offering a glimpse of cleavage.

"Striking, isn't she?" Haley turned to her cousin and saw him mesmerized, watching Elizabeth's every step as she moved toward the ballroom. "Jay? Jay!"

He jumped. "What?"

"I said, doesn't Elizabeth look pretty?"

"Yes, of course she does." His gaze ventured off to find her in the crowd again.

"Who is with her? Isn't that Phillip Mayfield?"

Jay's expression darkened, and his shoulders squared. "That's the third time she's been out with Mayfield. What is going on?"

"Well, you're the one who said you two should see other people," Haley pointed out.

"Seeing other people does not mean seeing one person three times."

"Maybe they're getting serious."

Jay looked down at her, shock drawing the lines of his mouth taut. "Serious? You don't think…"

"What does it matter to you? Elizabeth smothered you. You hated it. Remember how she used to show up at your office uninvited?"

Jay shrugged. "It did brighten my day."

"And how she used to always bring your lunch— more food than even *you* could eat."

"She's a very good cook."

"What about those suppers at her mother's house? Every Sunday after church, every holiday, there you sat with Elizabeth and all her family."

"It was nice, in a way. I get lonely, you know, especially with no family in town, except now for you."

"You did the right thing by putting some distance between the two of you." Haley nodded wisely. "Why, before you know it, she'd have had you at the altar, just like you thought. And there you'd be with Elizabeth fussing over every detail of your life, loving and caring for you, providing a warm, comforting home. I'd say you're lucky to be rid of her."

Jay looked down at her. "Do you really think so?"

"Certainly." Haley smiled broadly and patted Jay's arm. "Where is your escort for the evening?"

Jay cleared his throat. "I didn't invite anyone."

"No? Well, not to worry. Every eligible young lady in Sacramento is here this evening. Go meet them. Forget about Elizabeth. You're better off without her."

His shoulders sagged. "I suppose so."

"Run along, then. They're all waiting for you." Haley watched from the staircase as Jay descended the steps and crossed the lobby into the ballroom.

A heated rush suddenly swept through Haley, and she felt a presence around her. Adam. She knew he had arrived. She spotted him coming through the entrance, and already his gaze riveted her. Her heart thumped against her breast.

He was devastatingly handsome in his tuxedo; his face looked tanned against the starched white collar and tie, and even from this distance his eyes sparkled like jewels. A head taller than everyone else, Adam crossed the lobby toward her. Haley gathered her skirt and walked down the stairs.

Adam paused at the bottom step, knowing that if he went up to meet her, he'd keep right on going and his weeklong plan to gain her trust would be shot to hell in about five minutes.

She stopped on the step beside him, and his knees weakened. Her hair was all done up in an artful confection that begged to be pulled free. And that gown—her breasts nearly spilled completely out of the thing. Adam gritted his teeth. A week. Seven days. His innocent, inexperienced wife needed that much time to learn to trust and accept him, regardless of what her gown did to him.

Adam offered her arm. "Shall we?"

He felt strong and sturdy; Haley needed the strength to bolster her wobbly knees. She'd never attempted to lure a man into bed before, and the fact that this one was her husband didn't make it much easier. After the demanding trolley schedule she'd outlined for him, she wondered if Adam would ever be receptive to her unpracticed advances. But she loved him, and she wanted her marriage to succeed. She'd make this plan work.

The ballroom teemed with guests, mingling, talking, beneath a dozen crystal chandeliers. The musicians occupied one end of the massive room, and already several couples were dancing. Small tables set with pale green linens and rich bouquets of spring flowers lined the edge of the room. The lavish buffets were already crowded.

Adam paused at the entrance of the ballroom. "You're the most beautiful woman here."

"Thank you." She slid her arm from his. "But you know, this gown is cut so close, I couldn't even wear all my underthings tonight. Excuse me, there's Aunt Harriet."

"You what?" Stunned, Adam stared at her backside as she disappeared into the crowd. She wasn't wearing her underthings! That fortress of stays and wires, and those yards of fabrics, gone! She was nearly naked under her gown! Adam gulped hard and plunged into the crowd after her.

Isabelle appeared in front of him. "Adam, dear. There you are. My, but you look handsome this evening. Doesn't he look handsome, Virginia?"

At her elbow, Virginia Mason smiled. "Good evening."

Adam watched the top of Haley's head disappear among the guests and managed a smile. "Good to see you ladies."

Isabelle leaned closer. "Is your father here yet?"

"He'll be here later." Martin hated these things and always arrived late, allowing for only enough time to be seen by people who expected a man in his position to attend such functions. But tonight the

McKettricks would be in attendance, and he would surely use the opportunity to talk business.

"We'll keep an eye out for him." Isabelle nodded wisely and glanced at Virginia. "You know your sister isn't coming tonight."

Adam shrugged. "I didn't expect she would. Gwen avoids these things."

"I stopped by the house and heard her and your father arguing." Isabelle cringed. "Very bad auras. I had to go."

"What were they arguing about?" Gwen and Martin rarely even spoke.

"Martin wanted her to come to the gala tonight, so of course she—"

"Wanted to do just the opposite." Adam eased away. "If I see Martin, I'll tell him you're looking for him."

"Oh, don't do that." Isabelle smiled broadly and touched Virginia's arm. "We want to surprise him."

At the buffet table, Haley spotted Jay with a plateful of untouched pastries, staring at the dance floor.

"Having fun?"

He spared her a glance and a heavy sigh. "Loads."

Haley followed his line of vision to where Elizabeth was whirling in Phillip Mayfield's arms. She ignored the forlorn look on her cousin's face.

"Come along, Jay, it's time to make introductions." She relieved him of his pastries and guided him to a table in the ballroom. "Excuse me, Iris. I'd like you to meet my cousin, Jay Caufield."

Iris McKettrick looked up from her seat at the table, relieved to see a welcoming face. "Please, join me."

"Where is your husband?" Haley asked as they sat down.

"Talking with your father-in-law." Iris nodded toward Johnny McKettrick, who was locked in conversation with Martin, near the punch bowl. She turned to Jay. "I believe my husband has an appointment with you on Monday, Mr. Caufield."

"Yes, we're going over the plans Sacramento Building has prepared." Jay cleared his throat. "Haley has told me of your concerns over the plans."

Iris nodded. "Actually, Mr. Caufield, I'd like to see the entire project scrapped."

"I understand your position. But Sacramento Building has come up with something unique, and we'd like you to be present when we go over the plans. Could you arrange that?"

Her brows rose. "You want me to review the plans with you and my husband?"

"Certainly."

From beside the musicians, Adam finally spotted Haley, seated alone with Jay. Damn this crowd of people. He'd looked for her everywhere. Dodging swaying partners, he cut across the room, only to see Mildred Price's husband escort Haley onto the dance floor. Adam's chest swelled. There was his wife, in practically no underwear, held in the arms of another man. If it hadn't been that old geezer George Price, he'd have cut in on them immediately. Instead, he sank into the chair beside Jay.

"Was that Iris McKettrick you were just talking to?" He kept his gaze glued on his wife as he spoke.

Jay, equally distracted by Elizabeth in the arms of

Phillip Mayfield, didn't look at Adam. "I'm meeting Monday with her and her husband."

Adam drummed his fingers, gazing at Haley. Six days. Yes, the more he thought about it, the more he realized six days would be adequate time to court his wife. He looked up suddenly at Jay. "Both of them?"

"Everyone knows Iris is largely responsible for McKettrick's success." Jay's shoulders sagged as he saw Elizabeth smile into Phillip's face as they whirled in front of them. "Women…"

"And you think Iris will sell her husband on your plans?"

"Absolutely." Jay planted his elbow on the table and propped his chin on it, still watching Elizabeth.

"Jay, have you ever considered working for Harrington Construction?"

When the song ended, Haley applauded politely and hardly noticed George Price being elbowed aside as Adam appeared before her. He slid his hand over hers. "I'd like to dance with my wife."

"I'd like that, too," Haley said.

Adam fought the urge to crush her against him, and managed to keep a respectable distance from those lovely bosoms of hers as he guided them though the other dancers. Holding her in his arms caused his need for her to grow fiercer. He drew in a deep, steadying breath. Six days. He'd have to stick to his schedule.

"Are you enjoying the evening?"

He was now. Content just to look at her and feel the fine lines of her body in his arms, Adam strained for some thread of conversation. "Yes, but I don't think your cousin is."

Haley glimpsed Jay, still sitting at the table where she and Iris McKettrick had left him. "He's pining over Elizabeth Denning. He told her to see other men, and now that she's actually doing it, he's upset."

"Why doesn't he just ask her to dance?"

"Something about his pride, I imagine."

Adam grunted. He certainly knew how that felt.

"Did you see the Olivers here tonight?" Haley asked.

Images of their own wedding, which had taken place at the Olivers' reception, bloomed in Adam's mind. Haley in his arms, then in his bed, the room they'd shared, just overhead. Adam's gut tightened. He'd never look at the Madison again without thinking of rolling around in bed with Haley.

"I didn't know Harry and Laurel were back from their honeymoon."

Haley nodded. "I invited them for supper."

"Good. Harry's been gone a long time. Things down at the courthouse have been a mess without him. I've missed him." And he envied him for being able to wile away these past months making love to his wife. Adam's chest caught. He should have done the same.

The song ended, but Adam didn't release her. She smelled delicious, and he couldn't pull himself away. He wanted to dance every number with her, keep her to himself all night.

"I have to speak with Leonora Montgomery, Adam. Excuse me."

Quick as a wink she slid from his embrace and slipped behind him. His back suddenly ignited as he felt her breasts brush against him. He whirled, but she melted into the crowd. Desire wound deep within him.

Five days wouldn't be rushing her too much, he suddenly decided. Five days was plenty. Adam mentally adjusted his schedule once more. Five days.

Adam eased through the crowd toward the buffet table, looking for Haley, but spotted his father instead.

Martin joined him. "I talked to McKettrick. It looks good. Real good."

Adam slid his hands into his trouser pockets, scanning the crowd, not the least interested in the McKettrick project. "He has two more builders to talk with."

Martin waved away the notion. "We've got it."

"I don't know. Sacramento Building—"

"Forget them!" Martin scowled at him. "I've had enough trouble this evening with Kip and that sister of yours. I don't want any more."

Tolerating his father's foul moods had begun to wear on Adam lately. "What's wrong now?"

"Kip told me about your talk with him. I'm telling you to keep out of it. Understand? I don't want you seeing that headmaster, getting the boy out of trouble. He left school over some silly nonsense about dancing, and he'll have to be punished for it. He got himself into trouble, he can get himself out."

Anger tightened Adam's chest. "Kip needs somebody to stand up for him. That headmaster—"

"You can't go fighting his battles for him. He's got to stand up for himself. It'll teach him to be a man."

"He's barely thirteen years old."

Martin nodded curtly. "The sooner he learns, the

better. I told him so tonight. I told him I wouldn't let you talk to the school for him.''

Adam squared off in front of his father. ''You told him *what?*''

Heads turned at the buffet table. Adam lowered his voice. ''You're wrong on this one, Martin.''

''And what makes you the expert on Kip all of a sudden? That wife of yours?''

Maybe it was Haley, and the things she'd noticed in Kip that no one else saw. Or maybe it was that for the first time in his life, Adam had actually spent time with his brother, and he could thank Haley for that, also. Maybe those things caused him to realize what Kip really needed.

Adam pointed an accusing finger at his father. ''You've ignored Kip since he was born. You'd better think about what you're doing before you have no sons left at all.''

''Haley, you've got to help me.''

Jay latched on to Haley's arm and pulled her into a corner of the ballroom, behind some potted palms.

''Gracious, Jay, what's wrong?'' He looked absolutely frantic. ''What happened?''

He gulped hard. ''I've made the biggest mistake of my life. It's Elizabeth. I was a fool to let her get away. I realized it just now, watching her with that bastard Mayfield. I've got to get her back, Haley. I've got to!''

''Calm down, Jay.'' Haley took both his hands. ''First of all, are you sure this time?''

''Oh, God, yes.'' He pulled his hands from her and paced fitfully in the tiny space behind the palms. ''I

love her with all my heart, Haley. I was just too stupid
to realize it. What am I going to do?''

Haley smiled. ''Tell her, Jay. Tell her what you've
just told me.''

He stopped short, his eyes bulging. ''Tell her? Just
like that? Blurt it out—here? In front of everyone?''

''Why not?''

''Mayfield is here.'' He pointed through the palm
fronds. ''What if she loves him? What if she laughs
in my face? What if Mayfield beats me to a pulp?''

''You have to talk to her.''

''Mayfield won't let her out of his sight. They've
been on the dance floor all evening.''

''All right. Let's think a minute.'' Haley pressed
her lips together while Jay paced. ''I know. Come
with me.''

''Where are we going?''

She took his arm. ''Stay alert. We'll get her in the
clear, then you grab her.''

''*We?* I can't—''

''Be quiet and pay attention. Go stand beside the
refreshment table.''

Haley sent Jay on his way, then turned in a circle,
searching the room. Only one person could help her
now. She found him quickly.

''Come here, Adam. I want you.''

He choked on an hors d'oeuvre and looked down
at Haley at his elbow. ''What?''

She slid her hand into the crook of his elbow.
''Please, it's a very delicate matter. There's no one I
can turn to but you.''

Adam coughed and handed his plate to a passing
waiter.

Haley lifted her shoulders. "It must be something about the Madison that brings out this sort of thing."

His belly clenched. "I know just what you mean."

"Then you don't mind?"

"Oh, God, no." His knees almost gave out.

"Good." She urged him across the room. "Let's hurry."

Hurry? Adam nearly heaved her over his shoulder and raced upstairs with her before he realized they were walking the wrong way. He froze in his tracks. "Where are we going?"

She frowned up at him. "To help Jay, of course."

"Oh." His shoulders sagged.

"He's finally realized he's in love with Elizabeth, but her escort for the evening is making a nuisance of himself. We've got to separate them."

Hardly the couple he'd envisioned getting together this evening, but helping Haley couldn't do him any harm. Adam forced his own ardor to cool. "What can I do?"

"This is my plan." Haley whispered the details as they skirted the edge of the dance floor.

When they reached the other side of the room, Adam nodded and waded into the crowd of whirling partners. He tapped Phillip Mayfield's shoulder. "Pardon me. Cutting in."

Surprised, Phillip and Elizabeth separated, and Adam swept her into his arms. Haley appeared immediately and cupped her palm under Phillip's elbow.

"Good evening, Mr. Mayfield. So nice to see you again."

Phillip glanced at Elizabeth and Adam, then offered Haley a smile. "Good evening, Mrs. Harrington."

She urged him away from the dance floor. "Have

you had the opportunity yet to speak with my husband's aunt? She has the most fascinating stories from her recent travels. Come with me—she'd love to share them.''

''But...''

She ignored his protest and hauled him to the far corner of the ballroom, where Isabelle stood chatting with several other ladies. Haley made quick introductions.

''Aunt Izzy, Mr. Mayfield was just saying how fascinating your travels sounded. Could you tell him about your trip?''

Her eyes rounded and she hooked his arm, pulling him into their circle. ''Certainly, certainly. First, I'll start with the day I left...''

Haley craned her neck to see Adam deposit Elizabeth at a table, then leave, with Jay hovering only a few feet behind her. Minutes dragged by, and Jay didn't move. Haley glanced at Isabelle; her story was still going strong. Adam caught her eye, and they both shrugged, wondering why Jay hadn't approached Elizabeth. He stood in the corner, shuffling his feet. More precious minutes slipped by—even Aunt Izzy couldn't talk forever. Finally, Haley started through the crowd. Jay needed a little push.

As she drew near, she saw Adam approach Jay and confer with him for a moment before the two of them walked to the refreshment buffet. Their backs to her, they hovered together, heads bobbing, before Jay finally walked to Elizabeth.

Surprised, Elizabeth looked at him.

Jay extended a crystal cup. ''Punch?''

Frustrated, Adam stood on the sidelines, his gaze combing the crowd. Where was she? He'd hardly seen her tonight. He'd felt like a hound pursuing a rabbit all evening, catching a glimpse of his wife occasionally, cornering her momentarily before she scurried away to attend to something or speak to someone. She was his wife, damn it, and he wanted her beside him. He wanted to hold her in his arms and dance with her. He wanted to take her upstairs and—

Adam folded his arms across his chest and reined in his lustful thoughts. Five days. He'd shortened his plan to five days, but even that period of time seemed interminable at the moment. He'd never make it if he kept allowing such thoughts to creep into his mind. Too much was at stake for him to let his instincts take charge.

A familiar scent tantalized his nose, whipping his desire into an instant frenzy. His chest swelled as Haley appeared at his elbow. Adam grabbed her with both hands.

"Could I have the last dance of the evening with my husband?" She batted her lashes demurely.

The last dance, already? Adam wasn't sure whether to be disappointed that the evening was ending, or relieved that she would get out of that dress and into something that wouldn't drive him crazy with wanting.

Adam secured her hand in his and guided them onto the crowded floor.

Haley gazed up at him. "Have you seen Jay and Elizabeth anywhere?"

Since he was already having trouble keeping himself under control, the last thing Adam wanted to talk about was another couple off God knew where doing God knew what.

He cleared his throat. "No, I haven't."

"They must be here somewhere."

Haley turned quickly to look over her shoulder, causing Adam's fingers to brush against her breast. His hand ignited, flames racing up his arm, then down to the center of his body. Hot urgency claimed him.

Haley shrugged, as if she hadn't felt anything, and fell into step once more. "Well, I suppose they're all right."

They might be all right, but what about him? Adam ground his teeth together.

Suddenly Haley pressed herself hard against him. Her breasts melted into his chest, her thighs met his. Unchecked want charged his blood.

Haley blushed and dipped her lashes. "It's so crowded out here. Sorry."

He tried to respond, but his mouth went dry. All he could manage was a small smile as heat raged through his body.

He'd been desperate to dance with her, and now he couldn't wait for the song to end. He couldn't keep a respectable distance from her. She brushed against him with every step, her thigh against his, her knee between his, her breast on his chest. Somehow they shifted, and his hand eased lower on her back. He even imagined that her fingers, intertwined with his, were caressing him.

Adam fought to hold himself in check, sure that Haley would think him the biggest cad in the world for taking such liberties with her on the dance floor. And what would happen to his plan then? He'd have to back it up to seven days again. Adam gritted his teeth. There was no way in hell he'd last seven days.

Mercifully, the song ended, but, desperate as he was to escape the torture of Haley in his arms, he couldn't let her go. Her cheeks pinkened, and he finally released her.

"I have a few things to check on, then we can go. Are you in a hurry to get home?"

He was in more than a hurry—almost frantic. Adam stepped away, grateful for the distance between them. "I'd like to go as soon as possible."

She nodded and hurried away. Adam milled around, talking with a few people, grabbing a bite from the buffet, forcing his thoughts away from the room upstairs and concentrating on his five-day plan. The ballroom was nearly empty before Haley appeared again.

"Your father is quite the topic of conversation," Haley said as they made their way across the lobby.

"Martin? What did he do?"

"He danced with Virginia Mason all evening. Everyone is talking."

Good. If everyone was talking about Martin, that meant no one had noticed how he lusted after his own wife all evening. A public embarrassment like that might send her running back to San Francisco. Adam's stomach clenched. He had to get Haley home. He had to start on his plan. His body couldn't take much more torment.

Cool night air swept them as they stepped out of the Madison. Golden streetlights glowed in the darkness. A group of people waited at the curb to board the last few hansoms. The older patrons of the gala gone hours ago, this boisterous younger crowd laughed and talked freely; a flask passed among them. All acquaintances of Adam's and Haley's, they drew them into their midst easily.

Jostled by the crowd, Haley rubbed against him, but didn't seem to notice as she talked with her friends. Adam sucked in deep breaths of the night air. He felt like a banjo strung tight enough to pop.

He craned his neck looking off down the street. "Where the devil is Edward with the carriage?"

"I sent him home with Chrissy and my things, but he should have returned long ago. I can't imagine what's taking him— Oh, dear." Haley leaned closer. "Edward and Chrissy are probably having an indiscreet moment in the carriage house right now."

His insides flamed again. "What?"

"I caught them out there once. They were groaning and moaning, and her skirt was—"

"I get the picture."

Annoyed, Adam pushed his way to the front of the crowd. Fine thing, his own driver off having his fill, while he waited on the curb, panting like a monk. Adam commandeered the last hansom cab and pulled Haley along with him.

She stopped at the door and turned back to her friends. "There won't be another cab along for some time. Come ride with us. We'll drop you off."

A cheer went up, and everyone piled in. Adam took a seat in the far corner, with Haley beside him, while three other couples squeezed onto seats designed for far fewer people. Just before the door closed, Haley jumped up.

"Oh, there's Estelle Padgette—I've got to speak to her."

In a flash, she disappeared out the door and cornered the young woman and her husband as they exited the Madison. They spoke for a moment, and then all three walked to the cab.

Derek Padgette stuck his head inside. "Got room for two more?"

A chorus of welcomes rose from everyone as Derek and Estelle Padgette joined them. Skirts rustled, elbows jostled, bodies shifted, until they settled in. A round of laughter broke out as Haley stood looking inside.

"Oh, dear, we've forgotten Haley!"

She laughed with them. "Not to worry. I'll just sit with my husband."

Adam braced himself as she climbed in and headed toward him. No, she couldn't mean to—

Her soft, round bottom settled on his lap, taking the breath out of him. Casually she rested her arm on the seat behind his head, thrusting her breast into his face. She shifted suddenly and wedged her legs between his, pressing her thigh solidly against him. The physical contact nearly drove him straight out of the seat.

"Am I making you uncomfortable?" she asked softly.

She was making him crazy. Adam curled his fingers into fists. The Padgettes lived only a few blocks over, and once they left the cab, Haley could sit beside him. He could make it that far.

Haley leaned closer. "I know you're anxious to get home, so I told the driver to drop us off first, even though we live the farthest from town."

The cab lurched forward, shifting Haley on his lap. Her knee caressed him boldly. Adam gulped hard and closed his eyes. Five days...five days...

Chapter Sixteen

To hell with five days. Four days. Four days, and not one damn minute longer.

Adam squirmed beneath the exquisite torture of Haley on his lap. His legs spread wide, hers wedged between them, she plied him steadily with her thigh. Gently at first, then with increased pressure, and then gently again. Slowly, then faster, and slower once more. For a moment, Adam thought she did it purposely, not simply undulating with the sway of the cab. But Haley was an innocent. She couldn't know what she was doing to him.

Nor could she help her breasts hovering in his face. Full and ripe, nearly spilling out of her gown, they called to him, taunted him, begged him to lean forward just a few inches.

Adam curled both hands into fists, thankful for the darkness of the cab and the fullness of her skirt. Everyone else—including Haley—laughed and joked, unaware of his excruciating agony. For a moment, he feared a repeat of the time Sally Winthrope had explored him in the closet at her thirteenth birthday party; he'd never been sure which of them was more surprised.

Adam ground his teeth together. Tonight, there could be no such surprises. Haley was delicate and innocent. He'd stick to his plan. Somehow.

The hansom cab finally rolled into their driveway, and Adam nearly dumped Haley on the floor in his haste to end his torment. He gulped in deep breaths of the cool air as the cab pulled away, the laughter from inside fading into the night.

Haley glanced toward the rear of the house as they climbed onto the porch. "Do you think you should go out to the carriage house and see about Edward?"

That was just what he needed, to walk in on his driver and wife's maid, locked in the throes of bliss. Adam opened the front door for her. "I'll see to it tomorrow."

Haley shrugged as she walked past him. "To hear Chrissy talk, they'll probably still be at it then, too."

Adam groaned and followed her swaying hips inside.

"Could you come with me, Adam?" Haley asked as she crossed the foyer. "I want to check on the sitting room before I go up."

"Tonight?" If his plan had a prayer of working, he needed to get her out of his sight immediately.

"Jay worked on the new window seat while I was at the Madison today, and I wanted to see if it's turning out as I asked." She gave him a tiny smile. "I'd like your opinion on the workmanship. You know I trust you."

A trust that was hopelessly misplaced. Adam swore silently and followed her down the hall.

In the sitting room, Haley turned the gaslight low

and knelt to inspect the new cabinets under the window seat. She looked up at Adam. "Well? What do you think?"

He thought she was the most beautiful woman he'd ever seen. And the most alluring. A force he could feel but not see pulled him across the room to her. He gazed down at her soft white shoulders, her delicate arms, and the full view of her breasts. Desire swamped him once more.

"The work is fine. Get up, Haley."

She frowned slightly. "But you haven't looked closely."

"I have. Believe me, I have." If he looked any closer, she'd never make it up to her room tonight. "Let's go."

Slowly she got to her feet, but she made no effort to leave. She eased closer to him. "Are you ready for bed?"

Adam pulled loose his bow tie, suddenly desperate for a gulp of air. "Oh, hell, yes."

"Let me help you."

Haley pushed his hands aside and opened the collar of his shirt. He held his chin up and dared not move as her soft fingers brushed against his throat.

She raked her nails through the crisp hair curling out of his collar. "There, does that feel better?"

God, how he wanted her. Internal heat consumed him, melting away his resolve to stick to his four-day plan.

He captured both her hands. "You'd better go."

She eased closer, until her breasts brushed his chest. "Is that what you want, Adam?"

He swallowed hard. "Yes."

Haley slid her hands from his and splayed them

across his chest. He jumped. "All right. If you say so."

His knees weakened. Desire and need twisted an urgent knot in his gut. He wanted to press himself full against her, feel her body yielding to his. Adam strained for self-control. With supreme willpower, he pulled her hands from him. "It's for the best."

Haley smiled demurely and walked from the room. Adam dragged his hand over his forehead and followed. He forced his gaze onto the steps under his feet, ignoring her bobbing bustle just ahead of him, said a respectable good-night and hurried into his bedroom.

Four days. Adam ripped off his jacket and tie and plucked open the buttons of his shirt. Four goddamn days of pure torture. If he had another night like tonight, he'd never last.

Burning up, he threw open the window and shrugged out of his shirt and undershirt, letting the breeze cool his heated body. Adam braced his arms against the window casing and stared down at the moonlit lawn. He ached for her, absolutely ached. He'd never waited this long for any woman in his entire life. But no other woman had been this important before. No other woman had been his wife.

Adam shoved away from the window. He'd built his life by making and following specific plans and schedules. Now, when he was so close to having everything he wanted, wasn't the time to change. No matter what his body demanded.

Adam yanked down the covers and sat on the edge of the bed. A cold soak in the tub. It couldn't hurt. He pulled off his shoes and socks and headed for the bathroom.

A soft knock sounded on the connecting door. Haley. He stopped still on the thick carpet. Wanton desire surged through him again.

For a moment, he considered not answering her knock, thinking she'd just go away. But then the door opened.

"Adam?"

He waited, his bare chest heaving, as she stepped into the dim light of his room. She still wore her gown, but her hair, released from its combs and pins, hung loose. She turned her back to him and pulled her thick tresses over her shoulder.

"Would you help me with my gown?" She glanced back at him.

Adam ran his sweaty palms down his trousers. "Where is Chrissy?"

She lifted her slim shoulders. "Still with Edward, I suppose."

Great. Just what he wanted to be reminded of.

"I took off everything else that I could. My slippers and stockings." Haley lifted the hem of her gown, displaying her shapely ankles and bare feet. She shook her hips. "My petticoats, too. I wasn't wearing any drawers, but you already knew that."

He knew it, all right. The thought had been burned into his mind all evening.

"All that's left is my gown. Could you unfasten it for me?"

He stared, mesmerized by her shapely backside. "That's all you want me to do? Just unfasten it?" If that was all, maybe he could manage it.

She looked over her shoulder again and grinned. "I don't want to sleep in the thing, and who knows how long Chrissy and Edward will be?"

Adam said a silent prayer and approached her cautiously. She stood very still as he worked the fasteners of her gown. One by one they opened until the bodice loosened. Haley folded her hands across her middle as it sagged away from her.

Sweat broke out on Adam's forehead. He stepped back. "There. It's done."

"Thank you."

She took a step away, then stopped.

Adam's heart stopped too.

"Oops. I forgot about my corset."

Haley shimmied, and the gown sank into a pool around her feet. She unfastened the sash of her bustle and let it fall, then stepped out of them both and turned to face Adam.

His knees nearly buckled. Haley stood before him, clad only in her corset, which barely covered the tops of her shapely legs, cinched her waist tight and pushed her round bosoms higher.

Haley turned and backed toward him until her bottom settled lightly against him. She leaned forward ever so slightly. "Just pull the strings and it will come loose."

Heat radiated from her soft, round bottom, seeping into him. Adam squeezed his eyes shut. "Haley, I don't think..."

"Then I'll slide it down." She swayed her hips across his fly.

He opened his eyes and gulped hard. "I can't..."

Haley straightened and turned to face him. She'd done everything she knew to get him in bed with her and get their marriage back on track. She'd pressed every body part she had against every part of his body all evening, she'd connived to send Edward home early, she'd planted herself on his lap, and now here she stood in only her corset—and Adam still wouldn't have anything to do with her.

Haley sighed inwardly. Maybe it was hopeless. Maybe her marriage really didn't stand a chance. "Fine, then. I'll go."

"No!" Adam grasped her upper arms as she moved away and pulled her against him. His flesh burned with the heat of desire, the passion of love.

Haley gazed up at him with bewildered eyes. She'd never seen such a tortured expression on anyone's face before. "Adam, what's wrong with you tonight?"

"Nothing. It's just that I didn't want to rush you into anything." His big hands caressed the flesh of her arms. "I, uh, I had a plan—a schedule for us to..."

"I see." Adam and his schedules. She should have known. Haley circled his waist, settling her breasts firmly against him. "And how long did you schedule for?"

His tense muscles quivered. "Four days."

"Four days, huh?" Haley slid her thigh upward along his. "Well, today is Saturday, so that means we'll wait until Wednesday. No, that's not right. It's after midnight, so actually today is Sunday, and that means we'll wait until Thursday. Is that your schedule?"

He caressed her soft, pliant flesh with his thumbs. "Well, yes, that was it, but now—"

"Now...what?" Haley rose on her toes and nuzzled a kiss against his neck.

His heart hammered in his chest. "Now, I'm thinking of altering the schedule. Making it, say, three days.''

Haley stretched higher and closed her mouth over his.

He responded greedily, then pulled away. "How about two days?''

She glided her palms across his hard chest.

Adam groaned. "How about one day?''

"How about now?''

"Oh, God, yes…'' The last shred of self-restraint flew right out the open window. Adam locked his arms around her and pulled her off her feet. "I'm never going to make another goddamn plan or schedule as long as I live.''

Adam moaned low in his chest and covered her mouth with his. He kissed her deeply, hungrily, and she responded eagerly, rising on her toes to meet him. He inched his hands across her back and fumbled with the strings of her corset until they pulled free. The garment fell to her feet.

Desire consumed him as he moved his palms downward, along the fine lines of her body, cupped her softness and pulled her tight against him. Heat raged within him, too strong to control.

His blatant want for her pressed hard against her belly. For a fleeting instant it startled her, but his strong arms around her, and the demands of his lips, drove that fear away. Haley looped her arms around his neck and shifted to capture him intimately. A shudder racked her, and she moaned.

Adam stopped suddenly and cradled her face between his palms. In the moonlight slanting through the windows, he gazed at her lovingly. They'd done this before, at the Madison, and he wasn't certain Haley remembered. But he did. The memories scorched his mind and tormented his body. He swept Haley into his arms and carried her to his bed.

The mattress felt soft beneath her as she stretched out and Adam sat beside her. He covered her palms with his and pressed them gently against the pillow, then lowered his head and touched his lips to her forehead. He trailed hot kisses down her face, across her lips, and into the hollow of her neck. Yearning, deep and hot, coiled within her. Haley turned her head to meet his lips.

He spared no time on a leisurely feast; his hunger was too strong. Adam shucked off his pants and drawers and climbed into bed beside Haley. She curled into him immediately, and the sweetness of her flesh drove his desire higher. Greedily he covered her body with his hands, cupping her breasts, caressing them, then tasting them, until she moaned and writhed against him. Her legs entwined with his, stroking him. He rose above her, desperate for the intimate relief only she could provide, desperate to show her the love his heart and soul held only for her.

She welcomed him in her, seeking to satisfy the strong craving that claimed her. Haley slid her hands over the strong muscles of his arms, through the crisp hair of his chest and the tiny, tight disks buried there. There was such joy in the feel of him. He moved rhythmically within her, slowly and gently, then deeper. Her body tightened, and her need grew. She flung her arms around his neck and grasped a fistful of hair as his thrusts lifted her higher.

Lost in the heat of his own desire and her need, Adam strained for control. Throbbing, aching, he curled his hands into the pillow beneath her head, willing himself to hold back. He'd never felt so swollen in his life, never wanted fulfillment so completely. He'd never wanted a woman as he wanted Haley. His wife.

She tossed her head fitfully on the pillow and held tight to him, as desire built steadily, fueled by his exacting movements. He took her higher and higher, until at last great waves of pleasure broke over her again and again. She cried his name and twisted her hand into his soft, thick hair.

Beneath him, sheathing him, her body tightened and blossomed, driving her hips against him violently. Adam groaned and held back, waiting until he knew she was ready, then drove himself into her. He called her name and buried himself deep inside. Over and over he poured out his love, in an aching release, until he was drained of everything but the warmth in his heart as it beat steadily with her.

Moonlight bathed the room in soft shadows as Haley roused from a light sleep and saw Adam staring down at her. Locked in his arms, he held her tight against him, cradling her head on his wide shoulder. He looked as though he'd been awake for a while.

She felt her cheeks pinken. "I fell asleep. I guess I was...overcome. Sorry."

Adam ran his finger along the curve of her jaw. "Don't apologize. I wanted you to be overcome."

"It's a good thing?"

He grinned. "Oh, yes, honey."

She rolled to face him, content in the security of his strong arms. "This is all new to me, you know."

He draped his leg over hers. "Not exactly. Our night at the Madison. You remember, don't you?"

Haley shrugged. "No."

"None of it?" He touched his hand to his forehead.

She shook her head. "None of it."

Every moment of their lovemaking etched deep emotion in his mind. The recollections had driven him crazy. "But you must. How could you not remember?"

Haley threaded her fingers through the crisp hair on his chest. "I guess we'll have to keep at it until something jogs my memory."

Adam looked down and saw her grinning at him— that special grin only lovers share. He laughed low in his chest. "I guess we will. And I want you to know I'm committed to restoring your memory, no matter what it takes."

Haley snuggled closer. "Who'd have thought coming to Sacramento and attending a wedding would lead to so much?"

"Next time I'm in San Francisco, I think I'll look up this Farnsworth character and thank him personally."

She laughed aloud. "If it hadn't been for Reginald, I'd have never left San Francisco. But I don't think he'll be very happy to be reminded of me."

Adam pushed himself up on his elbow. "All right, now. I've waited long enough. You've got to tell me exactly what happened between you and Farnsworth."

"I caught him with my best friend the morning of our engagement party."

"Ouch. That hurt."

She shrugged. "At the time, yes. He begged me to forgive him, said it meant nothing. Mother had planned a huge wedding, our families were both prominent, and to break it off would be a scandal nobody wanted. So I went along with it.''

"Until…''

"Until the engagement party got under way. Three hundred guests, crystal, china, the finest hotel, champagne Grandfather Hasting had sent from France. And when I was presented as the happy bride-to-be, I knew I could never go through with it. So, right there in front of everyone, I informed Mr. Reginald Farnsworth that I'd rather die a shriveled-up old maid than be tethered to a lying, cheating skunk like him for the rest of my life. I dumped the cake into his lap and left.''

A deep laugh rumbled from Adam's chest. "I wish I could have seen that.''

"Mother was quite beside herself, but I wouldn't change my mind. I wouldn't marry someone I didn't love.''

Adam stroked his fingers through her hair. "No wonder you were so shocked when you woke up at the Madison married to me.''

"You mucked up my plans pretty good, that's for sure.''

He planted a kiss on the end of her nose. "I hope you'll let me make it up to you.''

She grinned. "So far this evening, you're doing all the right things.''

"Oh, honey, there's a lot more where that came from.''

"Good.'' Haley looked up at him suddenly. "Do you think Jay and Elizabeth are doing what we're doing?''

Adam shrugged. "If he's smart, he'll get that woman into his bed and not let her out.''

Her chin went up a notch. "Is that what you intend to do to me?"

"Hell, yes."

"Good." Haley kissed his cheek. "But what about work? Won't Martin wonder where you are, day after day?"

"I'll get your cousin to cover for me. I offered him a job tonight, you know."

Haley sat straight up in bed. "What? You offered Jay a job with Harrington Construction?"

Adam rolled onto his back. "What's wrong with that?"

"Jay would never abandon Sacramento Building. Our fathers built that company together. It means the world to him."

"Maybe." Adam reached over and coiled a lock of her hair around his finger. "Running your own company is hard work. It's risky. You can lose everything over one bad deal."

"But he's put his whole life into the company."

"Your cousin might want the opportunity to take it easy now, let somebody else take the risks." He sat up and slid his hand around her shoulders. "Being cradled in the protective arms of Harrington Construction isn't so bad, is it?"

Adam's arms certainly felt enticing. Haley leaned against him. "I think I'll need more information before I can make a decision."

He grinned. "Is that right? Well, let me demonstrate."

Adam lowered her onto the bed again and covered her mouth with his in a deep, loving kiss. His hands moved over her slowly, leisurely, bringing her senses alive. She responded readily, touching him, seeking out places their earlier frantic lovemaking hadn't allowed time for.

He groaned as she stroked him, and parted her thighs for him. Both of them were eager to once more know each other fully. They melded together easily, then urgently, moving in an anxious rhythm until ecstasy overcame them both and they fell, spent, in each other's arms.

"Mr. Harrington! Mr. Harrington!"

Frantic knocking drove Adam from a sound sleep. Dazed he sat up. "What the hell—?"

Haley lifted her head from the pillow. "What's wrong?"

The bedroom door burst open. Haley gasped and pulled the sheet up to her chin as Bernard barged into the room.

Adam leaned forward, sheltering Haley. "What the devil is going on?"

Light from the hallway outlined Bernard as he stepped into the room, his hair sticking up, his robe tied askew.

"Mr. Harrington, something dreadful has happened."

Adam sprang from the bed and grabbed his drawers. "What is it?"

"It's your brother, sir. He's been shot."

Chapter Seventeen

"Shot? Who shot him?"

Adam shoved into his trousers and charged across the room.

Bernard fell back.

"What the hell happened?"

In the shadows, Haley sprang from the bed and slipped into Adam's shirt. "Where is Kip?"

Trembling, Bernard pointed down the hall. "I put him in the last bedroom."

Adam fastened his trousers. "How did he get here?"

"Send for the doctor, Bernard, and get Mrs. Ardmore up here with water and bandages. I'll be right there." Haley disappeared through the connecting door to her bedroom.

"Yes, ma'am. I've already dispatched Edward for the doctor and Mr. Harrington." Bernard gulped hard, then turned to Adam. "The man who brought him here is waiting downstairs."

Adam shoved him aside.

"Sir?"

He turned back. In the pale light, Bernard's face was ashen. Adam's gut knotted.

"It's your father's guard from the construction site. He shot him."

A string of filthy curses tumbled from Adam's lips as he hurried down the staircase. In the foyer, the front door stood open, and deep in the house he heard shouts and running feet. A man stood in the corner.

His eyes bulged in his colorless face as Adam advanced on him. He fell back against the wall, wringing his hat in his hands.

"I never meant to hurt the little fellow, Mr. Harrington. I didn't know it was him—I swear, I didn't know."

Adam's chest heaved, and he stopped short. "What the hell happened?"

"Your father—he said to shoot. Said he'd fire me if I let one more piece of Harrington equipment get damaged."

Adam's breath caught. "It was Kip? He vandalized the work site?"

"Yes, sir. I guess it was him doing it all along." He shook his head. "Who'd'a thought a kid like him—a kid with everything—would tear up his own father's business? But I swear to you, Mr. Harrington, I'd have never fired that shot if I'd known—I swear. I tried to take him to the doctor, but he's bleeding so much I got scared. I brought him here because it was closest."

Adam cursed again and ran back up the stairs, his bare feet silent on the carpet. He stopped outside the last bedroom. In the dim light, he saw Haley bent over the bed, working. Chrissy and Mrs. Ardmore, in dressing gowns and mobcaps, held extra lanterns, basins of water. Haley's calm voice bolstered all of them.

Between the hovering women, Adam caught a glimpse of Kip. He lay perfectly still. Frightfully still. Blood was everywhere. Soaking his shirt, streaking his face, seeping into the quilt and linens. On Haley's hands, the sleeves of her dressing gown. Adam's stomach heaved. Damn Martin and his armed guards.

He forced himself into the room. "Where the hell is the doctor? What's taking so long?"

Haley looked up at him as she pressed a fresh bandage against the wound. "It's his shoulder."

Adam stopped at the foot of the bed. Kip looked so tiny and fragile, his eyes closed, mumbling incoherently. He wanted to grab him up, hold him tight, take the wound into his own, stronger body and make him well again. "Is he going to be all right?"

"Why don't you go downstairs and wait for Dr. Mather? Get him up here as soon as he arrives."

Adam nodded quickly. He knew he was being sent away, but he felt so damn useless just standing around. At least now he'd have something to do. In his room, he pulled on his shoes and a shirt, then hurried downstairs and paced the foyer, smacking his fist into his palm. A few minutes later, when Edward whipped the horses up the drive, Adam yanked Dr. Mather from the carriage and hustled him upstairs.

The bedroom door closed ominously in front of him, blocking out the sight, but only muffling the sounds. The doctor's deep voice, Haley's softer one. Adam began pacing again.

Shouts came from the foyer, and footsteps on the stairs brought Martin and Gwen into the hallway.

Adam's hands clenched into fists at the sight of his father.

"What the hell happened?" Martin demanded.

Beside him, Gwen looked pale, afraid. She touched Adam's arm with her trembling hands. "How is he?"

Adam shook her off, his gaze riveting his father. "One of those damn guards you hired shot him. I told you something like this would happen."

Martin's face reddened, and he ground his teeth together. "You're saying this is my fault?"

"I sure as hell am!"

"I had every right to protect Harrington property!"

Gwen pressed her hand to her forehead. "Kip vandalized the work sites? Kip?"

Adam spared her a glance. "Yes, it was Kip." His gaze impaled his father once more. "And he was very nearly killed because of it!"

"You wait just a damn minute! I didn't know—"

"You didn't try to find out!"

"Don't preach to me! This isn't my fault! I—"

The bedroom door opened, and Haley stepped into the hall, glaring her disapproval at the two men going at each other. They fell silent at the sight of Kip's blood on her hands as she wiped them with a linen towel.

Gwen pressed her palm against the wall, steadying herself. "What is the doctor doing? Is Kip going to be all right? What's happening in there?"

Haley raked her gaze over the three of them. "I don't know, but this certainly isn't helping anything. The doctor will be out as soon as he knows something."

Gwen wrapped both her arms across her middle and turned away. Adam and Martin glared at each other, then paced in separate directions. Haley waited beside the door, feeling more needed here as referee than inside, assisting the doctor; Chrissy and Mrs. Ardmore had the situation in hand.

Minutes dragged by in tense silence. Neither Adam nor Martin spoke; they just paced, avoiding each other. Haley had expected such a reaction from the two of them, men accustomed to controlling every aspect of their lives, now helplessly unable to control something so vital. But she hadn't expected Gwen to look so troubled, so lost in the depths of worry. Maybe Kip meant more to Gwen than she'd realized.

The foyer clock chimed the hour, the tolling faint below them. Bernard brought up coffee, but the tray sat untouched. Time crept slowly in the silent house until finally the bedroom door opened and the doctor stepped into the hallway. Everyone surged forward.

Dr. Mather held up his hands, silencing their questions. "It doesn't appear to be serious."

"Oh, thank God." Gwen bit into her knuckles and turned away.

"But time will tell. He needs rest. Lots of rest." Dr. Mather turned to Adam. "I don't want him moved. He'll have to stay here."

"Of course. Is he awake? Can I see him?"

Martin stepped forward. "I want to see him."

Dr. Mather adjusted his glasses. "The boy's awake, but the only person he wants to talk to is Haley."

Martin glared at her. "Her?"

"Why not her?" Adam demanded. "She's shown him more kindness than you have."

"Like hell she has."

Gwen gulped. "Please, Dr. Mather, I have to see him."

"Quiet down, all three of you." Dr. Mather shook his head in disgust. "I'm sure not letting any of you in there, snipping at each other like this. The boy wants to see Haley, and that's who he's seeing. Now, keep it quiet out here."

Aware of the hot stares on her back, Haley followed the doctor into the bedroom. Chrissy and Mrs. Ardmore left.

Kip lay beneath the stained sheet, wrapped in white gauze, his bare chest rising and falling in shallow breaths.

"I've given him something to make him sleep. He'll be out in a few minutes." Dr. Mather turned to the bedside table and began packing his equipment into his bag.

Haley sat down carefully on the edge of the bed and slid her hand over Kip's. His eyes opened; soft light from the lantern darkened the circles under his eyes.

"You gave us quite a scare." Haley brushed back the hair from his forehead. "But you're safe now. We're going to take good care of you. You'll be home in no time."

Big tears pooled in his eyes, and he shook his head frantically. "No, no! Don't make me go home. Father will be so mad at me."

Haley glanced over her shoulder at the faces of Adam, Martin and Gwen, staring in from the hallway. She wiped away a tear as it rolled down Kip's cheek.

"No one is mad at you. We just want you to get well."

"It was me." He squeezed his eyes shut. "I was the one tearing up Father's work things."

"That doesn't matter now, Kip."

He looked up at her with pleading eyes. "Don't make me go home. I want to stay here. With you."

"But, Kip, your family wants you."

"They hate me." Tears flooded his cheeks. "All of them. They all hate me."

Stunned, Haley gasped. "No, they don't."

He drew in a ragged breath, sobbing. "Yes, they do. It was my fault. She died on account of me."

A moment passed before Haley realized what he meant. "Do you mean your mother?"

"I caused it, and they all hate me. They've always hated me." Racking sobs shook his small body. "It's my fault."

"Oh, Kip…" Haley tucked his hand tight in hers and leaned forward, pressing her lips against his forehead. Her heart ached.

She held him until his pitiful tears stopped and he fell asleep. Slowly she rose and looked at Dr. Mather who was standing in the corner. He shook his head and followed Haley into the hallway.

Martin shoved his hands in his pockets and turned away. Gwen pressed her hand to her forehead and swayed against the wall.

Adam gazed helplessly at Haley. "How could he think that? How could he believe we blame him?"

Haley shook her head. Adam turned to Dr. Mather, but he had no answer, either.

"Who knows what the boy was thinking?" Martin grumbled. "Hell, why was he vandalizing our work sites?"

Adam turned on him. "Maybe if you'd paid some attention to him, we'd know."

Martin's jaw tightened. "What are you saying?"

"I'm saying if you'd acted like his father, none of this would have happened."

"You're not blaming this on me!" Martin's fist clenched. "You're the one filling his head with promises to get him out of trouble at school! You should have kept your nose out of it!"

"Somebody had to do something!"

"And look where it got him!"

"If you hadn't been so bullheaded and hired armed guards—"

"I wasn't going to stand by and let—"

"Shut up!" Gwen pushed herself between the two of them. "Shut up!"

Stunned, Adam stepped back. Gwen rounded on Martin and struck him across the chest with her fore arm.

"This is your fault! Nobody's but yours!" Hot tears flowed down her cheeks. "You think you're so smart. You think you know everything, that you can control everyone's life. Well, look what you've done now! Gotten another one of us killed!"

Silence fell in the hallway. The color drained from Martin's face.

"Mother died because of *you!* Peter wasn't good enough, you said. You bought him off. Sent him away, so I couldn't see him."

"You were sixteen years old. You didn't know what you wanted." Martin waved away her words with his hand.

"I loved him! And he loved me!"

The lines of his face were hard. "The boy took the money. How much do you think he really loved you?"

"He didn't know about the baby!" Sobs shook

Gwen's whole body. "I hadn't told him. He'd have stayed, if he'd known."

"I did what was best for you."

"No. You did what was best for *you*. The great Martin Harrington wouldn't lose his first grandchild. You wanted everything—and you didn't care how many lives you destroyed getting it!"

Adam grasped Gwen's arm and turned her toward him, his face ashen. "What are you saying?"

Tears poured down her face, choking off words.

Adam looked at his father. "Martin?"

Jaw set, he stared at them both and squared his shoulders, but didn't answer.

Frustrated, Adam shook Gwen. "What happened?"

She curled her fingers into the fabric of his shirt. "He told everyone Mother was pregnant. But it was me. He sent us away so no one would know the truth."

Adam swallowed hard. "Kip? Kip is…"

"Mine!" Gwen swayed against his chest, sobbing uncontrollably. "He's mine…my baby."

"All these years?" Adam held her away from him, searching her face. "All these years you've pretended differently? You've lived under the same roof, watched him grow up, and never acknowledged he was your child?"

Gwen fell against him, sobbing harder.

Adam locked her protectively in his arms and pivoted to face Martin, his gaze demanding an explanation.

Undaunted, Martin held his stance rigid. "When your mother died in that fire, it was too late to change our story. Everyone already thought she was carrying the child, not Gwen. The fact that she died changed nothing.''

Disgust and revulsion roiled through Adam. "You bastard…''

Dr. Mather stepped between the two men. "She needs to lie down.''

His gaze locked on Martin, Adam didn't respond.

Haley touched his shoulder. "Adam?''

A long moment passed before he looked down at her, raw emotion showing in the taut lines of his face.

She closed her hand around his arm; his muscles were coiled tight. "Help your sister,'' she said softly. "She needs to lie down.''

Dumbly he looked at Gwen in his arms, then nodded. Haley held Adam's elbow, and they all walked down the hallway together.

Dr. Mather gave Gwen a sedative, and Adam sat beside her on the bed, holding her hand while she cried, until she finally fell asleep. He rose, looking numb and dazed, and walked blindly into the hallway. Haley followed, relieved to see that Martin was gone.

She went down to the foyer with Dr. Mather and listened to his instructions for both Kip and Gwen, then thanked him. The normally unflappable Dr. Mather—accustomed to witnessing all sorts of family problems—seemed stunned by what he'd seen and heard tonight.

Haley found the servants gathered in the kitchen and explained Kip's condition; about Gwen she told them only that she had been overcome with worry. Chrissy and Mrs. Ardmore followed Haley upstairs, to watch over them both until the nurses Dr. Mather had promised arrived later in the morning.

Haley went into her own room, swamped by fatigue, wishing for Adam's strong arms around her. But she didn't know where he was, or if she should try to find him. Maybe he needed time alone.

She pulled back the covers of her unmade bed; her brief time in Adam's bed seemed days ago, not just hours. Haley sank down on the edge of the mattress, thinking how unappealing the cold bed suddenly seemed.

The connecting door to the sitting room swung open. Outlined in the light behind him, Adam's big frame filled the opening. Haley came to her feet, resisting the urge to run to him; the thread of their newfound love seemed too fragile to test.

"Come to my bed, Haley." Adam held out his arms. "Please."

She rushed to him, and they clung to each other for a long moment. He looked beaten and bruised, emotionally numb.

"Let's go lie down."

He nodded, and they went into his room. Adam undressed down to his drawers and rolled into bed. Haley slipped out of her dressing gown, noticing for the first time the bloodstains up the front. Surprised, she realized she still wore Adam's shirt beneath it. She climbed in beside him, and he pulled her hard against him. They both fell asleep.

Sunlight through the drapes told Haley that she'd slept until late morning. She lifted her head from the hollow of Adam's shoulder and heard the deep, even rhythm of his breathing. In sleep, he looked content, and it was odd seeing him this way—his big muscles relaxed, his expression peaceful.

The temptation to wake him nagged at her, but Haley didn't give in to it. A long day lay ahead, and it was good that Adam was resting while he could. She eased out of bed and went into the bathroom.

Haley wrapped the fabric of Adam's shirt closer, cool now, without the heat of his body against her. She filled the tub and bathed, then swathed herself in a towel and went into her own room.

Chrissy looked up from the bureau drawer. "Oh, Miss Haley, I'm worried as a blue hen over little Kip. You reckon he's going to be all right?"

"The doctor didn't seem to think there would be any permanent damage. He's young and healthy. He should recover."

Chrissy shook her head. "What do you suppose happened? How come he got shot in the first place?"

Haley turned away and slipped into a fresh dressing gown. This was a question they would hear many times today, she was certain. "It was an accident. He was mistaken for an intruder at the construction site."

"Poor little fella." Chrissy pulled a gown from the closet. "That Constance Porter lady finally showed up. She came by earlier this morning. I didn't see any sense in waking you up."

Haley sat down at her vanity. "Where was she yesterday?"

"That telegram didn't get to her until late, then the train busted, or something. I showed her the gown, though. She said it looked real good." Chrissy stepped behind her, studying her reflection in the mirror. "I know this isn't the best time to say so, but that Miss Porter said my stitching looked good as snuff, and not half as dusty. She said for me to come work for her, if I wanted to."

Haley turned on the bench to face her. "Work for Constance Porter? Really, Chrissy?"

She nodded, her curls bobbing. "She said she'd teach me everything there was to know about seamstressing. Don't get me wrong now, Miss Haley. I like it here, and all. But, well, I wouldn't mind making those fancy dresses."

Haley nodded. "I'd hate to lose you, Chrissy, even if it is a wonderful opportunity for you. But what about Edward?"

Chrissy waved away the thought. "Oh, him. He's just a pair of pants, if you get my meaning. There's lots more of them to be found."

Haley smiled at the maid's unconventional approach to men and such delicate matters. She knew Chrissy would be all right, no matter where she went.

"I think you should do it. And I'll be your first customer."

Chrissy laughed. "You already were, Miss Haley. That gown of yours got me the job."

Haley dressed and went to check on Kip, leaving Chrissy daydreaming by the window. The nurse Dr. Mather had promised was on duty; a broad-shouldered woman wearing a stark uniform, she sat at his bedside. Colorless and drawn, Kip slept, fading into the white pillow beneath his head, jerking occasionally and mumbling.

He looked frail. But the nurse, a Mrs. Mattingly, assured her that Kip's progress was as to be expected. She exuded a warmth that comforted Haley and assured Haley that Kip was being well taken care of.

"Let me know if anyone needs anything," Haley said as she opened the door to leave. "Kip *or* Gwen."

"Miss Harrington is gone."

Gwen had been so distraught last night, she couldn't imagine her up and about so soon. "Where did she go?"

"She wouldn't say, ma'am. I advised her to stay, but she refused to listen to good reason."

Haley nodded. "Has Martin been here this morning?"

"Mr. Harrington? No, ma'am. He hasn't."

She wasn't sure if she expected him to visit or not.

Haley closed the door behind her and went downstairs, to the kitchen. Mrs. Ardmore and her staff had filled the room with delicious aromas.

"Thank you for your help last night," Haley said.

Mrs. Ardmore looked up from the dough laid out on the sideboard, sifting flour from the rolling pin. "How is the young man this morning?"

"As well as can be expected."

"How do you suppose such a thing happened?"

If Mrs. Ardmore was asking, that meant the servants hadn't overheard the airing of the family's dirtiest laundry in the upstairs hallway last night. Haley was relieved.

"A tragic accident."

Mrs. Ardmore shook her head sadly, then waved her hand around the kitchen. "I'm making him chicken soup. My mother's recipe. Fix him right up."

Haley smiled. "Thank you, Mrs. Ardmore."

A short time later, after church let out, people began to arrive. Word had spread, bringing a steady stream of friends to the house, expressing concern, asking questions. Haley told them all the same story. Most stayed only briefly, others hung on. Mrs. Ardmore served tea, coffee and pastries. Amid it all, Haley caught sight of Adam, dressed in a dark pin-striped suit, coming down the stairs. She excused herself and met him in the foyer.

"You look tired." Actually, he looked horrible, drawn, pale, emotionally exhausted. "Why don't you rest some more?"

He touched his hand to her elbow. "Only if you come with me."

She ached for the comfort of his closeness, and apparently he felt the same way. "I can't leave our guests."

Adam glanced around at the people clustered in the foyer, the hallway and the parlor, at the servants bustling everywhere. "I don't think anyone would notice."

"Probably not."

"I checked on Kip. He's still sleeping."

"That's good. He needs to rest. Gwen left before I got up. I don't know where she is, Adam. I'm worried about her."

He nodded grimly. "Has Martin been here?"

She hated to tell him that his own father hadn't arrived to check on Kip. "No."

His jaw tightened. "Good."

The front door opened suddenly, and Aunt Izzy barreled inside. She didn't need a reading to know something was wrong. Adam went to her and escorted her quickly down the hallway to his study.

Aunt Harriet and several of her friends arrived. She took over the parlor as if she visited the Harrington house regularly, impressing her friends considerably. Haley sat with her as long as she could stand it, then excused herself.

"Let me know what you need," Aunt Harriet instructed as Haley rose. "We're all family here."

"Thank you, Aunt Harriet."

Dr. Mather slipped upstairs unnoticed by the guests, but Haley caught him on the way out and had a quiet word with him. Kip was doing as expected, but he was concerned for Gwen. He promised to go by Martin's house and see if she'd gone there. As she stepped onto the front porch with the doctor, Aunt Izzy charged past without a word. Haley could only imagine where the woman was headed.

Thankfully, two very familiar faces appeared, and Haley took them into the sitting room. She was tired from sleeping so little and from the emotional strain, tired of the stream of well-intentioned callers, and tired of telling the same story over and over. Adam had looked so big and sturdy the few times she caught sight of him during the afternoon, and she wanted to melt into his arms. For now, she took comfort in visiting with Jay and Elizabeth.

"I'm so glad you're here." Haley closed the door to the sitting room and lifted her face to receive Jay's peck on the cheek.

"We just heard." Jay kept his arm around Elizabeth as they sat down on the settee. "How is Kip?"

Haley lowered herself into the chair across from them. "The doctor says he'll be fine."

"Thank goodness."

"Is there anything we can do?" Elizabeth asked.

They both were doing their darnedest to contain themselves, putting on somber faces for the occasion, but Haley could see that they were both about to burst over something.

"Yes. You can tell me what's going on with you two."

Elizabeth blushed and dipped her lashes. Jay

grinned down at her, as if her behavior were the cutest thing he'd ever seen.

"This is hardly the time," Jay said.

"This is most definitely the time." Haley pinched the bridge of her nose. "Believe me, I can use some good news. It is good news, isn't it?"

Jay beamed with pride. "This wonderful woman, whom I don't deserve, has consented to marry me."

Haley's eyes rounded. "Oh, Jay! That's wonderful!"

He gave Elizabeth a little squeeze. "Yes, she's going to make an honest man out of me."

"Jay!" Elizabeth's cheeks colored again.

"I'm so happy for you." Haley sat forward in her chair. "We have wedding plans to make."

Jay took Elizabeth's hand. "We've decided on something small, something simple...something soon."

The look they shared left Haley with no doubt about what they'd been doing all night. And suddenly she missed Adam very much.

Jay got to his feet, pulling Elizabeth up with him. "We won't keep you. I know you have guests."

They all hugged, and Jay opened the door.

"I'll let you know how it goes tomorrow morning."

Haley frowned. "Tomorrow morning?"

"McKettrick, remember?"

"Oh, of course." Jay was going over the plans with Iris and Johnny in the morning. How could she have forgotten?

Haley watched them cross the foyer, feeling the warmth of their love radiating around them. A profound longing coiled inside her. She couldn't wait another minute. She wanted her husband.

She found him alone in his study, both arms braced against the window casing, staring out into the rear lawn. Silently she closed the door. He turned, his profile outlined in the light outside the window. Haley's knees weakened. He really was a handsome man.

"He wanted to help me finish the gazebo. He asked a dozen times, but I put him off." Adam turned back to the window. "I should have paid more attention to him."

Haley crossed the room and laid her hand on his shoulder. Even through the jacket, she could feel his tight muscles. "You didn't know."

"But you knew. I should have listened to you." Adam gazed outside again, at the half-finished gazebo. He should have done a lot of things differently. The afternoon of their picnic, he'd scoffed at Haley's suggestion that they have supper in the gazebo and watch the sunset. Now, the idea coiled a knot of delight in his belly.

Adam pushed away from the window and looped his arms around Haley. She came against him willingly, and circled his waist with her arms. God, she smelled sweet. Her gown was a dark blue, nearly the same shade as the dress he'd taken off her last night. But today, while he still yearned for her, as he always would, the sight of her brought him a deep, abiding comfort he'd never known before.

"I saw you talking with your aunt. Where was she last night?" Haley asked.

"She stayed at Virginia Mason's house. Some friends dropped by after church and told her about Kip. She came straight over."

"How did she take the news?"

"Badly." Adam pursed her lips. "She lit out after Martin."

"Good. He deserves her wrath."

Adam lapsed into silence for a long moment. Gingerly Haley reached up and drew her finger along his jaw. "It won't help to hold it all inside."

He exhaled heavily. "I always—always—looked up to my father. When I was young, I wanted to be just like him. Even now..."

"You want to please him. That's pretty normal."

Adam spun away from her, his teeth clenched. "But it was all wrong. The things I admired about him have turned out to be all wrong. He's controlling, shortsighted, manipulative. Look what he's done to Kip. Look what he did to Gwen...to Mother."

He closed his eyes. The ugly picture of his father widened to encompass him, as well. He was on his way to becoming his father. Look what he'd done to Haley. Married her for his own convenience, with no thought of what she wanted, what she needed—the engagement he'd thought silly, the parties, the elaborate wedding ceremony he'd wanted no part of.

Adam rubbed his forehead. "I don't want to turn out like Martin."

Haley slipped around in front of him. His face had gone white. She eased herself into his arms and looped her hands around his neck. "You're not like him."

He gave her a hopeful smile. "You don't think so? Really?"

"Really."

He hugged her fiercely against him. "I'm going to do better. With Kip, with Gwen. I swear I will."

Haley rested her cheek against his big chest. His heart pounded steadily in her ear. Maybe some good had come from this tragedy. Maybe its effect on Adam would be a positive one.

Haley squeezed her eyes shut. Maybe, one day, he might even say he loved her.

Chapter Eighteen

"We got it!"

"What?" Confused, Haley stared at Jay's animated face across the threshold.

"The McKettrick job!" He pulled off his bowler and threw out both hands, turning his face skyward. "We got it!"

"We got it?" Haley's mouth fell open. She let out a whoop and leaped into his arms. "We got it!"

Jay spun around on the porch, swinging Haley with him. They clasped hands and danced in a circle.

"Oh, Jay, you're brilliant." She hugged him.

"No, you're brilliant. It was your idea."

"Yes, but you did the designs."

"I would never have thought of it if you hadn't suggested the whole thing."

Haley lifted her hands. "I guess we're both brilliant."

"I can hardly believe it." Jay clutched his chest, slowing his breathing. "The Sacramento Building Company won the most prized job of the year."

"We did. Even— Oh, dear." Haley's excitement cooled. "If we won, that means Adam didn't."

Jay's enthusiasm dimmed. "Right. Too bad."

"I wish you both could have gotten the project."

"I'm afraid it doesn't work that way."

The late-morning breeze ruffled her skirt. "Does Adam know yet?"

"Probably. He'll be disappointed."

Haley considered the thought. In truth, when he left the house this morning, work had seemed the farthest thing from his mind. He'd asked her to come into his room last night, and they'd made love. Slow, healing love that drove away the images of Kip and Gwen and Martin that had haunted them all day. Then, just before dawn, playful, exhausting love that had sent Adam off to work with a big, goofy grin she'd never seen before.

Jay drew in a deep breath. "I hate to be crass, but I need money. McKettrick wants to start immediately."

"I'll go to the bank and arrange for the funds, then come by your office and let you know it's all been handled." She'd go by Harrington Construction while she was in town and see Adam, too.

Jay popped his bowler on. "Sounds perfect, partner."

"Wait. Before you go, I have something for you." Haley scurried back into the house and returned to the front porch a moment later. She passed a thick envelope to Jay. "I did this for you, but now you can consider it a wedding present."

He eyed the packet. "What is it?"

"Open it and see for yourself."

"I don't like that smile on your face, cousin." Jay slid it open and unfurled the long document. He read it once, then again. His jaw fell slack. "This is the deed to Leonora Montgomery's house."

"It's your house now. You deserve it, Jay. So does Elizabeth. Live in it, enjoy it, raise the next generation of Sacramento Building Company owners in it."

Jay just stared at her. "I don't know what to say."

She grinned. "Say thank-you."

"Thank you."

She turned him toward the hansom cab waiting in the drive. "Run along, now. You've got lots of work to do. I'll be down later this afternoon."

Dazed, Jay tucked the packet into his jacket pocket. "Things are working out for both of us, aren't they? Sacramento Building is growing, Elizabeth is going to marry me. Your living with a Harrington has turned out all right."

Haley smiled. "Nice, huh?"

He nodded. "I feel like nothing can go wrong now."

"I can't imagine what it would be."

"I've been cut off!"

Frantic, Haley collapsed into the chair in front of Jay's desk, her face white, her hands trembling.

He jumped to the edge of his chair. "You've been what?"

"Cut off!" Haley gripped the edge of the desk. "I went to the bank to get the money, and they wouldn't give it to me. Nothing! Not a dime!"

Color drained from Jay's face. "But it's your money."

"Grandfather Hasting cut me off, and that pompous, arrogant banker took great pleasure in telling me so—as if the money were his to hold on to. Grandfather just returned from Europe. He found out about Reginald.''

"Oh, God, no."

"He was furious. He cut off my funds."

Jay's eyes bulged. "What are we going to do? We have to start this project immediately."

Haley gulped down two big breaths of air. "Let's calm ourselves. We have to think. Now, you have money, don't you? I mean, you had the funds for the McKettrick project to begin with. You told me you did."

He gestured wildly at the plans spread out over his desk. "That was back when it was rows of tiny, ugly little houses. We changed all that. Your brilliant idea, remember? A community Iris McKettrick would be proud to have her name on. Now we've got two- and three-story homes. Churches. Stores and shops. A park. A lake. Swans! For chrissakes, Haley, we've got swans!"

Haley rocked back in her chair, her heart pounding. She waved her hands to calm him. "Let's just think—quietly."

Haley chewed a fingernail. Jay planted his elbows on his desk and buried his face in his palms.

Finally, he looked up. "Maybe, if we pull together enough cash to get the project started, the bank will give us a loan."

"I don't know." Haley squirmed on the chair. "That horrible Mr. Nobles I talked to this morning isn't likely to loan us anything. You don't think he'll tell the other bankers in town about it, do you?"

"Christ…" Jay covered his face again.

Haley's shoulders sagged. The other bankers probably had known about it before she did.

"I have my jewelry," Haley offered.

Jay peered at her through the cracks between his fingers. "Unless you own the crown jewels, it won't help."

"I could ask Aunt Harriet for a little something."

"Good, Haley. Let the whole town know we're in financial straits." Jay pulled on his neck.

"We'll have income from the easterners who'll buy up the land we bought."

"But that will take months. We need cash now." Jay exhaled loudly. "I'll sell the house."

"Leonora Montgomery's house? But it's your wedding present."

He gasped and sat straight up in his chair. "Good God, now I can't marry Elizabeth."

"What? Of course you can marry her."

"And live on what? When word of this gets out, the Sacramento Building Company will be ruined. No one will let us build a doghouse for them, let alone anything else."

Haley moaned and touched her forehead. "There must be some way to get the money. Surely, between the two of us, we know someone who has these kinds of funds."

Their gazes collided over the desk as the one truly viable option dawned on them both.

"Don't say it."

Jay slumped onto his elbow again. "I won't if you won't."

"I'm going home. I can think better there."

"I'll be here. I don't know why, but I'll be here." Jay raised his head and looked glumly around the office.

Haley rose and squared her shoulders. "We'll think of something."

Jay nodded bravely. "Of course we will."

Haley laid her head against the back of the leather chair and stared blankly at the ceiling. She'd racked her brain for hours, trying to come up with money for the McKettrick project. Seeking guidance by osmosis, she'd settled into Adam's study. Surely he'd solved many problems in this room. Maybe she could, too.

But her mind had drifted to Kip. She'd checked on him several times today. The one time he was awake, he'd only lain there, colorless and weak. She'd read to him for a while, and then he'd fallen asleep again. She wasn't sure what to tell him when he woke the next time. If he asked why his father or Gwen hadn't been to see him, she wasn't sure what to say.

"Having visions of taking over the company?"

Adam stood in the doorway. She vaulted from the chair. "Oh, no."

He came into the room and caught her in his arms. "How is Kip?"

Despite her own troubles, she snuggled close. It felt good to be next to him. "He's awfully weak, Adam. Dr. Mather will be over later tonight."

"Good. I want to talk to him about Gwen."

"Where is she?"

"Holed up in her room at home. Aunt Izzy came by to see me today. She tried to coax her out, but couldn't. I'm worried about her."

"What did Martin say?"

He frowned. "He didn't show up at the office today."

"He didn't?" Her eyes rounded.

Adam grunted. "Suited me all right."

Haley pressed her lips together. It would be a long time before the rift between Adam and his father healed.

Adam looked down at Haley, cradled against his chest. "What should we do about Kip? Should we tell him the truth about Gwen?"

"We should discuss it with Gwen, of course, but I don't think it would be a good idea. Not now, anyway. When he's older, maybe. When he can understand better."

Adam let a long moment pass, then bent down and brushed a kiss across her forehead. "I missed you today."

The feel of his lips on her skin warmed her, and sent McKettrick and money problems flying from her head. She gave him a provocative little grin. "Did you think about me?"

"Oh, yes." He dipped his mouth lower in a trail of kisses until he nuzzled her neck. Adam groaned and shifted his weight against her. "Guess what I was thinking."

She gasped as the hard ridge of his trousers pressed against her belly. Heat rolled off him, seeping into her, coiling deep inside her, reaching secret places.

Haley slid her hands inside his jacket and let them roam the angles of his wide, hard chest. He groaned and pushed himself closer against her.

"Supper will be ready soon," she said.

He closed his lips over hers, kissing her greedily, then pulled away. "I want dessert first."

"Surely you don't mean on the dining room table."

Adam grinned down at her, his eyes gleaming. "That's a hell of an idea."

"Maybe we should try it." Haley lifted herself on tiptoe, pressing herself intimately against him. "How about it? We'll give all the servants a week off, and try out every room in the house."

Adam moaned and pushed against her. "A week? The way I feel tonight, I'll only need about five minutes."

He pressed her backward over his desk and laid claim to her lips with a hungry kiss. Her breath felt hot in his mouth as he dipped his tongue into the sweetness. He circled her breast with his palm, then cupped it, stroking until it tightened and she arched forward.

He couldn't wait. He'd thought about her all day, and he hadn't gotten a lick of work done. He wanted her. Now.

With hot, heavy breath, he broke off their kiss. "Let's go."

Lost in the heat of desire, Haley only nodded dumbly. "Yes, now—"

"Begging your pardon, sir."

Adam froze, refusing to turn around. No, not Bernard. Not now.

"Sir?"

Haley gazed up at him with glassy eyes, her cheeks pink, her lips wet. Adam groaned and released her.

"Yes, Bernard?"

He gazed straight through them, as if not seeing the distress on both their faces. "The Olivers have arrived."

"The Olivers?"

"Yes, sir. They say they're expected."

Haley gasped and slapped her hands to her cheeks. "Oh, my goodness! The Olivers. I invited them for supper when I saw them at the spring gala and completely forgot about it."

"Have them wait in the parlor, Bernard. We'll be there...sometime."

"Yes, sir. And the doctor has arrived. He's upstairs." He left them alone.

Haley bit down on her lip. "I'm sorry."

Adam slid his arms around her again. "Harry and Laurel are newlyweds, too. I'm sure they'd understand if I explained the situation."

God help her, for a moment she was actually tempted. Haley planted her palms firmly against Adam's chest and backed him away. "You know we can't do that. But maybe, if we're really boring tonight, they'll leave early."

"Good idea."

Haley smoothed down her dress and touched her hand to the back of her hair. She gave Adam a sidelong glance. "You'd better...control yourself before we get in there."

He looked down at the front of his trousers. "Maybe it will give them the idea they're interrupting?"

Haley blushed. "I'll stand in front of you. Let's go."

"I don't think that's going to help." Adam followed her out of the room, his gaze glued to her swaying bustle.

Haley leading the way, they went into the parlor. Harry and Laurel Oliver were seated on the settee, holding hands, their heads bent together. Harry whispered something. Laurel giggled. Haley's cheeks pinkened. Adam's condition worsened.

"Harry, good to see you again." With Haley blocking him, Adam shook hands, and greetings were exchanged. Harry and Laurel settled on the settee again, and Adam and Haley took the wing-backed chairs across from them.

Adam crossed his legs. "How was New York?"

Harry and Laurel looked at each other again, and both of them snickered. "Great," Harry said. "Just great."

"Did you do much sight-seeing?" Haley asked.

This time, they both laughed aloud.

"No, not really," Harry said.

Laurel's face pinkened. "Harry, you devil."

"Well, they're newlyweds, too." He looked across the coffee table at Adam. "I can't get over it. You two actually got married."

"You'd know. You were there," Adam said.

Harry and Laurel both laughed uproariously.

"Oh, yes—the wedding." Harry turned to Haley. "I've never seen any man so taken with the sight of a woman before. Adam was going mad trying to find someone to introduce you to him. I thought he'd tear the place apart."

Surprised and pleased, Haley looked at Adam. He just shrugged helplessly.

"And then, when you two finally danced, well, I knew he was hooked," Harry said.

Laurel lifted her hands. "So what could we do but marry you two on the spot?"

"Not a bad ceremony, if I do say so myself." Harry adjusted his cravat. "I may have missed my calling."

The smile faded from Adam's face. "You mean, the ceremony Judge Williams conducted, don't you?"

Harry and Laurel both burst into laughter again.

"Judge Williams—that old goat." Harry slapped his knee. "Wouldn't he just rip me apart if he knew I could sign his name as well as he?"

Laurel fanned her face to calm her laughter. "Adam, I hope you realize what a friend you have in this new husband of mine. He left his own wedding reception to get a marriage license from the court house, just to get you together with Haley. Then performed a beautiful service right there by the punch bowl."

Harry wiped the corner of his eye. "And to think you two actually ended up getting married—for real."

"Who'd have thought it?" Laurel laughed.

He touched her arm. "Maybe I should go into the matchmaking business."

Haley's mouth sagged open as she stared at the Olivers, laughing on the settee. Slowly she turned her head, and her gaze met Adam's. His face had gone white.

Adam leaned forward. "Do you mean Judge Williams didn't conduct the ceremony?"

Harry laughed harder. "Of course not."

"It was us." Laurel giggled behind her hand. "We did the whole thing ourselves."

"Jesus..."

Haley surged to her feet. The room spun around her, and she touched her hand to her forehead. "I'm not well."

Adam jumped up and steadied her. "Haley, I—"

Harry and Laurel sobered.

"Maybe we'd better go," Laurel said.

"Good idea." Harry rose quickly. "We'll make this another time."

They clasped hands and hurried from the parlor.

Dazed, Adam stared at Haley. "This means we're..."

"...not really married." She lifted her gaze to meet his. Suddenly she felt chilled to the bone. Her heart swelled, her stomach knotted.

Adam's chest tightened. And right before his eyes he saw the slender thread that connected them snap in two. Haley pulled her arm from his grasp. Her gaze turned cold, as if he were a stranger.

"Haley, this doesn't mean anything. We'll just—"

"Of course it means something!" She pressed her fingers to her lips, then whirled away and ran from the room.

"Wait!" Adam went after her.

He charged up the staircase, taking the steps two at a time, and caught her halfway up. He grabbed her elbow. "Wait! Will you just wait?"

She turned, staring coldly at him, two steps below her. "Don't you see what this means? This is a farce. This whole thing!"

His belly twisted into a knot. He wasn't going to lose her. Not now. "Look, let's just sit down and talk about it."

"Let's draw up a schedule! Make a timetable! That fixes everything, doesn't it?"

He plowed his hand through his hair. "I know you're upset. I'm upset."

"I'm sure you are! Your whole plan is spoiled now, isn't it?" Fury coiled deep in her body. "You'll have to start prowling weddings again, searching for unsuspecting punch drinkers."

"Now just a damn minute! You know good and well—"

"All right now, you two, that's quite enough."

They both turned to see Dr. Mather descending the stairs, coat over his arm, black satchel in his hand.

He wagged his finger at them. "Let's not upset Kip."

"Oh, yes, Kip." Haley swallowed her emotion, forcing it down like a big lump. "How is he?"

"As well as can be expected." Dr. Mather frowned at Adam. "And don't you be upsetting this wife of yours, either. It's not good, given her condition."

Haley reeled backward and grabbed the railing. "What condition?"

Dr. Mather chuckled. "Well, we don't know for sure, but it could be we've got another Harrington on the way. I told Adam to have you come down to the office for a visit. Make it tomorrow morning. We'll find out for sure."

The doctor left, taking most of the air with him and leaving Haley panting. Her thoughts spun wildly as she tried to come to terms with everything. They weren't really married. Had Adam known? Possibly she was pregnant. Adam most definitely knew that.

The air left her lungs in a rush. He'd used her. All along, Adam had used her.

Her gaze riveted him, impaling him with hot anger. He backed down a step. "I hadn't had a chance to tell you yet, Haley. With Kip and everything, I—"

"It's just another part of your plan, isn't it? An heir. That's what you wanted me for all along."

He felt as if he'd been kicked in the gut. "No, Haley. That's not true."

Tears welled up inside her, but she refused to let

them fall. "Tell me a child wasn't on that mental list of yours."

He was losing her. He could see her slipping away. Still, he couldn't lie to her. "You know I thought about it. But it means nothing. We don't know if you're carrying a child or not. It was the doctor's idea. We don't know for sure."

Haley drew herself up to her full height and pulled in a deep breath. Fighting off the swirl of emotion, she looked down at him. "I may not know if I'm pregnant. But I do know for certain that I am not married."

She turned and walked up the staircase.

Adam curled his fist around the railing, his heart aching. "Don't go. Haley. Haley!"

Chapter Nineteen

"Now, now, don't worry. It's just a little tiff. All couples go through these things."

Haley clamped her mouth shut, wishing she could close out Aunt Harriet's well-intentioned advice. A week had passed since she left Adam's house, a week of living with her aunt, a week of staying in her room, refusing to speak of what had driven her here in the first place. And still Aunt Harriet insisted it—whatever it was—was only a tiff and would blow over soon.

Haley rose from her bed. She'd felt hurt. Wounded so deeply that she cried herself to sleep night after night. Up until today, that is.

And today, after her trip into town, she was just plain mad.

"Haley, dear, they are the Harringtons. We must remember that."

As if she could forget. Haley tamped down her anger. "Thank you, Aunt Harriet."

She smiled sweetly. "It's good you two are seeing each other tonight. You can patch things up this evening."

Adam would need to be patched up after she got finished with him. Haley forced a smile. "Yes, I think so, too."

Aunt Harriet heaved a sigh of relief. She stopped at the door. "Oh, by the way, your cousin is downstairs."

Haley soaked up the welcome silence as the door closed behind her aunt. Jay. She hadn't spoken to him in a week, either. Now she felt guilty facing him. She'd abandoned him. Left him alone to worry about the McKettrick deal. After all her talk about being a partner, she'd been too consumed with her own problems to consider him.

Well, no sense waiting any longer. Haley went downstairs to the parlor to get the tongue-lashing she deserved. Jay rose from the settee when she walked in.

"I don't blame you if you hate me."

He crossed the room and kissed her cheek. "Don't be silly. But I have been worried sick about you."

"You haven't heard? No one said anything?"

Jay lifted his shoulders. "No one has said a thing. I only knew you'd left Harrington's because I went by to see you."

The fact that word of her nonexistent marriage and possible pregnancy hadn't made the rounds brought her some comfort. It wasn't the kind of thing she wanted advertised.

"Feel up to talking about it?"

"If I could talk to anyone about it, Jay, it would be you. Adam's taking me out to dinner tonight. That should decide things." One way or the other.

"He looks pretty bad."

Haley's stomach knotted. At once, she was glad he was upset, and worried about him, too.

Jay shrugged. "Well, then, I guess I'll just get down to business."

Haley sat on the settee. "I have to apologize for leaving this whole McKettrick situation on you, Jay."

"It's all handled." He sat down across from her.

Her stomach clenched. "Don't tell me you gave up the project."

"On the contrary, I still have it."

She sat forward, grateful for the first good news she'd heard in a week. "Jay, that's wonderful. But how did you get the money?"

"I found someone who could afford both the project and me." Jay lifted his chin. "You're looking at the newest employee of Harrington Construction."

"Oh, Jay, no..."

"It's for the best, Haley, really it is." Jay stretched across the marble coffee table and touched her hand. "I'm in charge of the project but I don't have to worry about anything else. Adam and I discussed it at length. I have a good feel for it, honestly I do."

"But Sacramento Building... Our fathers..."

Jay sat back. "It had been withering for a long time. It was destined to die. At least this way, I can salvage something of it."

Haley closed her eyes, letting the full impact sink in. She looked up at Jay. "Are you sure?"

"Absolutely. Now I can marry Elizabeth and keep the Montgomery house. I can see the McKettrick project through, with lots of new ones on the horizon. It's the only sensible thing to do, Haley."

Sensible. The very last thing she wanted to be at

this moment. Haley swallowed hard. "Yes, of course you're right."

Jay rose. "Well, I've got to go. I'm having supper with Elizabeth at her mother's this evening. We're picking out flowers, or china, or something."

A smile crept onto Haley's lips, the first she'd felt in days. "You're enjoying it, aren't you?"

He grinned. "Yes, I am."

She kissed his cheek and went back up to her room, a strange sadness tugging at her. A myriad of emotions had assailed her these past few days, turning, changing, driving her from anger to tears in a heartbeat. But now, after what had happened this morning, all she could think of was confronting Adam. He thought he was taking her to supper this evening; he had no idea what was in store for him.

Aunt Harriet's gleeful face appeared at her bedroom door several hours later, announcing Adam's arrival.

"He's here, he's here!" Her smile fell as she looked at the gray silk dress Haley had chosen for the evening. "Don't you think that's a little drab, dear?"

Haley pinned her hat in place. Actually, she'd considered wearing black. It didn't matter, anyway. She didn't intend to have supper with Adam, only a few well-chosen words guaranteed to spoil anyone's appetite.

Haley turned away from the mirror. "I don't want to keep him waiting, Aunt Harriet."

She gasped. "Oh, yes! Of course!"

Following her aunt, Haley went downstairs. She caught the scent of him, musky and masculine, as she crossed the foyer. Then he stepped out of the parlor. Her heart skipped a beat. Damn. He was handsome and strong and sturdy, and she wanted to run to him. But Haley stopped short and hardened her feelings as the morning at Dr. Mather's office came back to her.

"You two run along and have a wonderful evening." Aunt Harriet twittered and smiled, as if that could make everything all right between them.

Adam edged next to her, and she could feel the heat emanating from him. She fought the natural urge to melt into it and walked out onto the porch. Evening shadows stretched across the lawn as they crossed to the carriage. Adam cupped her elbow to assist her inside.

She jerked away. "Don't touch me."

He dropped his hands to his side. "Yes, ma'am."

A little grin tugged at his lips, and that sent another wave of anger through Haley. She climbed inside, unassisted, and settled onto the leather seat. The interior of the carriage shrank as Adam sat across from her and stretched out his long legs. Haley clamped her mouth shut until the carriage lurched forward and the last sight of Aunt Harriet, waving from the porch, disappeared. Then she couldn't hold it in any longer.

"You have no business interfering with my life. I want you to stop it. Do you understand me?"

Adam spread out his palms. "It's only a dinner invitation."

"You know what I mean!" Haley gripped her handbag in her lap. "I went to see Dr. Mather this morning."

"Oh, yes…that." Adam nodded slowly. "And?"

His calm, solicitous attitude infuriated her further. "You know what he said. He refused to see me—on your instructions!"

Adam nodded again, making her angrier.

"I am not your concern any longer. Why did you tell the doctor that? Why?"

He looked across the carriage at her, his expression solemn. "Because I didn't want to know."

Haley's chest tightened. He didn't want to know. She could be carrying his child at this moment, and Adam didn't want to know.

She gulped down a lump of emotion. "Take me back to my aunt's. Now."

Adam shook his head. "You promised to have supper."

"I've changed my mind! I don't want to be with you. Where are you taking me?" She looked out the window at the familiar scenery. Anger pushed its way through her churning emotions. "No. I'll not go to your house. Let me out of here! I'll walk back to my aunt's!"

Adam sat forward and reached for her hands, but remembered himself and propped his elbows on his knees instead. "Kip's been asking for you. I promised him you'd come by and see him tonight. It won't take long."

Her jaw tightened as she jerked her chin away. She could hardly say no. "All right. But just for a few minutes."

Adam nodded and leaned back against the seat.

They rode in silence, the sway of the carriage diluting most of Haley's anger. She hadn't let herself think about it until now, but she'd missed Kip. She'd worried about him, too. In fact, everyone at Adam's home, in Adam's family, had been on her mind. In the short time they were in her life, they'd all wound their way into her heart.

Haley looked across the darkening carriage at

Adam. He was there, too, in her heart, though she was loath to admit it, even to herself.

An eerie feeling of calm swept over Haley as the carriage came to a stop in front of the house. The windows were ablaze against the twilight sky. Edward smiled pleasantly as he helped her to the ground. Had he been doing all right since Chrissy left? Did he miss her? She wished she could ask.

Bernard waited on the porch, looking proper and dignified, as always. Who had overseen the servants this past week? Had they missed her? Was she penciled on the schedule tucked inside Bernard's pocket?

Haley accepted Adam's hand on her elbow as they went up the walkway, stopping at the foot of the steps; here, at this house, it seemed foreign to do otherwise.

"Good evening, sir, madam." He looked down at them from the porch. "Everything is prepared, sir, as you instructed."

Adam nodded and gestured toward the path that led around the house. "There's something I want to show you."

She dug in her heels. "I'm only here to see Kip."

Adam grinned. "It's something special. I want you to see it."

Not wanting to make a scene in front of Bernard, and somewhat intrigued, Haley allowed herself to be guided to the rear of the house. There, Adam stepped back and waved his hand at the newly completed gazebo, settled under the boughs of the oaks. Its intricate latticework sported a gleaming coat of white paint, accented by lanterns strung under the eaves, casting soft light into the closing darkness. Inside, a table draped with a linen cloth and set with china, crystal and a lit candelabra waited.

"We finished it this morning," Adam said proudly. "Jay and I worked on it nonstop. Kip came down and helped, too."

"But you were supposed to start the McKettrick project."

Adam shrugged. "I told McKettrick it would have to wait. I had a more important job to finish. Come look at it."

He took Haley's hand and led her up the two steps into the gazebo. The lanterns and candles cast a soft pink light over them.

Haley gazed up at him. "You put the entire McKettrick job off so you and Jay could finish the gazebo?"

"For you. I wanted you to have supper here with me, so we could watch the sunset." Adam gestured to the purple-and-lavender clouds streaking the horizon. "Like you asked. Remember?"

The day of the picnic. A lump of emotion rose in Haley's throat. "Yes. I remember."

Adam took both her hands securely in his and hugged them to his chest. "There's a few things you should know. First, the doctor has recommended a sanitarium near Los Angeles for Gwen. He says it will be good for her. And Martin's leaving. He's going to Egypt with Aunt Izzy and Virginia Mason. Kip is staying here with me."

Her heart lurched. "You're keeping Kip?"

He nodded. "I want him here with me. We'll be good for each other."

Haley nodded. "Yes, you will."

"Jay is taking over most of the day-to-day work at

Harrington Construction so I'll be free to pursue other projects."

"Your skyscrapers. You can build your skyscrapers." She saw the excitement in his eyes, felt it radiate through his hands. "All your plans and schedules have paid off."

Adam grinned and shook his head. "Oh, no. I've sworn off meticulous schedules, since the night of the spring gala."

She flushed at the memory of that night, and saw it reflected in his green eyes.

Adam tightened his hold on her hands and inched closer. "I asked Dr. Mather not to see you because it was the only way I could think to convince you I wasn't after an heir. It's you I want, Haley, only you."

A wave of emotion engulfed her. Her throat closed off.

Adam went down on one knee, still holding her hand. "I want to watch every sunset for the rest of my life with you in my arms. Marry me, Haley. Please."

With his other hand, he fished a velvet box from his jacket pocket and pried it open. A diamond ring sparkled in the soft light. "This is for you, Haley. A proper engagement ring. I know we can't have a big wedding, since everyone already thinks we're married, but we can have a reception. Whatever you want, Haley. Please say you'll marry me."

She wanted to. With all her heart, she wanted to dissolve into his arms and stay there forever. But she couldn't. He'd left the most important thing unsaid.

Haley pulled her hand from his and turned away. "I don't know, Adam."

Fear, cold and raw, chilled his gut. Adam rose and tucked the ring in his pocket. She couldn't say no. He couldn't lose her. He'd done everything—said everything. He'd—

Reason hit him like a kick in the head. He stepped toward her. "Did I mention that I love you?"

Haley whirled around, tears blinding her. "No, you didn't."

"Damn." Adam plowed his fingers through his hair. "You see? This is what happens when I don't write things down."

A giggle bubbled up through her torment of emotion. Haley pressed her fingers to her lips. "So, does that mean you love me?"

"Oh, God, yes."

He couldn't wait another minute. Adam pulled her into his arms, crushing her against him. "I love you, Haley. I want you to marry me. It doesn't matter if you're having a baby now or not. I only want you. Just you."

Haley curled her arms around his neck, soaking up the heat and maleness of him. "I'll marry you, Adam."

He kissed her solidly on the mouth, then stopped suddenly and looked down at her. "You do love me, too, don't you?"

She giggled. "Yes. I love you with all my heart."

They snuggled against each other, content in each other's arms.

"You know, Adam, maybe it would be a good idea for you to start making plans and schedules again. You seem to need them."

He kissed her forehead. "I was thinking the same

thing. Do you remember that schedule you worked out for me?''

She rolled her eyes. "The one you rebelled against so strongly? The one that made you feel like a trolley car? How could I forget it?''

"Well, I've rethought that whole thing. It might work for us, with a few changes, of course.''

She grinned up at him. "What sort of changes?''

"I'm thinking of scheduling more stops for this trolley." Adam snuggled her closer. "Lots and lots and lots more stops.''

*   *   *   *   *

The Jewels of Texas

Bestselling author

Ruth Langan

presents

Ruby

Book IV in
the exciting
Jewels of Texas
series.

The town marshal and the town flirt fall in love,
and join forces to save the little town of
Hanging Tree, Texas, from a killer.

The Jewels of Texas—four sisters as wild and vibrant
as the untamed land they're fighting to protect.

Available in September
wherever Harlequin Historicals are sold.

Harlequin® Historical

Take 4 bestselling love stories FREE

Plus get a FREE surprise gift!